SENTINEL

"He's making waves! Horror fans, Drew Starling should be at the top of your author-to-watch list!"

~ Best Selling Horror Author, Daniel Willcocks

"Well written, beautiful and haunting. If this is the authors debut, then I feel many good things coming from him in the near future."

~ PAN's Horror Book Reviews

SENTINEL

Paperback ISBN: 978-1-990245-10-7
Hardcover ISBN: 978-1-990245-11-4
Digital ISBN: 978-1-990245-07-7

Edited by Linda Nagle
Cover Design by Francois Vaillancourt
Book Formatting by Michelle River

For Candy

PART I

DAY 1

The Grand Elder stuck two fingers through the blinds, creasing the aluminum into an elongated diamond and sending a sharp burst of noonday light through the cavernous and otherwise unlit office. From his lofty vantage, Manhattan was a gray tableau of microscopic urban chum. Dirty rooftops of more modest buildings, tiny yellow taxis squirming through the streets, impossibly small blobs of pedestrians. Life was down there, life and an oblivious public, a breed of commoners blissfully ignorant to the world's most heinous and unbelievable secrets. Secrets which, if exposed, would disturb the very bedrock of civilization and send those same masses rioting.

Here in his gilded fortress on the 110th floor, the Grand Elder guarded those secrets. Only a handful of people in this dimension of reality were privy to such knowledge, and the way the Grand Elder saw it, that's how it should be. Easier for a lonely and loyal few to burden such complicated matters.

The voice of his secretary buzzed through the intercom. "Sir, your 12:30 is here."

"Thank you. Send him in."

The Grand Elder held watch over the city as the mahogany doors creaked open behind him. It was well-known within the Order of the Old Roses that you did not make eye contact with the Grand Elder. Decades of living under the weight of such harrowing truths and waking nightmares had done something terrible to him. Now, he took great pains to hide his face from the world, and his clerics, his deacons, his deaconesses, and his acolytes did not look upon him. He alone guarded the Order's most sensitive work.

The doors opened and the sound of quick footsteps on the hardwood floor caromed off the walls.

"Thank you for coming," the Grand Elder said, keeping his gaze locked on the cityscape below him.

"Yes, sir, my pleasure, sir," the other man said, his voice quick and decisive.

"Do you know why I've summoned you today, Deacon?"

"No, sir."

"You are aware of our activity in Bensalem, correct? At least vaguely?"

The room filled with a nervous silence, save for the maniacal ticking of a grandfather clock in the back corner recording the seconds like a timer about to go off.

"Deacon?" said the Grand Elder, his teeth grinding around the word.

"I—I am, sir," he stammered.

"We still have a small chapter in Bensalem. Dwindling, but still active. I just got off the phone with our cleric there.

She believes it's time to address our problem, update our equipment, so to speak. We've disagreed on some things in the past, but I fear she may be right. It's been more than forty years since we've done so."

"Our ... equipment, sir?"

"That's a rather crass way to put it. Either way, the details are laid out in the folder on the desk. Read it. We call it the Bensalem Project. The full history and scope of the ordeal is inside. It's imperative you understand this inside and out before you get there. I certainly wish my predecessor had demanded the same of me."

The man moved towards the Grand Elder's desk. The only item upon the sprawling, lacquered surface was a three-ring binder bearing the Order's logo: a gold, trefoil cross with a red rose in the center.

The Grand Elder paused for a moment, contemplating his next words with care. "I haven't decided yet, but I'm inclined to permit the transition. However, the cleric is impetuous, desperate even, and may go ahead before she is ready. I want you there to make sure nothing goes wrong. I want you to watch the cleric, monitor her actions."

"I'm not sure I understand. What am I looking for, sir?"

The Grand Elder turned around, and as he did, a ripple of shock washed over the man. It was not that the Grand Elder's face was in any way unsightly. On the contrary, his chin was smooth, his eyes were dull, and his flat features were quite ordinary. But after eighteen years of service, not once had the Grand Elder turned around to face his top deacon. Not one time.

"You'll know when you see it. The matters with which this cleric trifles are beyond even her understanding. This job worries me, and if I'm worried, you should be terrified."

The Grand Elder walked forward and planted his hands on the desk, glaring into the man's eyes.

"We operate within the margins of the known world, sometimes needing to cross the astral plane to do our work. Hundreds of years ago, an entity more terrible than you could ever imagine crossed that plane and came out the other side in the woods of Bensalem. If the world were to find out what's in Bensalem, well ..." The Grand Elder lowered his tone to a whisper. "The world cannot know what's in Bensalem."

Something stirred in the grayness of the Grand Elder's eyes, a flash of white that seemed to emanate from some deep aspect of his essence.

"That'll be all."

"Right. U—Understood, sir."

As the man left the Grand Elder's office, three-ring binder in arm, his shoulders were slouched in a way they hadn't been when he walked in, a new weight resting upon them.

• • •

Four hours earlier, an exhausted Aaron Dreyer was on the final leg of an eight-thousand-mile journey home. After a wild bachelor bash in India, three westbound flights from hell, and hours of airport drudgery, he found himself in a land where nature lived and man did not, on a flat and naked road in the rippling hills of the Virginia Piedmont. Cattle grazed on dewy grass, stout pines dotted the landscape, and a creamy summer sun hung over the Eastern basin.

Only when he stopped at the intersection of Route 45 and Virginia State Road 639, rolled down the windows and inhaled that sweet country air, did he feel like he was home.

To his right, a pale-green sign read: WELCOME TO BENSALEM.

State Road 639 led through a rookery of low-laying structures and country shops that made up Bensalem's downtown. No one was out, and the town would have seemed quiet at this hour if it were loud at any other. A few miles past town, a dense thicket all but obscured the one-lane gravel turnoff to Wickham Road. Besides old Hank Teakle on his horse farm, Aaron, Ellen, and their four-year old, Caleb, were the only residents on Wickham Road.

Coming around a bend in the road past Hank's place, Aaron looked up at the lonely, mammoth house standing in a sunny repose at the top of a hill. It faced north over a treeless front yard and peered down on Wickham Road, as if to ask passers-by, 'Who goes there?'

The entire valley could be seen from the front door of the house. That view was the reason someone had built a structure there in the first place, and, a century-and-a-half later, the reason the Dreyers bought it.

Aaron's SUV trundled up the long driveway and he parked by the door to the back patio. Ellen, Caleb, and his eight-year-old German Shepherd were waiting for him.

Within seconds of opening the door, he was assaulted by both his dog and a sweltering summer heat.

"Okay, okay! Cooper, down! Hey, down!"

Cooper licked and jumped and grunted at his master, knocking him back into the SUV and practically jumping in after him.

Caleb's laugh rang out and Aaron's heart erupted in love. The boy was beaming and running full speed towards Aaron, a toy dinosaur sticking out from his hand. He leapt into his father's arms and giggled again as Aaron pelted him with kisses on the forehead.

"Put me down!" Caleb cried.

"My goodness, chicken, I've only been gone a week, did you get bigger? Will you stop growing, please?" Aaron said, his face pressed into clumps of his son's thick, black hair.

Caleb wriggled free. "Did you get me a present?"

"Yes, but you have to wait, Mommy gets hers first."

Practically glowing, Ellen stood leaning against the door jamb, hands in the pockets of short-sleeved medical scrubs. Her jet-black hair hung in a braid, and her smile scrunched up her eyes and nose.

"Did you get me a present?" she asked jokingly.

"And you wonder where he gets his manners."

Aaron kissed her and they embraced, squeezing hard, as if doing so would extinguish the separation that lingered in their bones and in their hearts.

"I love you so much, Ellen," Aaron whispered.

Pulling away, he took a long look at the face he'd laid his eyes upon more than any other in his thirty-three years. The girl he'd met in college was still there, just with a few more crow's feet and laughter lines that deepened as she smiled.

Ellen wrapped a hand around Caleb's head and cradled him into her hip. "Glad to have your dad back, chicken?"

"Yeah," Caleb said. "Dad, Mom showed me India on a map. That's on the other side of the world, right?"

"It is. It's the farthest I think anyone could go from here," Aaron said.

"What's it like there? Do they have the same TV shows?"

"It's too hot out here. Let's go inside and I'll tell you all about it. How's that sound?"

"Okay," Caleb said before scurrying inside. Cooper followed, leaving Aaron and Ellen alone in the driveway.

"How long's your shift today?" Aaron asked.

"Just a half, I'm covering for Sandra. That okay? I should be back by dinner."

"Of course it is. I feel bad you burned vacation for this."

"Don't. We had a nice little staycation."

Aaron took Ellen's hands and rubbed his thumbs over her knuckles. "I missed you so much."

"How are you feeling? How was the London flight?"

"Awful. The whole fucking trip back was awful from the minute I left Goa. I've been a zombie for the last thirty hours. Half-asleep and half-awake. Breathing that recycled air. Christ, I never want to fly again."

"Why don't you take a quick nap? I'm not on until noon."

"Really? You don't need a Caleb break yet?"

"Just make it a quick one and then go do something fun with Caleb this morning, yeah?"

"Great, let me just get these bags real quick."

Aaron started towards the trunk of his SUV, but Ellen, still holding his hands, clamped down and pulled him towards her. "Hey," she said, her eyes wide and her voice soft, "You have a good time? Did I get you back in one piece?"

He kissed her on the lips. "Yeah. You got me back in one piece."

"Good. We're glad you're back."

• • •

Streaks of mid-morning dancing on Aaron's face woke him in

his bed thirty minutes later. His side of the bed faced a window that looked out on the front yard, Wickham Road, and the valley. A wire fence twisted from years of neglect, lined the perimeter of the property, allowing the Dreyers to let Cooper roam around unsupervised. They were more careful with Caleb.

Across Wickham Road, a flat meadow basined low against the tree line. A field of wheat grass coated a rippling meadow, each strand a golden string standing straight up, swaying back and forth in the summer wind. Blue and white wildflowers stippled the canvas in an almost intentionally sparse pattern. At night, moonlight dyed the golden grass a deep teal, and a hollow mist would rise on the surface just before sunrise.

The eastern and western edges of the meadow across the street were flanked by towering pine forests. So tightly packed were the trees it was difficult to make out their individual shapes, but their collective blackness provided stark contrast the shimmering meadow between them. The pines stood tall, perfectly aligned, standing guard.

But as boldly as the meadow and the forests regaled their admirer, the Blue Ridge Mountains to the north stood apart as the crown jewel of the view. To some, they might have seemed underwhelming as far as mountains go. No snowy peaks trying to scrape the heavens. No jagged, otherworldly rock faces.

From Aaron Dreyer's bedroom window, they were a five-layered set of sloping horizons, each one neatly pocketed behind the next and blending a little more into the sky with distance.

And then there was the sky itself. Depending on the time or the attitude of the weather, it could be any of a hundred different hues. During the day, it was a crystal-clear pool of flawless azure. At night, it faded into a navy-blue gradient littered with stars, planets, and, if cloudless, the Milky Way. When it stormed, white-hot streaks of lightning splintered the grayness, there one second and gone forever the next. Sunsets, wild with gashes of red, orange, and purple, served as celestial revolving doors, ushering out the last fragments of the day.

A knock on the bedroom door shook Aaron from his reverie.

"Hey. You awake? Gotta get going," Ellen said.

"Hey. Yeah, I'm up," he called back.

The door opened and Caleb charged through it.

"Dad! Mom said you'd take me to Hank's. Can we?"

"Oh, did she?" Aaron asked as Caleb draped himself over his father.

"She did," Ellen said.

"Okay, go put some shoes on. No flip-flops. Can you put Cooper in his harness or you want me to do it?"

But Caleb flew out of the room as quickly as he had entered it, thumping down the stairs and leaving Aaron's question unanswered.

• • •

Aaron considered Henry "Hank" Bartholomew Teakle, the only other resident on Wickham Road, to be one of his closest friends in town, and his only true neighbor. No agrarian farming occurred on the property, and per the name, horses were his only livestock.

When Hank was a younger man, he had bred competitive racehorses, but in the wake of both local racetracks shuttering, he was forced to narrow his offering to boarding-only.

He was born in Bensalem on the same day his father left for the Pacific theater. They never met, but Hank had a happy childhood and a productive adolescence under the tutelage of his mother, who left him the horse farm when she died.

Three years ago, Hank tested the waters of retirement when his wife passed, but went back to work when he realized that he had nothing to live for. His depression spiraled further when Ethel Thomasin sold her lonely old house on the hill to live with her daughter in Blacksburg. The house, like Hank's heart, sat cold and empty for two-and-a-half years until one day, Aaron and his young family from Charlotte drove up and bought it. The promise of new neighbors brought him a level of joy he had long since forgotten, and Aaron and Caleb's near-weekly visits became the light of his life.

Aaron left for Hank's fifteen minutes after Ellen left for work. In cooler weather, he would have walked Caleb and Cooper down Wickham Road to get there, but the morning had all the signs of an absolute scorcher in the making. The air was thick, the sun was bright, and not even the faintest hint of a wind drifted through the trees.

Hank's driveway snaked up a steep and tightly-wooded hill, the same wood that bordered the meadow across the street from the Dreyers'. It ended in a gravel courtyard that faced out on a hodgepodge of buildings in various states of disrepair, some for the horses, some for Hank. Two stables, one small and the other colossal, two sheds, and an old farmhouse that doubled as Hank's office.

Cooper leapt from the SUV into the woods, barking joyously at who knows what. While he worked to unbuckle Caleb, Aaron heard Hank warbling something from the house, his voice dimmed by the immense trees between them.

"Afternoon, boys!"

Hank held an oiled cloth in his hands and bore a huge smile on his face. He walked with a slight limp, but he kept his back straight and looked sturdy. His denim overalls looked ancient but fit him like a glove. There was a zest in his face and in his gait, more so than many men of his age, especially out here where the years were hard on people.

"Hello, Caleb! How's things goin' at y'all's place?" Hank said. He took off his hat, revealing olive-green eyes and a wafer of hair that somehow floated a centimeter above his head, and he wiped a fuzzy forearm across his sweat-covered brow.

"Mr. Hank, can I ride Cocoa today?" Caleb said.

"Well, you'd better believe it there, kiddo. Got her all set for ya. Here, go give 'er a treat for me."

Hank reached into his overalls and placed three sugar cubes in Caleb's outstretched hands. Caleb ran to the big stable.

"Aaron, how you doin', old man?"

"Doin' good, Hank," Aaron said. "We're just fine. Believe it or not, I actually just got back from a trip to India. My college buddy's bachelor party."

"India? Y'all went that far for a party?"

Aaron chuckled. "Pretty wild, huh? Was there for five days and just got back a few hours ago."

"Shoot. Tell ya what, I missed that train, boy. Ain't get no bachelor party or nothin' like it. Alls I got was dinner at the in-laws. Buncha 'Yes, sirs', 'no, ma'ams', and had to keep my hands to myself, if you know what I mean."

The two of them strolled to the big stable where an almost eerie quiet hung in the air. None of the horses were visible in their carrels, and they made no noise besides soft stomps and snorts. The walls of the building were dank and musty, dark with age, and there were three yellow circles painted over the batwing double doors. The earthy smells of straw and manure and old wood filled Aaron's nostrils and wormed their way into the fabric of his clothes. In the center of the stable, Caleb stood gazing up at a chocolate-brown mare.

"You wanna try and do her bridle today?" Hank said.

"Yeah, but can you help me?"

"I wouldn't be much of a horse farmer if I couldn't."

Hank handed Caleb a web of leather straps and clutched the boy under his arms. With incredible ease and care, he lifted Caleb up to Cocoa's head and began whispering instructions.

"Okay, let me do the bit. That's the yucky part. You take this strap and put that around her ear. There ya go."

Caleb lifted a strap over the horse's ear at a slow and deliberate pace, his brow etched in concentration.

"Go ahead, you got it," Hank said. "Now do the other one. That's it. That's it."

With the bridle secure, Hank hoisted Caleb into the saddle.

"And you're ready to ride, cowboy! Feel good up there?"

"Yeah," Caleb said.

Hank guided Caleb and Cocoa twice around the whole of the property, and Aaron towed along in a calm silence.

When the Dreyers were ready to leave, Aaron packed up the SUV and whistled to the dog. Cooper came back happy and smelling of something vaguely metallic. Before Aaron started the engine, Hank leaned in through the driver's side window.

"Aaron, one more thing before ya go. You've, uh, been

here, what, 'bout, mmm, six months?"

"It'll be six months in a couple weeks, yes sir."

"Good, good. Well, I'd love to have ya over for dinner one night. Over here, that is. Just the two of us. Man-to-man sorta thing. You know, I just love you boys comin' over. Means the world to me. Daughters don't call much anymore, so, you know. It means a lot."

"Oh, gosh, well yeah, I'm flattered you'd ask. I'd really love that, sir. Let's see, what day is it? I've completely lost track."

"Today? Tuesday, last time I checked."

"How's Thursday? I think Ellen's home that night. That way it'd just be me."

"Oh, good. Yeah, that works great if it's just you. I think, uh, yeah, Thursday works perfect fer me. Like barbecue?"

"Man, I love it. I can't wait, Hank."

"Yeah, that's good. That's good. Say, uh, one more thing."

Hank reached in and put a hand on Aaron's shoulder. Something erased the joy in his face, and he glared at Aaron with a focused and stony gaze.

"There's things you'll need to know about this place if you plan to live here."

"Of course. Well, uh, I appreciate that."

"Good. Good. Okay, I'll see ya Thursday, then."

"See ya Thursday."

Hank's grin returned, and Aaron kept his eyes on it as he backed down the driveway.

• • •

Instead of heading home, Aaron forked right and got on the main road. The noonday sun rained down a fiery heat that rip-

pled the road in front of him into an oily illusion. The cab of
the SUV had baked to a crisp at Hank's, even under the shade
of the trees in his driveway. Cooper panted from the cargo
space in the back. He grinned crazily, tongue whipping up and
down, lips dripping with drool. From his car seat in the back,
Caleb's bangs quivered under the blast of the air conditioning,
which Aaron cranked to its maximum setting.

"Where we going?" Caleb asked.

"I gotta get something. We're going into town," Aaron
said.

"What?"

"I gotta get Mommy a present."

"Can I have a present, too?"

"I already gave you yours. Remember? The little train
from India?"

"Yeah, I remember, but if you're buying Mommy a present, can't you get me one, too?"

Aaron shook his head. A smirk snuck across his face.
"We'll see, chicken."

"It's my birthday soon, right? Isn't it Sep-Sep-Set—"

"—Sep-tem-ber. Try it slow. Sep-tem-ber."

"Sep-tem-ber. Dad, is that soon?"

"Kinda. Not for a couple months, though."

Caleb took a long moment before replying. "And you said
Carmen and Diego can't come to my party, right?"

Aaron sighed. "We can send invites, but they probably ar-
en't gonna be able to come. It's just too far. What about Marco
from your new school? Didn't you want to invite him?"

Caleb gazed wordlessly out the window. He sniffled, and
Aaron watched him rub a tear from his eye in the rear view.

"Oh, my buddy," Aaron said. He pulled the SUV over to

the shoulder and spun around to Caleb.

"Hey. We talked about this, remember? People move all the time. I know it's hard. Carmen and Diego are still your friends. I promise. They just live far away."

"I—I know," he sniffed.

"Listen, believe it or not, this is hard for me and Mommy, too. We're all new here. But it's okay because we have each other. You have a new school. Mommy has a new hospital. And Daddy's gonna get a new job soon." He wiped a bead of sweat from Caleb's brow, his bangs still blowing in the air conditioning. "Remember, chicken? We're in this together, right?"

Caleb nodded.

• • •

Like many small-town commercial centers in the Piedmont, Bensalem's Main Street had been reduced to a shadow of its former self. Empty boutiques cried out for help through dusty windows and faded signs. In some, forsaken wares still littered the shelves: clay jars, gaudy fridge magnets, hand-carved keychains, and other unsellable things left to rot because newly-bankrupt store owners were too exhausted or too distraught to finish the job of moving out.

The stores that did remain tried to put on their best faces, but they looked beat-up and worn-out, like mourners at a funeral. They were struggling and everyone knew it.

D.C. area tourists escaping the humidity and the traffic would swing by searching for a cute souvenir, but they didn't want "I <3 Bensalem" tee-shirts or novelty teaspoons. Women from the city would walk in, touch a few necklaces, realize they could pay half-price for something similar at a box store or online, smile, and wave goodbye.

Most of the store managers were used to those kinds of customers and stopped expecting anything from them ages ago. One of those managers, Jane Harcourt, was seventy-one and still in business at M&J Fine Gifts.

The aluminum wrapped glass door smacked a bell when Aaron swung it open. Scents of lavender soap and teak oil flooded into his nose, and the store's air conditioning coated his skin in a cool blanket of relief. Everywhere, aisles and end caps were packed to the brim with seemingly random merchandise: crystals, soaps, oils, porcelain figurines. Every inch of wall and shelf space seemed to be occupied with either an object, a picture, or a gaudy wallpaper design.

Jane manifested from behind an aisle of potted succulents and greeted the Dreyer boys, Cooper included, with sky-blue eyes and a broad smile. Two long locks of gray hair hung over her shawled shoulders.

"Sorry, I was in the back. Wrapping up a phone call with a very old friend. Help ya with somethin' today?" As if pulled by an invisible gravitational force, Jane's head cocked down towards Caleb when he came into her view. "Oh! And who is this young man?"

Caleb stared up at his father for approval. "Go ahead," Aaron said.

"Caleb."

"Why, you are quite a handsome fellow. My name is Jane. How old are you, Caleb?"

Caleb opened his mouth to speak, but Jane whipped a finger up to silence him. "Wait! Let me guess. You look like you're ... four?" she said.

"Four-and-three-quarters."

"Four-and-three-quarters! Why, you're practically as old as me!"

"Dad, can I go look at the toys?" Caleb asked.

"No, buddy, stay with me. Why don't you hold Cooper's leash for me like a big boy?"

Cooper had been sniffing everything his snout could reach since he entered the store. Aaron handed a length of the leash to Caleb but kept hold of the looped end himself.

"Now," Jane said to Aaron, "what can I help with?"

"I was hoping to buy a pair of earrings for my wife."

"Any occasion?"

"No, not really. Just want to get her something nice."

Jane steered Aaron towards a long, rectangular jewelry case. Caleb, one hand in his father's and the other holding the leash, followed quietly. Cooper was a considerably less subtle presence: panting, sniffing, lurching his great head from smell-to-smell.

Inside the case, hundreds of shimmering objects beamed up at their overhead admirers.

"Wow. A lot to look at here," Aaron said.

Smiling, Jane looked at Caleb again, and in response, Caleb glanced away and squeezed his father's hand.

"Well, what's her sign?" Jane asked.

"Her what?" Aaron asked.

Jane placed a hand on top of the case. The fingers were mangled into a lame and knotty mess, possibly crushed by some incredible force long ago or broken under the grip of a decades-long battle with arthritis. Aaron stared at those fingers a second too long before shifting his eyes up to the gold cross she wore around her neck.

"Her birthday, dear?" she asked.

"Oh, right, December 21st."

"Ah, a child of the winter solstice, then. I have just the pair for your Capricorn."

With her other hand, which appeared to be in fine physical shape, she reached for a pair of cerulean blue stones cradled in a pewter bezel.

"Now, this here, they call blue topaz. Topaz starts out a kinda murky brown, but it can turn bright blue with the right exposure to heat and light. Think she'll like these? This lighter shade, they call it Swiss Blue. Perfect for a winter solstice baby."

Aaron took the earrings from her and flipped them over. He blinked twice at the "86~" written on a sticker on the bottom of the box.

"You're local, aren't ya'?" Jane said.

"We live up on Wickham Road. The old house on the hill."

"Oh, I know the one. Ethel Thomasin lived there for many years. Quite the old soul, that one."

"Yeah, that's us now. Us and my wife Ellen. The Capricorn."

"Well then, how 'bout we call it sixty?"

"Oh, no, I can't—"

Jane smiled as she closed the jewelry case, the wrinkles around her eyes spreading the entire length of her pale cheeks. "We take care of each other here in Bensalem. You're one of us now. You, my new friend Caleb, and Ellen the Capricorn. Consider it a welcome gift. What d'ya say?"

"Wow. You've got a deal. And I'll definitely be back. Thank you, Jane, and thanks for the welcome."

Aaron paid her sixty dollars, and all three Dreyer boys left

M&J Fine Gifts, venturing into the blistering heat once again. Within minutes of being back on the road, Caleb fell asleep in his car seat. Unable to resist stealing glances of his sleeping son in the rearview, Aaron was reminded of a similar vision from five months earlier, except it was Ellen cradling the sleeping Caleb, not the car seat. They were driving from Charlotte to Bensalem, and Ellen was comforting a little boy grappling with the brutal reality of what it meant to move. He'd cried himself to sleep that day. Aaron dug his fingers into the steering wheel and watched a mirage of moisture ripple on the road ahead of him.

• • •

None of the Dreyer boys fashioned plans for a productive afternoon. Aaron was tired from jetlag, Caleb from horseback riding, and Cooper from being a long-haired dog in sweltering heat. When Ellen arrived home from work, she helped Aaron with dinner, and they put Caleb to bed as the summer sun began to set.

Aaron and Ellen soon found themselves splayed out in the Adirondack chairs on their back patio. They faced a circular firepit and rested on a bed of smooth white stones that offered Aaron's bare feet a hint of coolness. Ellen poured two generous glasses of pinot noir. They clinked glasses, kissed, and sat in silence for a succulent moment, gazing at an auburn sky, listening to millions of frogs and insects sing into the night. Cooper, catatonic on the stones, grunted at something in his sleep.

"Caleb asked about his birthday again," Aaron said.

"Oh no. Invites again?"

"Yeah."

"Poor baby. We just need to get through this year. He'll have new friends up here with a full year of school under his belt. This one's just gonna be tough."

Aaron took a big sip and craned his head back. Although summer days were hot, evenings tended to be blissfully temperate. Bensalem's elevation high above the swampish muck of the coastal lowlands meant heat didn't settle in the basin at night.

"Well?" Ellen asked.

Aaron lifted his head. "Well, what?"

"How was everything? Glad you went?"

"Honey. You know what they say. What happens in India stays in India."

"No one says that."

"It was great. The guys are great. But I feel like shit. I passed out during TV time with Caleb before I started dinner, but I'm still exhausted. My body has no idea what time it is."

"Yeah, I think jetlag's worse coming back. You need a sleeping pill tonight?"

"I don't know. Hope not."

"Well, let me know."

A gnat had fallen into Aaron's glass and drowned in the goblet of burgundy liquid. He tilted the glass and fished out the gnat, smearing its impossibly weak body against the inside of the glass. When he examined his fingertip, all that remained was an ambiguous smudge.

"Hank said something weird to me today," Aaron said.

"Huh?"

"He said he wanted me to go over there for dinner alone. Said something about needing to talk to me about this place."

"What place?"

"I don't know. The neighborhood? The town?"

Ellen laughed. "What neighborhood? He's just lonely. He wants us to feel welcome. You should go. It'd mean the world to him."

Ellen took another long sip and closed her eyes.

"Speaking of weird things. Something kind of fucked-up happened at work today. Want to hear about it?"

"Do I want to hear what an emergency room doctor considers to be a fucked-up day at work? No. No, I'm good."

"So, this kid, sixteen or seventeen I think, comes in after a four-wheeler accident. Mudding."

"I already don't like this. Can't you see we're having a pleasant evening out here? You're gonna upset the dog."

"Broken hip, broken femur, six fractured ribs, lacerations all along the left side of his body. He was separated from his friends when his accident happened. We're guessing he went into shock because he wasn't discovered until this morning. Somehow he was able to drag himself over to the side of a road and a driver called 911 for him."

"Jesus Christ. Is he alive?"

"Well, he's in a coma now, but that's not even the weird part."

"Of course that's not the weird part."

"When he came in, his vitals were so low that consciousness would have been essentially impossible. But Dr. Mirsa said that during triage, he woke up, opened his eyes, took off his oxygen mask and looked at her and said—"

The bugs weren't holding back now. They teemed with life, their rhythmic crescendos cascading over one another, building a million little murmurs into a roar. Cooper flicked an ear and twitched his paws from the depths of his unconscious.

"He said, 'It's running in the back of my dreams,' and then he put his oxygen mask back on and went out again."

"Is that the weird part?"

"Yeah. That's super weird. His brain was … off, basically. I don't know how he could have said that. I mean, people wake up all the time, but I guess it was just the way he said it. It's weird to me because Dr. Mirsa found it weird enough to tell me about it in the first place. That woman's seen some shit."

"I thought the weird part was that he was able to get himself to the side of the road with all those injuries."

"Not totally weird. Not for a teenage body in shock. You'd be surprised."

Ellen poured herself another glass. She passed the bottle to Aaron. A pale moon now poked out of a vast and quickly darkening sky. Aaron walked over to her chair and drew the jewelry box from his pocket.

"I have something for you."

Ellen gasped. "What? Aaron!"

"It's nothing. Just something I picked up. A little thank you for being cool about me taking off and going to India for a bachelor party. From me and the chicken."

She opened the box and grinned at the earrings. Her cheeks went instantly flush with blood. She became very still, save for the dropping of her head to peer intently into the crystal blue water of the stones.

"Swiss Blue topaz," Aaron said. "Topaz apparently starts out a real dark color and then turns that bright blue. You like them? I didn't know if—"

"I love them, Aaron. I love them and I love you."

"Really? Even though I'm a deadbeat and don't have a job and run off to India with my friends?"

Ellen lifted her head. Some part of the shine of those stones had been instantly captured in her eyes, and it magnified her beauty as Aaron gazed upon her.

"I know who you are," she said. "You have great friends. You're a great dad. A great man. I love you. We're in this together. All of us. You know that."

She closed the case, put a hand on his cheek, and kissed him.

"Now take me upstairs."

In one motion, Aaron rose from the ground with his wife in his arms, her long black hair draped over him. A pop in his knee caused him to stumble briefly before getting his bearings again. He put her down and they smiled bashfully at each other.

"Are you weaker or am I fatter?" Ellen said.

"I'm weaker," he said.

"Smart answer. Come on, party animal."

Aaron led her inside.

• • •

Hours later, Aaron had still not fallen asleep. Ellen laid on her side, faintly snoring next to him. He got up, went downstairs and opened the door to the patio. Ellen's half-full wine glass still sat on the arm of her chair.

The sun had set long ago and now the moon waxed gibbous in the sky, its paling light drenching the terrain in a glow for miles in every direction. Around him, the symphony of little creatures continued in the shrubs, clicking and wailing and chittering over each other. An owl twit-twooed, and swallows and bats swooped in and out of the tree line. Behind it all, the

Blue Ridge Mountains stood in the background, watching over everything in the valley.

Those mountains had seen more sunrises and sunsets than one could ever fathom. They'd seen countless cycles of life and death only to wake up and watch it all unfold again. They'd seen things humans would never believe. Things that shouldn't have existed in the first place, that even they were not meant to see.

He picked up the wine glass and went back inside to grapple with the reality of being wide awake at 2:00am. The old floorboards whined in the silence of the night as he tip-toed to the living room. He collapsed on the couch. Windows overlooking the front yard and the valley lined the wall behind him, pulling in blue light from outside and splashing it across the room in random, almost alien shapes.

On the opposite wall, a television hung over a fireplace. Aaron surfed channels until miraculously stumbling upon the same Bollywood movie he had fallen asleep to during the flight from Mumbai to London, 'Dilwale Dulhania Le Jayenge'. The main character, Raj, was in the middle of a Jerry Lee Lewis impression so painfully embarrassing, the cheese practically leapt off the screen.

When the movie ended, he laid silently in the dark. One at a time, he unshackled himself from the burdens of his long trip home. The stress of those mad house international airports, the cruel stiffness of two dozen hours of being sardined into economy-class window seats, the worry of his bags ending up halfway around the world from him. But all was right in the Dreyer household. His son and his dog were safe and happy. His wife was as strong and beautiful and wonderful as ever. He stared at the blank ceiling. He listened to nothing. He thought about nothing.

But from that nothingness, something arose. A click-clacking of claws on hardwood, perforating the stillness. It started faintly and grew louder, closer, until a pair of glowing, yellow eyes suddenly stared back at Aaron from the center of the room. Cooper's eyes. Cooper stood there watching, alert. Aaron pushed himself up off the couch.

"You okay? Come here."

But the dog did not heed his owner, instead lumbering through the living room to the front door. The door, too, faced the front yard and the meadow across the street.

"You need to go out?"

With his nose an inch from the solid oak door and his eyes staring right into it, Cooper's ears pinned themselves back, and his upper lip curled, exposing a trap of lethal white teeth. His tail, which usually bounced along as he walked, divined itself straight down towards the ground, and his back legs began to quiver. Cooper glared at the door, shaking slightly, growling in a triggered rage.

"Cooper, knock that off."

Aaron stood and faced the living room windows. Nothing seemed out of place in the front yard or the meadow, but Cooper continued to growl, his volume low enough not to wake Ellen or Caleb, but so downright out of place for a dog of his character that Aaron kept his distance.

Then, like a photo somehow coming alive, a dark object moved on the perfectly-still canvas. A shadow at the edge of the pine forest on the right-hand side of the meadow pulled itself out of the thick black trees.

Aaron tried to look closer, to look harder, but he was more than two hundred yards away from whatever it was. But even from such a distance, its scale against the trees told Aaron it was of some unnaturally great size. He walked softly to within inches of the window and squinted. The moonlight was weak, and from this far, the shadow resembled only a dark gray blob.

He crossed behind Cooper, who paid him no mind, and into a room the family intended to use as an office but hadn't furnished yet, save for a desk and a landline phone. An analog clock on the wall read 4:03am.

Rifling through a box in the corner, he pulled out a pair of binoculars. He returned to the living room, put the binoculars to his eyes and guided his thumb over the focus dial to sharpen the picture. Finally focusing on the object, Aaron gasped at what he saw.

An utterly baffling and gargantuan organism plodded through the meadow's wheat grass. It appeared to be walking on two legs that supported an upright frame, almost humanoid, but definitely not human. Some sort of ethereal mist floated around its body, blurring the specifics of whatever was underneath.

A bitter chill trundled up Aaron's spine, starting in his lower back and resting at the base of his skull, where pressure began to build. Cooper began mixing low barks in with his growls.

The binoculars nearly slipped out of Aaron's sweaty hands when he raised them to his eyes for a second time. The picture was still cloudy, poorly lit, and too far away. All he was certain of was its immense size. Deer in that exact spot in the meadow would have looked like rodents in comparison.

The creature continued to trudge through the meadow, and the pressure in Aaron's skull became so great he winced in pain. He dropped the binoculars and fell to his knees, clutching his head with both hands. A shrill ring inside his eardrums began to build, and Cooper's anxiety only compounded the vicious cacophony in his head.

"Ahh, God! The fuck is happening?"

The room spun. His eardrums throbbed. His heart rate ticked up, and up, and up, so much so that his lungs couldn't keep pace and he started hyperventilating. The noise from Cooper took an odd turn towards howling, as if he was attempting to communicate, but he didn't budge from his station at the door.

Aaron reached a hand to the windowsill to steady himself, and he opened his eyes for the first time in minutes. The volume in his ears began to decrease and a sudden release of pressure in his skull gave him the strength to stand again. Cooper simmered to his initial register of tepid growling.

Aaron picked up the binoculars and searched the hazy meadow for the creature, but no sign of it could be found. Cooper stopped growling altogether and stood motionless at the door, still staring into that hard oak, still unwavering in his defensive stance. Then, he simply turned around and click-clacked back upstairs.

All that resided in the meadow at that moment was a tranquil, pre-dawn mist that hovered on the grass. Aaron scoured the mist through the binoculars, up and down, forwards and backwards. Nothing. The edges of the forest, too, were smooth and unadulterated, doing well to hide evidence of whatever chaotic presence had just passed through them. The moon was gone now, recently replaced by a thin line of redness tracing along the edge of the mountains.

Aaron had gripped the binoculars for so long and with

such force that a dry layer of sweat peeled off his palms when he finally put them down, as if they were now a part of his anatomy and reluctant to be severed from their host.

"What in the ever-living fuck was that?" Aaron said.

He returned upstairs and laid sleeplessly in bed until the sun rose over the mountains.

DAY 2

Whatever fragments of sleep Aaron stole from the early morning hours left him ill-equipped to deal with the headache that struck him just before 8am. Muffled voices and thumps from the living room floated up from downstairs, and Aaron threw off the duvet. He kept his feet planted on the floor for a moment, making sure to find his balance before heading to the bathroom. After splashing cold water on his face and taking an anti-inflammatory, he joined his family. Ellen sat slouched in an armchair with a mug of coffee in both hands and a half-smile on her face. Caleb's head rested in her lap as he stared up at the squawking television.

"Morning," Ellen said.

"Morning," Aaron replied.

Aaron leaned over the pair and kissed them. Caleb swatted his father away in annoyance for blocking the television.

"What's going on with you guys?" Aaron asked.

"You're lookin' at it," Ellen said.

"Where's the dog?"

"I dunno. Around somewhere."

The tiniest of reflections from the sun glinted in the lens of the binoculars, sitting on an end table by the couch. Aaron picked them up and turned them over in his hands, studying them and screwing his face into a scowl of confusion. He began to draw them upward but stopped halfway.

"Hey. Can I talk to you for a second?" he said.

Ellen yawned. "What's up?"

"In the kitchen."

"But look at how comfortable I am."

"Only be a minute."

Aaron took the binoculars with him and set them on the kitchen counter. He fixed himself a cup of coffee. Ellen shuffled in and sat at the table.

"Bird watching?" she asked.

"I wish."

"What's up? You didn't get any sleep, did you?"

"No, and my head is killing."

"Get some sleep today. I'm working tonight, so use the day to rest up."

"That's not what I wanted to talk about." Aaron joined her at the table and took a long sip of coffee. "This is gonna sound wild," he sighed, "but I saw something fucking crazy last night."

"Huh?"

"I don't know what it was, but it looked like a gigantic person or creature or something out in the meadow across the street."

"Might have been a bear."

"Do bears walk on two legs?"

"Not naturally. I mean, I'm not an expert on bears." Ellen shifted in her chair and put down her mug.

"Listen, remember how you said a few weeks ago you heard Cooper growling in the middle of the night?"

"Oh yeah. Constantly. Usually around four when I'm getting ready for morning shifts."

"I was down here last night, and he started growling. It was crazy. I couldn't sleep from the jetlag, so I tried to relax on the couch, and all of a sudden Cooper just came right up to the front door and started growling. I looked outside and I saw this ... I don't even know how to describe it. It was huge, and it was walking around out there."

Aaron paused to let his wife reply, but all she offered him was a baffled look.

"But listen to this," he continued, "while I was looking at it, I had this really fucked up physical reaction."

"What ... kind of reaction?"

"Like my head started pounding and I could barely see straight. My ears started ringing. I felt like I was gonna pass out."

"Could be your blood sugar's out of whack. Your body is on virtually no sleep and doesn't know what time zone it's in."

"Did you not hear any of this last night?"

"No. I was dead last night."

Aaron dropped his head into his hands and rubbed his temples. "God, this hurts. I still have a headache from it."

"You seem worried."

"I am. I think something's out there. Watching us ... I don't like it one bit."

"But you don't know what it is."

Aaron shook his head.

"I don't know what to tell you. You're locking the doors, right?"

"I think I want to set some lights up. Cooper obviously sees something, or senses it, at least. Maybe in the light, I can get a better look at whatever it is."

Ellen's face broke into a grin before collapsing into an uncontrolled burst of laughter.

"What?"

"Nothing," Ellen said, shaking her head. "You do you. If I were you, I'd get some sleep. I think that's your problem."

• • •

Two hours later, Aaron's eyelids felt like lead weights as he struggled to stay awake on the interstate. The inside of the SUV baked him in a dry, static heat, even with the air conditioning at full blast.

"Jesus fuck, it's hot," he said.

Markers of a civilization grander than the one in Bensalem populated the sides of the four-lane road. Fast-food chains, car dealerships, strip malls. A concrete-walled office building with black-tinted windows reminded Aaron of the hotel he'd stayed at in Mumbai with his friends. The rest of them were there for another two days. Only Aaron had left early, and right now, they were either in that hotel or had just left for another night on the town. Where would they be partying tonight? What old story would they be laughing about while Aaron installed a rag-tag security system in his front yard?

He pulled into the asphalt tundra in front of Home Depot and parked by a sad little oasis of an island where a single sapling offered the SUV meager shade. Upon opening his door, the stuffy summer promptly wrapped him in a blanket of agony, as if chastising him for pursuing such an endeavor.

Two sets of motion-activated double doors slid open, and the elements of the place engulfed him. Smells of wood, paint, dust, and dirt. Sounds of random clanking and 70's soft rock.

He lapped the entire store, including the outdoor gardening section, several times before procuring the necessary items: three 500-watt halogen flood lights, a half dozen industrial strength 100-foot extension cords, and a three-way grounded power tap. In a less beleaguered state, he would have swung by the power tools just to see what looked cool, but every time his mind tried to relax, the creature from the meadow crept back in.

A cashier — named Patti, according to the magic marker script on her apron — rang him up.

Power-walking through the bustling box store had kindled an energy within him he did not have on the way in. He practically bounded to the SUV, barely noticing the cab was so hot he began sweating within seconds of closing the door.

Not once did he consider the ways in which this could prove disastrous.

• • •

"Dad! Dad, come look!" Caleb cried from across the front yard.

Aaron turned around to see Caleb scampering towards him. The afternoon sun shimmered off his shirtless chest, lacquered with water from his inflatable water slide. His black hair formed a damp skull cap over his ears and forehead, and neon-green swim goggles hugged his face. Even with the lenses completely fogged over, he seemed able to see.

"Watch me slide down!"

"Hold on, bud," Aaron said, crouched over a floodlight. With both hands on its frame, he shoved his bodyweight down, driving a stake attached to its bottom further into the earth.

"Come watch me!"

"Hold on, I need your help. I need your muscles to get this into the ground. Think you can do it?"

Caleb beamed, and he trotted around to his father's side.

"Hop up there," Aaron said, pointing to his back.

Caleb slipped and squirmed his wet body onto Aaron's back. Aaron's tee-shirt was already soaked from the heat with sweat.

"What do I do now?" Caleb asked.

"Push down on my back, really hard. You be the hammer and I'll be the nail. Ready?"

Caleb thumped his chest down onto his father's back, who in turn pressed down on the floodlight.

"One more time," Aaron said. Caleb thumped himself down again.

"Is it working?" Caleb said.

"Almost! One more. Make it a really big one."

Caleb took a deep breath and closed his eyes. With his arms around his father's neck and his legs wrapped around his waist, he slammed his chest down so hard that it bounced a grunt out of him.

"Hey boys!" Ellen's voice called down from the house, cutting through swarms of overlapping cicada calls and filling the front yard. "What's happening here?"

Caleb whipped his head towards her and yelled. "I'm helping Daddy!"

"Wow, bud, great job," Ellen said, not masking her disbelief.

Aaron rose with Caleb still attached to him. He wiped his palms on his jeans. "You headed to work?"

"Yeah," she said, walking towards them. "I'll be back around eight."

When she reached them, the smell of her perfume cut through the swell of natural scents, of grass and dirt and sweat that had settled in Aaron's nostrils. She planted a kiss on Caleb's wet forehead and Aaron's cheek.

"I love you," Aaron said.

"Love you, too. Don't get heatstroke."

"Mom!" Caleb cried. "Can you come watch me slide?"

• • •

After setting up the lights and enjoying a late dinner, Aaron persuaded both Caleb and Cooper to snuggle with him on the sofa in the living room while they watched television. Caleb fell asleep on his dad's chest and Cooper fell asleep at his feet. Aaron stroked the hair back from his son's forehead over and over again. He looked at the boy's face, free from care and the hardness of time, his little wet lips open in a sleep-induced frown, a stuffed dinosaur glued to the inside of his elbow.

With Caleb tucked into his proper bed a few hours later, Aaron took Cooper out back one last time to pee. An army of night crickets roared. The air was still warm, but cooling fast, and soon it might even be chilly. On any other night, Aaron would have gotten the firepit going and killed a bottle of wine by himself. But looking at Cooper and remembering the way his yellow eyes had peered at him in the darkness wrapped a cold hand around his heart. He felt goosebumps rise on his forearms and the back of his neck. Triggered by nothing but his own ruminations of massive, misty creatures in the woods, he swiveled his head from side-to-side, scanning the terrain for any sign of disturbance.

"Come on, Cooper. Hurry up and pee. I don't wanna be out here."

Back inside, he paced over to a power outlet lodged next to the front door and under the living room window. The window was cracked open a half-inch, and through it, the male end of an extension cord hung and rested on the floor. He plugged it in, and a blanket of white light poured into the front yard and every corner of the meadow across the street. It even lit up the edges of the forest, dipping their blackness in a layer of dark green paint.

"Let's get a good look at you, motherfucker," he whispered.

Cooper laid half-asleep on his side at the foot of the stairs. Aaron rested one hand on the dog's skull and scratched his belly with the other.

"Good boy. You're such a good boy. You tell me if the bad guys come."

Cooper pushed a heavy breath through his nostrils and closed his eyes, and Aaron returned to the couch. He sank into the cushions, but unlike the night before, physical comfort did not unshackle him from his mental burdens. He sighed, and, staring up at the ceiling, searched to no avail for the same nothingness he had seen in it the night before. That nothingness was gone, instead replaced by the dull glow of floodlights from the front yard. The hum of the night bugs seeped in through the window, still open slightly over the extension cord.

• • •

A shattering clang jarred Aaron from his sleep. It stopped, clanged again, and only now did Aaron realize it was landline telephone in the office. Its shrill and sudden shriek ripped through the quiet night like a crazed banshee, and in first few moments of Aaron's confused state of waking, his heart rate started skyrocketing.

"Jesus! Fuck!"

Cooper sprang from his spot on the floor and started barking. He did not approach the door but paced about the room shooting his canine cries in all directions: at Aaron, at the phone, towards the floor and up at the ceiling. Unlike last night, the look in his eyes was not one of a focused and assertive rage. This time they bulged, the whole of his irises visible against a white backdrop of fear, and they darted madly back and forth in their sockets. The room itself appeared unchanged from when Aaron had closed his eyes to sleep. Soft light on the ceiling, deep light on the yard and the meadow. Caleb was still upstairs, thank God, and hopefully able to sleep through the madness.

Unable to help himself to a peek at the meadow on his way over to the phone, Aaron saw nothing he hadn't seen out there before he went to bed. Nothing in the yard, nothing in the meadow, all the lights working. No moon, no mist, and no sign of any creature. As he strode over to the office, his legs still stiff from such a sudden conjuring, a dull chill began working its way through his body, and his heart pounded so hard he could feel the individual valves opening and closing as blood surged through them.

But as he picked up the receiver and lifted it to his ear, Aaron knew it was not the cacophony of sound alone that had sent his heart racing at a breakneck pace. Rather, it was the collection of every natural instinct he possessed, screaming at him that something about this phone call was deeply, horribly wrong.

He choked out a whisper. "Hello?"

Waves of odd, rough static echoed through the phone. Its swooping tone and hectic pattern reminded him of listening to a far-off AM radio station, where it seemed like something clear existed somewhere but was being warped out of control by a much more powerful intervening force. Cooper's barks continued to rip through the house.

"H—Hello? Who's there?" Aaron said into the void.

But only that howling static replied, until finally another sound, an awful sound, broke through above the static.

"... ohhhh ... gayyyyeee ..."

Aaron gulped down a lump of fear, his throat clicking as it passed through him. "What? H—Hello?"

"... ohhhhpahhh ... gayyyyttteee ..."

The voice Aaron heard was dreadful, alien, like a robot trying to speak with a mouthful of gravel. It didn't even sound like a real voice, more like a loud whisper or a thousand muffled cries trying to corral themselves into a single scream. It was a stiff, guttural drone, low and otherworldly, and it stripped Aaron of any sense of physical security. Cooper's incessant barking, growling and snapping didn't aid the situation.

"... ohhhh-paahhnnn ... theee ... gayyyyttteee ..."

The swooping static behind the voice had been getting louder since the call started, and now it was almost deafening. The voice struggled to push through it, as if its owner hadn't used it in a very long time.

All at once the line went completely silent, and a second later, in perfect clarity, the voice from the other side of the universe boomed into his ear.

"OPEN THE GATE!"

The line went dead, and a tinny dial tone jeered at him through the receiver.

Fear engulfed him where he stood. He released a punctured gasp. Goosebumps popped on his arms and the back of his neck. His ears rang and throbbed with blood, and his heart was a huge, hot coal burning inside his chest.

With the phone still in his hand, the dial tone still cackling at him from the abyss, Aaron watched Cooper growling through the window. He hung up the phone and put the binoculars to his eyes, and he could feel his throat tighten as his thumb fumbled over the focus. Here and there, a blade of wheat grass twitched in the wind, and moths flitted with fascination in the beam of the floodlights. But besides that, nothing. He glanced at the analog clock on the office wall: 4:08am.

Beside him, Cooper relaxed his posture and began panting, indicating that whatever had just happened was over as far as he was concerned, and the house fell silent again. So silent that Aaron had to stare at his dog for a beat to make sure the whole episode hadn't occurred in his head.

"Caleb," he whispered.

Flipping on every light switch in his path, Aaron darted upstairs to Caleb's room. Miraculously, the boy was still asleep, but Aaron's relief evaporated when he moved closer and saw Caleb's lips quivering. He appeared to be mouthing words in his sleep, and under the paper-thin, veiny skin of his eyelids, his eyeballs rocketed back and forth. A thick band of sweat had formed on his concerned and focused brow.

Aaron sat down on the bed and jostled Caleb's shoulders. "Caleb. Hey, Caleb. Caleb!"

Caleb's eyes shot open, and his face went bone-white. He seemed to be looking through his father, still entranced by whatever visions had held him in his dreams.

"It's me. It's Daddy. You okay? You had a bad dream. It's just a dream. I'm here. Daddy's here."

Caleb burst into tears and Aaron scooped him up in his arms. Caleb wailed into the night, Aaron sniffled into the crook of his son's neck, and they gripped each other tightly in the darkness.

PART II

DAY 3

In the waning hours of that day, another phone call took place in Bensalem, this one on the other side of town and under very different circumstances.

The cleric, after determining she'd encounter no one else for the evening, walked over to the wall where a long tapestry hung. She brushed it back with one hand and twisted the hidden doorknob it exposed with the other. The door's hinges creaked under the strain of being activated after a long slumber, and dust from the plaster supporting its frame fell to the ground.

She followed a short, cold hallway lined with moldy brick to a dark and cavernous room. The stench of mildew and decay would have withered less hardened olfactory receptors, but she was no stranger to smells both fantastic and vile. Her craft required such tolerances.

Three dust-covered candles sat merged together by their melted wax on a small, wooden table by the room's entrance.

She lit them, and then she sent a sharp blow into the fingerplate of an old rotary phone clamped to the wall over the table. One-by-one, she dialed the numbers. The call's recipient picked up on the second ring.

"Yes?" said the voice on the other side.

"Good evening, Grand Elder."

"Good evening to you, Cleric. It's been quite some time since I've seen this number. The lab phone, if I recall correctly?"

"You recall correctly."

"Then I take this call to mean you've decided to move forward with the transition?"

"We have."

"We?"

"Myself and our remaining members. We're not all gone yet."

"I'm glad to hear that. It may be no secret to you that your depleted ranks are a worry to me, especially under the circumstances, but I understand the need for—"

"You do not understand our needs. You never have. That's not why I'm calling."

"Alright. Why are you calling, then?"

"Because after this transition is complete, I am going to New Atlantis. I'm too old. I'm too heartbroken. All I want is my son back, no matter what state he is in. I'm close to death, and the only sight I desire to see before I meet the New King is that of my son."

"If you leave, who will continue the work of the Bensalem Project?"

"That won't be my problem. After this transition, you'll have forty, maybe fifty years to figure it out."

The Grand Elder sighed. "You've identified a viable replacement for the sentinel?"

"I have."

"Set on a cover story?"

"We are. You may not remember, but we have ties to enforcers of mortal law here. He's not a member of the Order but he's agreed to help us many times over the years."

"And you still have access to the chemicals and materials required? Will you be performing the alchemy yourself?"

"You forget with whom you speak, Grand Elder. Do not meddle in our affairs, in my affairs. The years have dulled many parts of my being, but not my skills in the lab. I will perform the transformational alchemy myself, and I have everything I need."

"Yes, I apolog—"

"You would do well to remember that our chapter has always had everything we've needed out of necessity. This work is so rooted in the history of who we are that you or anyone from the headquarters could never possibly understand."

The Grand Elder grumbled. "That may be so, but it is you, Cleric, who would do well to remember that the mistakes of your ancestors created this problem in the first place. Do not pretend to know my place within the workings of the history of the Order. Yours is but one of the situations throughout the world that I am responsible for handling, just one of the secrets that is incumbent upon me to protect."

The cleric blew out the candles and began to hang up the receiver, but the Grand Elder continued.

"And if you were to fail, it is not you who would have to clean up the mess, but me. Because by the time I hear about it, the world will already know what you've been hiding there all these centuries, and you'll be dead. In fact, you may be the first one it comes for."

"I would welcome it! I do not fear the one of which you speak. I know the composition of the pestilence and my people rattle in the gale of its movement. I see it in my dreams, and I see it through the eyes of my son. I walk alongside it in the earth's darkness. I have seen the contents of its black being because it has lived in my mind for forty long years—oh, and it has ravaged me. But here I stand, still defiant, still alive, still fighting it. Where are you? Locked in your gilded tower? Will you stay there regardless of what happens to me, or to my son, or to my town? I spit at your fear. You fear it because you do not know it. That's the difference between us."

The cleric hung up the phone.

• • •

Deputy Sheriff Cheryl "Mac" McNamara flicked on the flashers. In front of her, a derelict and low-riding sedan swerved through multiple lanes on the interstate just north of Bensalem. Gazing at the red and blue lights whipping through the Saturn decal on the back of the car, she remembered the company's old slogan.

"'A new kinda car company'", she said aloud.

The sedan pulled over and Cheryl steeled herself as she approached. A gross, brown gas choked out from its muffler. She shone her flashlight at the driver, a mousy-looking young man with his eyes closed and his mouth open. She tapped on the glass. No reaction. She tapped again.

"Scoot, roll down this window, please."

The driver rocked his head forward, as if jarred into coherence, and obeyed.

"Ahh, I'm—I'm so sorry, Mrs. McNamara, I—" he said.

"Deputy McNamara, please. We're not on the baseball diamond and I'm not Lenny's mother right now. Do you know why I pulled you over, Scoot?"

"Well ... I ... I'm pretty drunk." His eyes drifted shut again and his jaw flung open, as if all the muscles in his face suddenly deactivated. A wild stench of bourbon and old-car-smell wafted out from the cab as Cheryl leaned her head closer. Shining her light in the passenger seat revealed a few strewn-around CD cases, and in the passenger side wheel well, two empty beer cans.

Walter "Scoot" Hampton had it tougher than most kids in Bensalem. His parents had split when he was a toddler, and his mother had been in and out of rehab for most of his teenage years. He played baseball with Cheryl's son, Lenny, all the way from the under-10's up to varsity at Bensalem Senior High. He was a sharp third baseman and fast as hell on the base paths, which was how he'd acquired his nickname. He set a school record for stealing home four times his senior year, earning his name an etching onto a plaque alongside other names of boys and girls who'd peaked before the age of 18. The plaque sat in the back of a dusty plexiglass trophy case where no one would ever find it unless they sought it out.

"At least you didn't lie. Woulda made this a whole lot harder," Cheryl said to a now-sleeping Scott. She leaned forward, ready to push him awake, but a deep, content snore stopped her. Instead, she buzzed into her walkie. "Dispatch, ten-fifty-one southbound on Route 231. Walter Hampton again. Room at the inn?"

"Copy, there's room," buzzed back Officer Derek Brady.

In her view, Brady was a talented young cop with a good heart, if not sometimes a little rough around the edges. Only because she liked him did it not bother her that he was ahead of her in line to be Sheriff, at least as far as the electorate was concerned. Even though she had about twenty years on him, he had the connections and a politician's charm. Plus, he wasn't a transplant. Brady was one of the few kids in Bensalem who was going to both turn out okay and stay in town.

Lenny McNamara only achieved one of those things. He was in his third year of a five-year Civil Engineering program at Virginia Tech, setting him on a very-much-okay path far away from a town he hated. That was Cheryl's reward for being a good mom.

Flipping the flashlight around in her hand, Cheryl rapped on the car door three times, sending a sharp series of metallic bangs rifling through the night. The muscles in Scoot's pencil-thin neck gave out, and his jaw swung from pointing straight out to plummeting into his chest. He belched into his lap.

"Jesus Christ, man," she said.

Cheryl stuck her head through the window, careful not to put her face within firing range of a potential firehose of vomit. She shined her light over his seatbelt buckle and jammed her thumb on the big red button, releasing the belt with a snap.

"Come on, Scoot. Time's a wastin.'"

With Scoot's arm draped over her shoulders, Cheryl led him to her patrol car and spilled him in the back seat. Some kind of dirty residue now coated her hands. She cringed and wiped them on her standard issue pants.

With Sheriff Duke Quinlan on vacation at Nags Head

through the next week, Cheryl was the commanding officer of the Bensalem Sheriff's Department. Originally from Vermont, her lack of Bensalem birthright required her to try harder to be viewed as an equal in the community. As an officer, she'd had to work a source a little longer than most to obtain usable info. As a mom, she'd had to bake a few extra cupcakes for the bake sale.

"They're just gettin' used to ya, bug," her husband Rick would say.

Back on the road, the sight of Scoot's reflection in her rear-view mirror forced her to ask herself how a boy like that could ever find his way out of the woods. Jail? Military? Seeing him back there reminded her of Lenny again. Her son was probably just as drunk right this minute, but "safe" in a frat house or somewhere else on campus.

The thought of one child's safety naturally led her to wonder about the other. Skylar McNamara was five years Lenny's junior and Cheryl's most relentless source of worry. Cheryl felt an aching in her gut every time Skylar stayed out too late, came home smelling like pot, or started tongue-lashing her mother for no apparent reason.

The radio crackled on. "Deputy McNamara? Come in, please."

"Copy. What's up, Derek?"

"Yeah, we've got a, um—",

"Come on, now, what's up?"

"It's, uh, officially, it's a CPR call, but sounds like the caller says it's a homicide."

"You askin' or tellin', Derek? Talk to me."

She figured he was tellin' but never had to call in anything like this before. He may never have even seen a dead body in his life. Homicides happened in Bensalem once a decade or

so. The only one Cheryl had seen in her twenty-one years with
the department was an open-and-shut meth deal gone wrong.
Years before that, the town had achieved brief notoriety for
the Loveless Murders, when Elliott Granger murdered his
business partner's family over money. Granger had broken into
the Loveless' house in the dead of night, and one-by-one, shot
Patton Loveless, his wife Beverly, their three children, and even
the dog. That bloodbath happened before Cheryl's time.

"I'm tellin', Deputy. Hank's Horse Farm on Wickham
Road off 639. Know it? Stable hand went up there to start
work and found the owner outside. Apparently, it's … I don't
know, kinda nasty."

A ball of stress formed in Cheryl's right foot, causing
her to errantly tap the gas pedal and send Scoot's lifeless torso
forward into his taut seatbelt with a drunken grunt. The stress
rose up through her legs and hips and into her chest where it
settled, pressing on her lungs and shortening her breath.

"Let's keep it professional," she said into the radio. "Public
channel. Is the area secure? You call Virginia State Police?"

"Yes, apologies, ma'am. No, I don't believe the area is
secure. I just got the call. I was gonna send Officer Nelson out
there since she's here with me. I can call VSP right now if you
want."

"Don't love the idea of sending Monica out there, six
months' pregnant and all. Might be a welcoming party waitin'
for us."

"Ten-four. What do you wanna do, then?"

"Is EMT over there? What's the scene look like?"

"Witness was alone when we spoke. Sounds like a lot of
blood. Heavy lacerations. She didn't get too close, understand-
ably. You want me to call Duke?"

"Sure don't. Let's see if we can't handle this ourselves. Though I already don't like the sound of this. The messier it is, the more people, more paperwork, more cleanup it'll be for us."

A thud from the backseat told her Scoot had slid sideways and smacked his forehead against the window.

"What's the witness' name?" she said.

"Taylor McMurray. She works, er, worked for Hank as a stable hand. Female Taylor, just to clarify," Brady said.

"Ten-four. Okay, send Monica and instruct her to secure the witness but wait on the crime scene. If you can, call Taylor back and tell her to get to a safe place until Monica arrives."

"Ten-four."

"Now, she'll get there before me, but I'm gonna ride out there now and send my ten-fifty-one back with her, then I'll go up. Don't want a drunk boy or a pregnant woman hangin' around there."

"Ten-four. You sure you don't wanna call Duke?"

"Depends on what I find. In fact, wait on calling VSP until I get there, too. Should be there by 6:30. Reckon we'll end up calling both, though."

"Ten-four. Here if you need me. Good luck, Deputy."

Cheryl put down the radio and sighed. On the road in front of her, an orange semi-circle poking above the mountains beckoned her forward, and a chill from the last vestiges of night sent a shiver across her skin.

• • •

A faint voice called to Aaron from the depths of his unconscious. "Daddy. Where were you?"

When he opened his eyes, morning light streamed through the bedroom window. Under the warm duvet and back in his own bed, his limbs felt weightless and rejuvenated in a way they hadn't felt in days, not quite rested but getting there. He pulled his right knee towards his chest, but something blocked it, something hard, and Aaron opened his eyes.

Caleb was kneeling on the bed beside him, silhouetted in front of the mountains through the window that overlooked the valley.

It took a moment, but a memory from last night crept into focus as he stared at his son: Aaron carrying Caleb to the master bed upon relenting to shared sleeping arrangements for the rest of the night. Aaron had tried to coax the contents of the nightmare out of his son, but Caleb locked it away and fell swiftly asleep, cradled by the scent of his mother and arms of his father.

Over Caleb's shoulder, the neon red digits of Aaron's alarm clock read 7:26 a.m. His hair, usually straight and flat against his skull, sprang outward in all directions and a delicate yellow crust lived along his eyelids. He wore only the tee shirt Aaron had dressed him in last night, his bottom half completely naked. "I'm sorry," Caleb said. In his outstretched hand, he held a bar of soap from the bathroom.

"What's that, chicken?"

Caleb swallowed and looked down at the bed. "I winkled."

Aaron pulled away the duvet to reveal a darkened circle in the sheets on Ellen's side of the bed. "Oh ..."

Every muscle in Caleb's face hardened and his cheeks swelled with redness. He burst into tears.

No matter the circumstance, that look on Caleb's face would never fail to send his father's heart reeling. Aaron felt something in his chest drop, as if a new dimension of gravity had suddenly opened up inside him, and all of his emotions converged into a fierce fire of love for his son. He wrapped both arms around Caleb and pulled him into a tight hug, lodging his mouth on his head and kissing it through that jungle of hair.

Aaron didn't respond with words at first. He shushed into Caleb's ear while the boy cried into his father's chest.

"Oh, my sweet, boy. My boy. I love you so much, baby. Hush, baby. Hussshhh."

But Caleb did not heed his father's words. His cries grew louder, his little chest heaved heavier, and Aaron felt his minnow-like arm muscles turn to stone.

"Don't you worry about that. Daddy's not mad," he said with a laugh. "I love you so much."

Finally, Caleb squirmed his head free and pulled back, his face beet-red and his nose and mouth covered in snot.

"Don't worry about that, okay?"

"But I'm a big boy and that's baby stuff."

"No, no. Accidents happen, it isn't your fault. We won't tell Mommy, okay?"

Caleb nodded.

"Hey, you were having some nightmares last night. That's why you slept in Daddy's bed, remember? Do you want to talk about it? Do you remember them at all?"

Caleb shook his head. "No. Can we have McDonald's?"

Aaron laughed at his son's sudden change of focus.

"Sleeping in Daddy's bed, and now McDonalds?"

"Well, but, you said you're not mad!"

Aaron put a hand to Caleb's face and wiped another tear.

"I'm the furthest thing from it, chicken. Go get dressed and we'll go to McDonalds. Let's try and get back before Mommy comes home. She should be ..." He twisted towards his nightstand, releasing two dry cracks from his spine, and pulled his alarm clock towards him: 7:34 a.m. "I think we'll just make it home in time before she comes back."

· · ·

When Cheryl made the turn onto Wickham Road, she saw Officer Monica Nelson's patrol car parked neatly in front of Hank's long driveway. She released a heavy sigh of relief after scanning the entrance to the property and noticing nothing grisly from down here on the road.

Monica sat on the hood of her unit, and Taylor McMurray, the stable hand who'd called it in, sat next to her. Black streaks of mascara ran down Taylor's cheeks and Monica held one of Taylor's hands in both of hers.

The two young women already knew each other well, having played volleyball together in high school. Monica was a prolific libero on the court and the captain of the team when Taylor, two years younger, got called up from J.V. A few years ago, they were plotting to beat Quincy Central. Now they were trying to grapple with what might be the ghastliest crime Bensalem had seen in decades.

Cheryl had never contained a homicide crime scene before, but she knew exactly what to do, even if it required a little improvisation. She strode up to them with a straight back and a stiff jaw.

"Officer Nelson, good to see you," Cheryl said. "Do me

a favor and take the ten-fifty-one in the back of my unit, cuff him, put him in yours and ask him to take a nap."

"Yes ma'am," Monica said, sliding off the hood of the patrol car before Cheryl had even finished her command.

"Ms. McMurray, I'm Deputy Cheryl McNamara. I'm the commanding officer of the Sheriff's Department. You're not in any trouble. Can I ask you a few brief questions?"

Besides the black thunderbolts of teary mascara on her cheeks, Taylor's face was ghost-white, giving her the appearance of some undead specter existing in an eternal state of acute shock. The heat of the day was already building, but the young woman's skin was completely dry, even her cheeks, which had presumably been covered in tears not long ago. On her neck and forearms, thin blue veins networked under near-translucent skin, and her hands shook feverishly. Cheryl, shorter than most, stood at almost perfect eye-level with Taylor, taller than most, seated on the hood of Monica's patrol car. After a few moments of waiting for Taylor to answer, Cheryl tried again.

"Okay, Taylor, you with me?"

Taylor's eyes looked quite literally dead, unable to focus, unable to move. They stared straight ahead and did not seem to change their depth of field when Cheryl approached. Cheryl moved her head to the side just to solicit a reaction, but none came.

"Tayl—?"

"It tore him apart."

The words came out broken and quiet, but something about their coldness, their sheer vacancy, hit Cheryl like an avalanche. She swallowed and moved closer to Taylor.

"Can you tell me what you saw and where you saw it?"

With all the haste of a tortoise, inch-by-inch, Taylor

turned her head towards Cheryl. Her mouth hung open and her eyes still bulged, and in those bulging eyes, now focused and present, Cheryl saw the fire of hell itself. She'd only seen that look one time before, when she was a young girl and her father recounted his killing of two Viet Cong soldiers.

Monica crossed into Cheryl's vision, the heavily pregnant young officer struggling mightily to guide the jelly-legged Scoot into the back seat of her unit.

"Okay, we'll talk later. I'm gonna ask you to go sit in the front seat of my patrol car while Officer Nelson and I contain the scene. We won't be long, and I'll lock the doors. That sound ok?"

Taylor nodded and carefully pushed herself down from the hood of Monica's car. Her face changed when she stood, her mouth closing and her eyes relaxing. She walked slowly in front of Cheryl to the other patrol car and didn't say a word upon sliding into the passenger seat. Before joining Monica, Cheryl looked at Taylor again, this time through the glass of her windshield. Whatever bedlam had resided in Taylor's eyes moments ago seemed to have seeped into her neck and shoulders, riveting them with a tenseness that hadn't been there before and did not seem natural.

Finally pulling her eyes away from the traumatized Taylor, Cheryl met Monica by the trunk of the car she'd just deposited Scoot into. The vision of Monica was in every way a contrast to Taylor: Monica's eyes were focused, there was vivid color in her face, there was life in every fiber of her being.

"Jesus H," Cheryl said. "Did you talk to her?"

"Not much. I've known her for sixteen years and I've never seen her like this a day in her life."

"Alright, well, we need to see what this is all about for

ourselves. Are you comfortable going up there with me? We need to secure the crime scene before tech and whoever else comes. I'd rather not do it alone, but if you don't wan—"

"Of course, I'll go. Let's go."

"Okay. Thank you, Officer. Stay close and watch my six. Don't be afraid to talk. Once we secure the perimeter, you'll take Scoot back to the station and I'll stay here. You sure you're up for it?"

As if Cheryl's question sank farther into Monica's psyche upon its second asking, Monica paused and reflexively put a hand to her stomach. "I think so, Deputy."

"Okay. Good. You're gonna be fine. Just stay close and you'll be fine."

• • •

Vertical streaks of sunlight streamed through the leaves of lofty oak trees lining Hank's driveway, spearing patches of the gravel leading up to the property. Under different circumstances, Cheryl might have heard the songs of warblers greeting the day, but as the two officers trudged up the driveway, the crunch of their stony footsteps banged in her ears. She tried to walk in time with Monica to reduce their number, but found herself unable to concentrate after a coppery, organic stench — the stench of fresh blood — overtook the natural scents in her nostrils. The stench grew stronger with each step she took, as if her increased proximity somehow gave it power. Her heart began to pound in her chest; from the heat, from the climb, and from the fear of what she might be walking herself and a pregnant young woman into.

She blinked sweat out of her eyes in anticipation of

reaching the top of the hill, but a wet squish stopped her in her tracks.

"Oh God," Monica whispered. She lifted her left foot, and a red smudge of liquid dropped from the sole of her boot to the ground. It landed on what appeared to be the wreckage of a human eyeball. Somehow, its olive-green iris was still intact, capped over one of the thousands of white stones that coated the driveway. "I—I'm so sor—"

"It's okay, crime tech will take care of it," Cheryl said, beckoning her forward. "You still with me?"

"Yes, ma'am, I'm sorry, ma'am."

Cheryl finally cleared the crest of the hill and swallowed a ball of tension lodged in her throat. She scanned every object in sight with a feverish haste, and seconds later, her heart dropped when she landed on a dark, red lump at the end of the courtyard. "Monica. Stay back a second."

The eviscerated and crimson-stained body of Hank Teakle lay face-up in a pool of dark, arterial blood. All around it, little red spots and pink pieces of flesh littered the ground like some cannibalistic confetti. All his limbs were spread straight out, almost ceremoniously.

"Oh God," Cheryl whispered, yanking the inside of her elbow into up to her nose and mouth.

One eye was missing, and the bottom half of his jaw had been pulled clean off, freezing his face in a silent scream of torturous finality. Crazed flies circled around the corpse, the ocean of blood surrounding it and the archipelago of tiny remains scattered around the courtyard. Their buzzing sent the ball tension she had swallowed back up her throat, triggering her gag reflex on the way. A dark shadow quickly glided through the red mess, and she craned her neck to see a single buzzard hovering high above.

"Monica, call VSP. Need tech. One deceased. And come quick."

Hank's entire chest cavity had been hollowed out. Blood, bones, and organs that should have been inside it were gone, leaving behind a giant, square pit running from his shoulders to his waist, and only scraps on the ground. There were several holes in the bottom of that pit, indicating that whatever had cut him went all the way through in some places. Along both of the pit's vertical edges, lines of white dots were all that remained of rib bones that had been cut with inexplicable cleanliness.

All sense of time seemed to vanish while she gazed into Hank's empty body cavity. She could have spent ten seconds or ten minutes contemplating how this had happened. The only semi-logical conclusion she could draw was that an animal, maybe a bear or a mountain lion, had become spooked and attacked him. But the injuries were inconsistent with an animal attack. Maybe someone was after the horses, a confrontation happened, and things had escalated. Even then, why injure him this badly? And where did his organs go? If it was done by a person, were they still—

Cheryl drew the service weapon she hadn't fired once in her entire career in law enforcement.

She flinched her head over her shoulder to glimpse at Monica. Tears streamed down the young officer's flushed face. Her jaw was clenched in a frown and her eyes were white-rimmed geysers of shock. She held her radio out, as if she wanted to hand it to Cheryl, and her other hand rested on the holster of her weapon.

"It's okay, hon. You're okay," Cheryl said.

Monica's eyes narrowed and she nodded herself into composure.

"State's on their way?" Cheryl asked.

"Yes, Deputy."

"Okay good. Now, I need you to cover me because I need to search these buildings. Just stay close, watch my six, talk to me. That's it. Okay? You with me?"

"I'm with you, Deputy." Monica wiped her nose with her wrist and blinked away whatever tears she could. "I've got your six."

Cheryl let a cold beat pass between them and felt something resembling a smile form on her face. "I know you do."

A thud came from the direction of the main stable, and both officers whipped around towards it.

"Stables. Let's go," Cheryl said.

The two officers took slow, drawing steps through the courtyard to the stable, Hank's decimated mortal coil leering at them as they passed it. Both took deliberate care not to end up with more of the crime scene on the bottom of their boots.

One of the stable's batwing doors was open an inch, and Cheryl threw a backwards fist in the air to instruct Monica to stay put. She approached in absolute silence, each step slower than the last. Putting her ear to the door, Cheryl heard more nothingness. She took a deep breath, solidified the two-handed grip on her gun, and nudged the heavy wooden door open with her shoulder.

The cavernous halls of the stable saturated her entire field of vision in dense shades of brown and black. Inside, hot and static air drenched her in a creeping, deafening silence save for the occasional clicking of hooves. If only the horses could talk.

Cheryl whipped her arms to her left and to her right as she snuck silently past each carrel. Sweat poured from her armpits and dripped off the butt of the gun. All the horses appeared safe and calm but for a few passing brays, as if to ask, "What's your problem?" She reached the end of the stable and stared back at a miniature vision of Monica silhouetted in the stable's entrance, seemingly a mile away.

"Clear!" she shouted, and holstered her weapon.

They found nothing in the other buildings. The sheds were sealed by padlocks that flaked rust when she touched them, and the house was spotless. Cheryl put a hand on the hood of Taylor's car, parked next to Hank's house, before walking back to the body.

"You did good, Monica. Now, can you go back down and take the ten-fifty-one back to the station? Tell Taylor I'll be just a minute."

Monica obeyed. She drove back to the station with Scoot, and Cheryl went back to the courtyard.

What was left of Hank seemed to call out to her, the song of an inaudible siren over the wood warblers and finches. The flies had settled along the edges of his deep lacerations and were squirming on top of each other to gorge on his flesh. Two of them landed on his nose, raced each other over the curve of his nostril, and crawled in.

"What the fuck am I looking at?" she said, and, again covering her mouth and nose with her sleeve, marched back toward the driveway.

· · ·

The memory of Taylor's early morning discovery branded itself into the young woman's psyche. Relentless terrors began lurking in her subconscious during the day and stepped out of their mental cages at night. They came right at the precipice of sleep, the moment her brain finally relaxed and surrendered itself to darkness. Sometimes Hank would sit at the foot of her bed and whistle the way he used to do while clearing the tack. Sometimes he would have a face and sometimes he wouldn't. The worst was when he would appear to her as a little boy. He'd hide in corners, sit on ceilings. He'd whimper in the middle of the night and ask Taylor if she was his mama.

After Cheryl questioned her further in her patrol car, a questioning that morphed into the first of thousands of therapy sessions Taylor would require over her lifetime, Cheryl drove Taylor's car down from Hank's house and sent her home.

With that, Taylor was gone, and Cheryl was alone. Alone with the carved-up corpse of Henry Bartholomew Teakle, eternal son of Bensalem, and her scrambled thoughts.

She trudged back to Hank's house, struggling to lift her feet more than a few inches off the ground with each step up the slope of the driveway. Her utility belt had pasted a thick band of uncomfortable sweat across her waist, and its looseness chafed at her bony hips. She tightened it a notch to keep it from jostling and crashed down on Hank's porch steps when she reached them. She peeled her hat off and let her head fall into her outstretched hands.

Rubbing her temples, the pressure in Cheryl's skull began to subside and the sounds of the wilderness returned to her ears. Squirrels gnawed on late breakfasts while cicadas droned in the treetops. High above, the purity of the cloudless sky was hypnotizing. The buzzard was now joined by a companion, both death birds flapping lazily above, sizing up what would surely be a gourmet lunch if the humans would just leave it alone.

The realization that this would not be an open-and-shut case sank into Cheryl's mind. It would be long, it would be messy, and it would be painful. It would be exactly as Brady had said: kinda nasty. Really nasty, in fact. People were going to ask questions. People were going to get scared.

She slowed her breath and sat in the morning heat, soaking up the last few foreboding minutes of peace before all hell would break loose and she'd have to deal with the tsunami of shit on its way.

The Nokia flip phone strapped into her belt buzzed, and Brady's number flashed on the screen.

"Hey, Deputy, just checkin' in. Everything okay? Need any help up there?" he said.

"Shoot. Need more than a little."

"VSP's comin'?"

"Can't come soon enough."

"Good Christ. That bad?"

"Not good, Derek. Not good at all. Lord knows what I'm gonna tell the press."

"You reckon who did it?"

"I do not. Can't even wrap my mind around it."

"Well, what happened?"

"I have no earthly idea. Found him face-up in a pool of his own blood. Body completely ripped apart. It was like someone dug his chest out with a shovel and then sucked everything out of there with a hose."

"Good Christ."

"And his arms and legs stuck straight like a stick figure."

Brady paused and chewed something on the other end of the line. "You ever dealt with somethin' like this?"

"Not by a long shot. I've dealt with homicide, I dealt with some weird shit long ago in Vermont. This is something else. I don't know if this is murder or an animal attack or something very much beyond those things. Whoever did this to him knew what he was doing. Took his time."

"It ain't like Hank had any enemies. At least none that I know of."

"Must've pissed somebody off real good."

Brady's lips smacked again, his chewing louder now. "Officer Nelson just got back. I've never seen her so pale. She didn't even say a word, just handed off Scoot and sat down at her desk and cried. Not sure what to tell her. She won't talk."

"I'll talk to her."

The howl of a distant ambulance poked through the natural serenity of steamy summer morning in Bensalem. Cheryl's empty stomach groaned.

"Deputy, you gonna call Duke? Reckon he should know about this?" he said.

"I really didn't want to, but yeah, I reckon. I'll handle it."

"Alright, well, I'm here if you need me."

"Ten-four."

A stiff breeze rolled through the tree trunks and cooled her sweat. The heightening crescendo of the ambulance's wail conveyed its haste. It was close now, and a second siren, sharper and shorter, laced in with the long and slow screams of the ambulance.

"Here they fuckin' come," she said to herself.

Cheryl began to put her phone away but stopped, instead opting to open it again and dial Sheriff Duke Quinlan. He picked up on the second ring.

• • •

Aaron called Ellen at the hospital before shuttling a dressed Caleb and a fed Cooper to McDonalds. As he stood in the office, holding the phone that his palm had nearly sweat through just hours earlier, a calm settled in his shoulders. The wheat grass shone golden in the meadow, not showing the slightest sign of disturbance.

"Hey," Ellen said, "How are you guys?" The din of hospital foot traffic rattled behind her and the exhaustion in her voice was palpable.

"Hey, sweetie. How's the floor?"

"Crazy tonight. Insane."

"Listen, you didn't try to call the landline last night, did you?"

She paused. "No. Did someone call the landline? When?"

"A few minutes after four. I don't know, it may have been a prank call. There was this weird voice. It was like a thousand whispers at the same time, and then they all merged into one voice. Something about an ... open gate? It just kept saying that over and over and then it hung up."

"That's super weird. Must have been some kind of prank or a weird automation. Not that many people even have our new number. Did you report it?"

"No, I don't know what I'd even report. I wish I could describe to you how messed up this call was. Just come home to us. It feels lonely without you."

"Did you see that thing you were looking for outside? Did the lights work?"

"I didn't. Nothing. Nothing but that phone call. Oh. Caleb had another nightmare last night. I let him sleep in the bed with me. Poor kid."

"My sweet boy. Did he tell you what it was?"

"No. I didn't press him. We're gonna head to McDonalds for breakfast to cheer him up."

"Ah, yes. Get me two Egg McMuffins and a side of hash browns, please."

"You got it. Love you. See you soon."

Cooper hadn't even settled into his den of blankets in the back when the SUV was met by a banner of POLICE LINE DO NOT CROSS tape stretched across Wickham Road. Aaron's jaw fell open. Two patrol cars and an ambulance were parked at the base of Hank's driveway.

A short, wiry female police officer scurried over, her sandy hair tied into a short ponytail. She held both hands high in the air, signaling Aaron to stop. The nameplate across the top of her beige shirt pocket read MCNAMARA. She had a hard-lined face with small features. The face of a woman who had seen a thing or two but still retained some kindness.

• • •

Cheryl looked at her watch and grimaced, realizing it was nearly 8 o'clock and the graveyard shift she'd started the night before had ended ninety minutes ago. But with a ruthless onslaught of names, cars, and people way above her pay grade above to bombard her small force, going home was the furthest thought from her mind.

The ambulance arrived first and pronounced Hank dead on the scene. Two officers from the Virginia State Police and the medical examiner arrived shortly after. A big swinging dick detective was on his way from Richmond. Cheryl tried not to think about how much of an asshole he was bound to be. It was only a matter of time before the press figured out what was going on and this was all over the news. Something like this would probably reach Richmond, and if there were any more bodies, maybe even national.

One of the VSP officers offered her some solace when he suggested she go back down the driveway and watch the road. She gladly accepted.

Within minutes, a civilian vehicle pulled up. It didn't come from the main road, but from the only other house in the area. It rolled to a stop and Cheryl put her game face on.

"Good morning, sir. My name's Deputy Cheryl Mc-Namara, with the Bensalem Sheriff's Department. Can I ask what brings you out here?"

"Hi there. What's happening here? Is Hank okay?" the driver said.

She peered at all three faces in the car: a smiling German Shepherd in the trunk, a jet-black-haired boy in the back seat with ten fingers laced around a sippy cup, and a disheveled driver maybe ten or fifteen years her junior.

"Sir, what brings you and your family out here this morning?"

"Oh, well, I live here."

He reached an awkward right hand across his body and pointed over his left shoulder.

"I live back there. 12 Wickham Road. My name's Aaron Dreyer. I'm Hank's neighbor. We were just on our way out for breakfast. That's my son Caleb, and the dog in the back is Cooper. He's harmless."

"Uh-huh." Cheryl paused, straightened her torso to peer over the top of the car, and quickly snapped back down. "Well, sir, there's been an accident. We're still working to secure the area, but for the time being, I'm going to ask that you head home. Got anything to eat for breakfast at the house? I might suggest you stay home until we can get this sorted out."

"Listen, I know Hank Teakle very well. He's a good friend of mine. Caleb and I see him every week and visit his horses. We were supposed to have dinner soon. Is he in trouble? Hank's in trouble, isn't he? This ... crime scene ... well, I've never seen anything like it. This can't be good, right?"

Cheryl let out a sigh that she hoped wouldn't give too much away. There was already something about Aaron she didn't like. "Well, we're still very much in the process of gathering information right now, Mister ... you said Dyer?"

"Dreyer. Aaron Dreyer."

"My apologies, Mr. Dreyer. Right now, unfortunately, this is a crime scene. Mr. Teakle was the victim of an attack in the early hours of the morning. I'm unable to comment on his condition. For now, it's best y'all return home." She tipped her hat and began to walk away.

"Officer! Wait a second! Do you know what happened exactly? I might know something."

That stopped her. "Know something?"

"Okay, I know this is going to sound insane, but I've been seeing some incredibly strange activity in this area lately. A couple of nights ago, I saw a very, uh, terrible-looking thing wandering around in the meadow across the street from my house. I don't know what it was, but it didn't look human, and it didn't look like any animal I recognized. I'm telling you, something about this thing gave me an incredibly bad feeling. My dog has been growling at things in the night and I think it's this thing. I think we have a serious predator on our hands."

Cheryl would have liked very much to believe his story. She would have liked to believe any story at this point. She'd seen Hank's body up close and couldn't fathom any man, woman, or animal carving him up like that. She shook her head.

"No, I—listen, Officer, I swear to God something is not right in this area."

Out of nowhere, a sharp gust of wind nearly blew Cheryl's hat clean off. She held it down with one hand.

"With all due respect, sir, we didn't need you to inform us that something is going on in this area. Mr. Teakle was found dead this morning on his property. His cause of death is unclear at this time but I'm sure we will be seeking official information quite soon. I am sorry, sir. I know Hank was a friend."

Aaron's lips peeled back along his gum lines in a look of confusion and disgust. "No! You can't be serious? This can't seriously be happening. You have to tell me what happened!"

"Mr. Dreyer, do you know if Mr. Teakle had any enemies? Anyone who might harbor a grudge against him?"

"Oh my God. No. Not at all. I'm sorry. He's seriously ... dead?"

"Sir, as you might expect, this sort of incident is uncommon in Bensalem, so please excuse me for being direct. The best thing you can do right now is stay home with your family and let us know if you can think of any reason someone may have wanted to harm him. We can't speculate about causes, and frankly, I'm only telling you this because you're a friend and a neighbor. I really shouldn't be."

"I ... I understand."

"You'll likely have a detective stop by later and ask you

some questions. If anything else comes to mind, please feel free to call me. They call me Deputy McNamara, but you can call me Cheryl. Sound okay?" She whipped out a business card and stuck it through the window.

"Wait, are—are you sure it was human? I mean, are you sure his death was caused by a human? Could it have been something else? You said you found him outside?"

"Sir, it's way too early to conclude anything. Now, please, I'm asking you to return to your home, and give me a call if you think of anything more substantial. I apologize for being the bearer of bad news."

She walked back towards Hank's driveway, this time determined not to turn around. Just as she suspected, this situation was already starting to get out of control. A worried neighbor wouldn't make it any easier.

"Hey! Wait!" Aaron shouted.

Cheryl summoned a level of patience found only in women who had raised teenage children, and turned around again.

"My wife is going to be coming home from the other direction soon. She'll be driving a magenta sedan. Will she be able to get through?"

"Of course. You can use that number on the card I gave you to report any additional information. Just call that number, it's my direct line. Does that sound okay, Mr. Dreyer?"

He sat stiff with his hands at 10 and 2, and a dumbfounded look plastered on his face.

"Mr. Dreyer? Does that sound okay? We'll let your wife through when she arrives. What did you say her name was?"

Staring blankly at his windshield, he replied, "Uh. Ellen."

. . .

As Aaron turned the SUV around, a gentle voice floated up from the back seat.

"Dad?" Caleb said.

"Yeah, buddy?"

"Are we still going to McDonalds?"

"No, I'm sorry. We can't today. We'll have pancakes. That okay?"

Caleb didn't answer. Aaron glanced in the rearview, but the only one returning his gaze was Cooper, grinning from ear-to-ear and panting his face off. Caleb fiddled with something in his hands and slanted his head towards the ground.

The golden grass of the meadow greeted the SUV as it reached the driveway to the Dreyers' house. Recalling the sheer size of the creature that had been there two nights ago, a dry chill ran over Aaron's face and neck. He considered its darkness, its debilitating power had somehow gripped him where he stood in his living room.

"Mr. Hank's dead, isn't he?" Caleb said.

"Hey, now don't say that. We don't know anything, buddy. He might be totally fine. Sometimes police come just to check on—"

"He's dead."

"Caleb! Stop saying that. That is not nice."

Caleb obeyed his father, not uttering another word the rest of the way home, nor during their impromptu pancake breakfast.

. . .

Black rainclouds crept over the western range as a thick pressure system escalated in the sky. The weather was turning — and fast — which wasn't uncommon in the summer, even in the morning.

Light rain danced on Ellen's windshield as she approached the caution tape blocking the final stretch of road to her house. The rain wouldn't stay light for very long.

A small woman in a full-length brown poncho with "BSD" screen-printed on the back jogged towards her car. Ponchos were supposed to run big, but this poor lady was swimming in hers. Thinking about ill-fitting work uniforms crudely reminded Ellen of how uncomfortable the drawstring waistline on her scrubs bottoms had become.

The small officer nodded in a business-like manner. "Hello ma'am. Are you Ellen Dreyer?"

"Yes. Is there a problem here?"

"My name's Deputy Cheryl McNamara, Bensalem Sheriff's Department."

Cheryl extended a wet hand through Ellen's car window. She shook it, manners being more important than cleanliness.

"Your husband Ethan let us know you'd be coming through. You just heading to your residence?"

"Aaron. Yes. We live down the road here. 12 Wickham Road."

Cheryl's phone buzzed.

"Sorry, hold tight here, Mrs. Dreyer."

With monumental effort, the officer clawed away her unwieldy poncho and pulled the phone out of her back pocket.

Ellen preferred Dr. Dreyer to Mrs. Dreyer. That people assumed a salutation relating to her marriage rather than her career never sat right with her, especially while wearing scrubs.

With Cheryl's back turned, Ellen assessed everything she could in her field of vision but there was nothing on the road besides vehicles. Whatever had happened must have occurred up on Hank's property. A second strip of caution tape, maybe forty feet in front of this one, blocked the road on the other side of his driveway.

Cheryl jogged back over, the muddy tail of the poncho dragging on the ground behind her.

"Alright, ma'am, like I said, this is a crime scene area, so I'm gonna lift this tape up and let you slide through. Once you do, I'd like you to immediately stop, wait for me to walk around to the front of your vehicle, and then trail behind me as I walk to the other side and lift the tape on the other perimeter. Sound good?"

"Understood, Officer. Although, I'm curious, why block the whole road off? My husband and I are the only ones who live on this road besides Mr. Teakle."

"Understand your concern, ma'am. This is just a precaution to make sure we can assess any people or vehicles for the moment. It'll be gone soon, I promise."

Ellen dealt with police all the time at the ER. She and Cheryl were both part of a class of people who kept the world glued together and understood the value of protocol.

Cheryl did exactly what she said she would, and Ellen followed her directions. The rain wasn't light anymore, but it wasn't quite a downpour. Yet.

"Thanks, Mrs. Dreyer. I gotta get back here, but I'm sure you have questions. I told your husband a little while ago that we're still very much gathering facts. We're asking that you stay inside for the time being. A violent crime did occur on this property late last night, but we have no specific reason to believe you or your family are in any danger. An investigator from the state police may call by later to visit you."

"Thank you, Officer. I'm an emergency room doctor at UVA and I just came off the floor. We didn't get any patients overnight who fit Hank Teakle's description. Hank's a friend of ours, so I—I'm sure I would have noticed his admission to the ward. He's the victim, right?"

"Yes. Unfortunately so, ma'am."

"Is there any way I can assist with treatment or with your investigation? If you need a doctor, I can—"

"I'm sorry to say, the victim was found deceased when we arrived. So ... yeah. I certainly appreciate the offer, but you probably won't be able to do him much good at this point, ma'am."

"Jeez. Wow. Okay, well, listen, if you come into contact of any family members who need a place to stay ... I think he has two daughters downstate ... we'd be happy to help in any way we can."

"That's mighty sweet of you. I'll do that."

"Wow. I can't believe this. And can you be reached to report any suspicious activity?"

"Yes, ma'am," Cheryl said, pulling out a damp card and batting away large swaths of poncho. "That's my direct line. I gave one to your husband, too. For now, please just stay indoors for the day and allow us to clean up here. We won't be more than a few hours."

"Thank you. Thanks for helping Hank. Good luck."

"Thank you, ma'am."

Ellen drove away with an ache in the pit of her stomach. She had turned down a lucrative residency offer in New York to be here, away from the chaos of the urban world. Surely, she wouldn't have to get used to a constant stream of violent crimes on her doorstep. Thunder rumbled softly in the sky.

• • •

Cheryl sat stoical in the front seat of her unit. She listened passively to police chatter on the CB and bullets of rain smacking her roof. Over the last two hours, the weariness in her legs and her eyelids battled against the responsibility burning in her heart to keep the crime scene at least somewhat intact for VSP. Now that they'd come and brought enough people, cars, and nervous energy to fill a football stadium, the scene was their problem no matter how wet it got. She had no desire to know what kind of bloody mud pit Hank's courtyard was turning into.

When Cheryl had called him earlier that morning, Sheriff Duke Quinlan said he wanted to come back as soon as possible but she'd talked him into taking his time, assuring him she had it covered. He'd leave Nags Head first thing in the morning and would be in Bensalem by sundown tomorrow.

She considered Aaron and Ellen, two people she had never met before, but both of whom jittered slightly with a kind urbanized nervousness not found in Bensalem's long-term citizens. Something about the pair struck her as odd, a starkness between them she couldn't quite put her finger on. She wondered which forces of the universe had brought together a man like Aaron and a woman like Ellen. She wondered whether they were happy, what their son was like, and what they might have looked like when they were young. It was only as she considered their nervousness — especially Aaron's — that she began to contemplate her own.

. . .

Ellen's windshield wipers whipped back and forth as she passed the same golden meadow her husband had passed a little less than an hour ago. This time though, no gold could be seen, only a murky brown haze beyond heavy torrents of rain. She wrapped her fingers around the steering wheel a little tighter when she allowed herself to think about the proximity of her son to what was sure to be a heinous crime. He was her everything.

She touched a hand to her chest, and with that little action, the memory of that day came flooding back.

Most young girls played with dolls and dressed up as princesses, but Ellen was born in a rural North Carolina community and was enraptured by the natural world — the real world. The Dalton family's thirteen-acre farm was the only playground she'd ever needed and the only friend she'd ever wanted. She spent day after day poring over every little piece of it — the grass, the dirt, the leaves, the trees, the plants, the bugs, the clay, the little black skinks that were always too fast to catch.

There were no natural paths in the woods behind the house, so she would forge them by running the same routes over and over again. One of those paths darted around a bulbous slab of granite sticking out of the ground that she covered in chalk drawings. At the end of that path stood a dead dogwood tree, a sprawling mess of twigs and branches poking in all directions.

One spring afternoon before dinner, a nine-year-old Ellen

climbed the dogwood tree and discovered an exquisitely craft-ed bird's nest with four powder-blue eggs. New discoveries in her queendom were always exciting but were typically simple. A rabbit darting through the yard, a creepy-looking bug under a rock, or, if she got lucky, a yellow-spotted salamander.

The blue eggs were otherworldly, and Ellen instantly felt a motherly spark ignite inside her, causing her nearly to believe the four chicks were her own.

It may have been that spark that persuaded her to pluck one of the eggs from the nest and put it into the front pocket of her overalls. She felt the shameful gaze of the forest's eyes on her, but she had to have that egg. She promised the mother she would take good care of it, slinked down the tree, and ran as fast as she could to the farmhouse.

At dinner that night, her father asked what had happened to her overalls. She looked down, saw a yellow ooze soaking through her denim, and ran to the bathroom.

The egg had been smashed, probably while she was run-ning from the shame of the forest's gaze. The baby bird was soaked in blood. Its naked, annihilated body sprouted feathers that resembled patchy hair. It had a stout little beak, the tiniest pair of wings she'd ever seen, and the ghastliest pair of venous eyes.

She screamed. When her father arrived, she fully expected him to take off his belt and spank her bare bottom, as he would often do when she got into real trouble. She almost wanted him to. This was an act of murder as far as she was concerned.

Instead, he put his hand on the back of her neck, drew her close, and pecked her on the forehead.

"Strip down and leave it all in the tub," he said.

She cried hysterically all night long and she didn't stop

the next day. School called after social studies class, asking for someone to come pick her up. Thinking about the mother bird was worse than thinking about the baby. She pictured her with her wings over her head, crying, wondering where her little baby could have gone. Would she hold out hope that her baby had beat the odds and made it? Did she think of him fondly soaring through the sky?

Ellen had carried that moment with her for decades — the ignition of that motherly spark trampled by the harsh reality of nature. That gooey baby bird was with her every day on the ER floor. Every now and then she would reflexively glance down or touch the spot on her chest where it died. Sometimes she could even smell it. It hung like a dirty cobweb in her subconscious through every waking moment with Caleb.

Caleb, who was her second chance.

• • •

Lightning cracked the sky as Ellen pulled to a stop in the drive-way. The rain had become a full-on monsoon. Sans umbrella, she sprinted to the patio as fast as she could, but running wasn't much use, as this was the kind of storm that only needed a few seconds to drench you. Her scrubs were already completely soaked by the time she got to the patio door.

Aaron shot his head up from his seat at the kitchen table when Ellen barreled in. The maddening sound of pelting rain came in with her, as did hundreds of huge drops that made it through the door just before she slammed it behind her.

"Ack!" she cried, her arms outstretched like a scarecrow and her hair dripping on the tile.

"Hold on!" Aaron jumped back from his chair and ran to the bathroom.

There was enough commotion in the kitchen to send Cooper rushing in from the living room, barking at the sky and jumping up onto a soaked Ellen.

"Down! Cooper, down!" Aaron said, handing Ellen a towel and relieving her of her wet purse.

She patted down her face, smearing mascara across her eye sockets. "Where's Caleb?" she said.

"Watching TV. We just ate. Hold on a second." Aaron left to fetch another towel and said something to Caleb on his way back to the kitchen. Upon returning to the kitchen, he wrapped the towel around Ellen while she squeezed water out of her long, black locks.

"My God, did hear about Hank?" she said.

"Yes! We drove up to it! That cop told me. I don't think she was supposed to. You think he was murdered?"

"Wow. Yeah, she said the same thing to me. She said it was a violent crime."

"Oh my God. This isn't real."

"Did Caleb see anything?"

"I don't know. I mean, he saw what I saw. What you saw. But he heard her say Hank is dead."

"Jesus Christ."

"What did you see? What did the cop tell you?"

"I couldn't see anything either. Whatever happened, it must have been up on his property. I didn't ask a lot of questions."

"What cop did you deal with? The short woman? Kind of mean?"

"McNamara?"

"I think so, she gave me her card."

"I'm sure she's just stressed. She seemed a little, yeah, brisk. I guess I would be, too."

Aaron pulled out a chair from the kitchen table and sat down. "What do you think happened?"

"No trip to McDonalds, huh?"

"What? No, the cop told us to come back home, but open the fridge. I've got a stack of pancakes in there for you."

"Oh, hell yes. I'm starving."

"Ellen, I have a really bad feeling about this. Do you think someone killed him? What other kind of violent crime could we be talking about here?"

Ellen shuffled across the kitchen floor and slid the plate of pancakes into the microwave. "Well, without seeing anything, it's impossible to say."

"I can't believe that cop told you it was a violent crime. Are you sure that's what she said? Who could have done this?"

Ellen sighed. She didn't turn around, opting to watch each second tick down. They eked by.

:10

:09

:08

"Ellen, what—"

"I don't know! What do you want from me? I'm not the police. I saw everything you saw and nothing more."

"But what do you think? You probably know a lot more about crime scenes than I do."

"Listen. Did you ever consider—"

DING!

"Consider what?" Aaron said.

"Maybe he … I mean, I hate to say it, but he's a pretty lonely old guy, right?"

"No way," Aaron said, slicing a hand through the air. "He was in an incredible mood the other day. There's no way he would hurt himself."

Ellen sat down and slathered the top pancake in butter. "He was probably in an incredible mood because you were there. You ever consider that?"

"We made dinner plans. I was going to see him on Friday. Wait, today actually! I was supposed to have dinner with him tonight! There's no way. Ellen, there's no way he would kill himself!"

Ellen closed her eyes and chewed.

Aaron leaned back in his chair and put his hands over his eyes. He wiped them down his face, pulling the skin like a stretched-out mask. "What do you think did it, El?"

"Could have been an animal. Bears, coyotes. A mountain lion."

"What are the chances of that, though?"

"Aaron, sweetheart, can I please eat?"

From the living room, thunderous little footsteps approached.

"Ellen, listen. This is going to sound crazy, but you know that thing I saw a couple nights ago? The thing Cooper's been growling at? I—I think it was what called last night. I don't know how or why, I just have a feeling. And I think it's what killed Hank. What else could have done it? There's no way an old guy like that has any enemies."

The little boy barreling towards her was a welcome distraction, but her heart dropped when he veered sharply towards his father and away from her. A pang of maternal pain exploded in her heart, as if a red-hot arrow had been shot through it.

"Daddy! Come see the town!" Caleb said to his father. Only to his father. Only ever to his father.

Ignoring Caleb, Aaron bored holes into his wife. Her anger ratcheted up a notch, but instead of letting it erupt, she pushed it down. Way, way down.

"What if it killed hi—"

"Please stop," she whispered, staring straight ahead at nothing.

Caleb tugged at Aaron's shirt. "Let's go! Daddy, let's go, come on!"

Aaron sighed, got up, and pushed his chair in. Caleb circled around him and planted his hands on his father's butt to shove him along.

Ellen finished her pancakes but was still starving. The yellow flash of a box of Cheerios caught her eye but feeling the drawstring on her scrub bottoms digging — and the tiny pouch of flesh hanging over them — she decided she could wait until lunch.

• • •

The rain diminished to a drizzle soon after and broke completely by the afternoon, leaving behind red ruffled clouds and a purple sky. Bugs and birds and other forest-dwellers shook off the storm and crept back to life in the wilderness around the house at 12 Wickham Road.

When a knock on their front door echoed through the house, Ellen was asleep, and the little creatures' dusk performance was in full swing, as if the rain had never fallen. Aaron peeled himself off the couch and answered the door.

Before him stood a skinny man wearing coke-bottle

glasses, a gray tweed blazer with elbow patches, and a pocket protector case with about thirteen things in it.

"Hi there," he said. "Detective Roland Pierce. How do you do, sir?"

"Oh, hi. Aaron Dreyer. Yes, please come in, someone said you might come by."

They shook hands.

"Ah, good. We try to move as fast as we can when something like this happens. You didn't already have a detective stop by today, did you? Sometimes we get our wires crossed."

"No, no sir. Uh, can I offer you anything?"

"Water'd be fine. Don't go to any trouble, please. This won't take long."

Pierce had an awkward way about him, a lack of balance or physical awareness Aaron assumed police detectives acquired through some sort of rigorous training regimen. He couldn't imagine Pierce running a city block.

Nevertheless, he guided the detective to the kitchen table where Caleb sat making Play-Doh mounds. Caleb didn't get up when Pierce sat down. He didn't even look at him, he just kept mashing a gross mixture of black, brown and yellow clay.

"What'cha makin' there, kiddo?" asked Pierce.

"Caleb, can you tell our friend what you're making?" Aaron said.

"Gremlins," said Caleb.

"Oh boy, scary stuff!" Pierce said, laughing. Caleb did not reciprocate.

"Detective, let's head into the living room where we can talk privately. Caleb, you stay here, okay?"

Caleb nodded, and the two left him to his creative devices.

"You have a heck of a beautiful home here, by the way," Pierce said as they walked. "Nothing beats central air, I'll tell ya."

"Oh, thanks. Yeah, we love it here."

"We?"

Aaron sat on the couch and Pierce sat on a chair by the fireplace. The detective sipped his water.

"Yeah, my wife Ellen's upstairs sleeping off a killer night shift. She's an ER doctor. Do you want me to get her?"

"Nah, only if you want to. I can always follow up."

"Oh, okay. Sure. Of course."

"So, I'll get right to it. Hank Teakle was killed last night. We believe murdered, right in his own front yard. We're still gathering information and we're just starting forensics, but we wanted you to be aware."

"Jesus. Okay. Do you have any idea who or what did this?"

"Well, Mr. Teakle at one point ran afoul of some high-profile horse breeders, and while it may seem extreme, our leading theory at this point was that some debt was unpaid. Or one of them had some kind of vendetta."

It took Aaron several moments to realize his jaw was hanging open.

"Sir?" Pierce said. "Does that surprise you?"

"Uh, that's an understatement. I never, ever would have guessed. Seriously? Good old Hank?"

"So, I take it he never mentioned anything to you? You ever get a whiff of something like that in your conversations with him?" Pierce pulled a steno pad out of the inside pocket of his jacket.

"No, never. I never would have guessed. Frankly, I'm totally shocked. Wow."

"Let me ask you another question, Mr. Dreyer. Have you

seen any suspicious activity around here lately? Specifically, around Hank's?"

Aaron felt a warm glow of comfort rise inside his chest. Was there someone in this world who would care about the creature? He adjusted his weight on the couch to square his body to Pierce's.

"It's funny you should say that, Detective. I have."

Pierce blinked as if coming back from somewhere far away. He took a loud sip of water. "Really?"

"This is gonna sound a little, uh, out there. Two nights ago, at 4:00am on the nose, I saw something very strange in the meadow out there." Aaron pointed behind him but didn't take his eyes off Pierce.

"A person?"

"I don't think so. No, it definitely wasn't. This thing was massive. At first I thought it was a bear or a horse but it walked upright."

"Walked upright how?"

"Well, I guess you could say it looked like a bear walking on its hind legs. I have no idea on earth what the thing was. Actually, it could have been bigger than a bear. I mean this thing was huge. You ever heard of anything like that? I'm telling you, it was unlike anything I've ever seen."

Pierce looked at him quizzically. He took another sip of water, his knuckles a tense white upon the glass.

"How close did you get? What did you see exactly?"

"I only saw it from the living room window. So, I guess pretty far away. A couple hundred yards."

"You said at 4:00am? So, it was dark?"

"Very dark, yes, but actually, you see those floodlights out in the yard? I just installed those to get a better look next time."

"So ... did you get a better look?"

"Last night? No, but—God, this is even weirder. At the same time, right at four, I got the creepiest phone call."

"Mm-hm."

Aaron made circles in the air with his hands. "It was this totally alien, totally demonic sounding voice."

"What did the voice say?"

"Something about opening a gate."

"A what, sir?"

"A ... a gate."

Pierce looked up from his pad. "I'm sorry, sir, I—I don't follow."

Aaron hung his head and sighed.

"Let's go back to the thing you saw, though. You sure it wasn't a bear? They've been known to walk on two legs every now and then. Rare, but it happens."

"I guess it could have been, but ... something told me it ... I don't know."

"Did this thing ... do anything? Hurt anything? Threaten you?"

"No, actually, it just walked through the meadow. It didn't stop walking, didn't come up here. I'm sure it didn't even see me."

"Well, no offense, sir, but what are you afraid of?" Pierce downed the last gulp of his water and set the glass on the coffee table between them. Cooper ambled over from who knows where to investigate the clank.

Aaron put a hand on the back of his head. He closed his eyes and winced. "I—I'm sorry. I'm just so tired. I don't know what's going on. I'm just scared. I'm seeing weird things. I'm getting these phone calls. Hank's dead. I'm jet lagged. I'm just—"

"Sounds like you need some rest, sir."

"Yeah. No, you're right. I definitely do."

"Well, look, it may be nothing, but I've made a note of it. If I were you, I'd just keep my distance from that area and try not to worry about it. If Hank's death occurred for the reason we think it did, there is absolutely no reason for you to worry about your family's safety. Although that is a perfectly natural response. Don't beat yourself up for it."

"Yeah. Yeah. I, uh, okay."

"Mr. Dreyer, I don't have any more questions. The local PD will be in touch if there's anything else. You got any more questions for me?"

He didn't. Pierce thanked him for the water and Aaron walked him to the door.

Watching the detective's sedan back down the long drive-way, Aaron felt strangely satisfied. Even if the conversation didn't yield or uncover anything, the sheer act of talking about it felt like progress.

He went upstairs to find a sleepy-eyed Ellen waking in bed. He took off his shoes and laid down next to her. She rolled her head into the crook of Aaron's shoulder.

"That was a detective," Aaron said.

"Oh. Okay. Did you learn anything?" she said.

"He said Hank was murdered."

"Really?"

"Yeah. Said he had some sort of mix-up with some breeders who might have had it in for him. Who would've thought, huh?"

"I never would have guessed."

"I told him about that creature I saw. He seemed kind of interested."

Ellen chuckled.

"What?" Aaron said with a hint of embarrassment.

"I'm telling you, it's nothing. It was probably a bear. Cooper sees stuff, hears stuff, growls at stuff. He sleeps weird hours and walks around in the middle of the night. He's a dog. It's his job."

"I really fucking hope you're right. I'd love to be wrong, I just don't think I am."

"Where's Caleb?"

"Downstairs. Wanna come join us?"

"Yeah. I'd love to. I miss my chicken."

That night, after a rousing round of a Caleb-conceived game called Raptor Fort, Aaron and Ellen tucked in their son together. They read him his favorite story, taking turns reading the pages while Cooper kept guard in the hallway. They hugged him, they kissed him, and they turned out his light.

Aaron and Ellen went to bed right after, and while Ellen snoozed blissfully with an arm draped over her husband, Aaron laid awake, staring at the ceiling, thinking about that creature and its power. It plodded through his brain like it plodded through the meadow: heavy, brooding, mysterious, but never close enough to actually see.

• • •

Darkness took Aaron until he found himself standing on the deck of an indoor swimming pool. He had been there before, long ago, but he couldn't place it. The water was tranquil. The building was silent.

In a dreamlike trance, Aaron's legs began to walk themselves towards the edge of the pool until he found himself in it. He passed the 3 FEET marker, then 4, then 5, then his lips touched the water and seeped into his nose. He kept walking, but he also somehow kept breathing. His eyes became submerged, and he saw something at the bottom of the deep end. It looked like a person. A young boy. Aaron got closer.

Closer.

And closer.

Caleb.

Aaron's little son, Caleb, lying naked and unconscious at the bottom of the pool. His eyes were open, and his face was blue. Aaron walked to within inches of the catatonic boy. Tiny air bubbles lined the contours of his cold, lifeless face. Aaron took him by the hand, and his feet began to walk again, this time right up the long wall of the deep end. Caleb felt weightless as Aaron dragged him out of the pool and laid him down on the deck. At no point during any of this did Aaron panic, or become scared, or even feel as though this was out of the ordinary.

Caleb blinked twice. Then his mouth swung open to reveal a gob of black slime that spewed out over his lips and down his chin. Without moving a muscle, Caleb's body slid along the concrete and plopped right back into the pool, leaving a trail of black slime and Aaron alone on the deck.

In the water, a dark mass began to take shape. It started in the center of the pool and grew outward until it poked out of the water. A dog barked faintly in the background of whatever world he found himself in. Aaron smelled metal and tasted ash.

The black mass rose further out of the water, nearly to the ceiling. All at once the thing recoiled and revealed itself to be the creature from the meadow. It was right there, in the pool, mere feet in front of him.

It must have been twenty feet tall, a titanic black body devoid of all but the most general of features. Its construction made it look like it had been crudely slapped together with mountains of pewter-colored mud. It had shiny skin, a rough stump of head and three — not two — tiny yellow eyes. Yellow eyes that looked through Aaron all the way into his soul. They saw his thoughts. They saw his fear.

But it wasn't the thing's size, metallic smell, or even the three yellow eyes that scared Aaron. Rather, it was its unsightly collection of long, tentacle-like fingers. Each individual finger, or claw, or whatever they were, must have been six feet in length, and they moved ever so slightly back and forth, not as flotsam in the water, but as sentient appendages quivering in some way that may have made sense to something somewhere in this universe or the next. They hung from the creature's elbows like old dead branches of a lightning-charred tree.

The barking grew louder.

Then, millions of flies rose up from the water and began spinning around the creature, hiding and protecting it in a dense and dizzying suit of insectile armor. The buzzing was deafeningly loud, and then the creature began to emit a guttural droning sound so loud it shook the entire building. The pool water rippled, and the ceiling tiles began to crash to the ground.

• • •

Aaron's eyes blasted open, and his skin stung from the chill of a coat of cold sweat. The blackness of the room told him it was still dark outside, and the crickets chirping outside told him the dream was over.

The creature, the pool, Caleb, were all gone. All that carried over was the sound of the barking dog. The bark was coming from outside, barely breaking through the crickets' roar.

He took a deep breath and looked at the clock on Ellen's nightstand. 4:08am.

Realizing the creature would be out there right now, Aaron desperately fought the temptation to look out his bedroom window. Hank was dead. Was Caleb dead, too? What was that dream trying to tell him?

He gave in, and looked.

There was the creature, making its moonlight trek, maybe two hundred yards away. Down by the road and halfway between the house and the creature, something else was moving, bobbing up and down towards the edge of the front yard fence.

"COOPER!" Aaron screamed.

Cooper stood like a gladiator at the edge of the yard in an absolute fever pitch, barking in his small ferocity at this monstrous interloper in the meadow.

"Oh God! Cooper, no! Cooper!"

Aaron heard Ellen stirring awake as he ran downstairs and plugged in the cord supplying power to the floodlights.

Whoosh.

As soon as the lights came on, the creature stopped in its tracks. It ceased movement altogether. It stood there, frozen mid-stride, almost exactly halfway across the meadow, between the two pine forests, under the starry sky with the eons-old Blue Ridge Mountains looking on.

Illuminating the creature had only further stoked Cooper's fury. Aaron darted to the front door and grabbed his leash. He had only acquired one shoe when Ellen's cell phone rang from upstairs.

"No! Ellen! Don't pick it up! Don't answer it, Ellen!"

Aaron diverted his entire focus back to his wife, willing her not to listen to that gaping portal to hell on the other end of the phone. He charged back through the house, maximizing every stride, every foot placement, every shift in body weight to shave off milliseconds.

Ellen was sitting on the edge of the bed with the phone to her ear, the whites of her eyes bulging around her irises and her jaw locked open. She handed the phone over without saying a word.

Aaron put the phone to his ear and kept his eyes on his wife. There was less static this time. Aaron couldn't immediately identify why, but that troubled him. It was as if the static had been masking what was really on the other end, and now the mask was off.

When the voice finally spoke, it was noticeably different than before. The voice was clearer, somehow familiar.

It was Hank.

"Open ... the gate. Open the gate."

Aaron ran back downstairs, leaving his wife behind to grapple with whatever thoughts ravaged her mind. He kept the phone to his ear. Hank sounded tired. The voice was strained, only a little more than a whisper against the static. It was Hank but it wasn't Hank, someone commandeering his voice and using it as their own. He kept repeating the same message.

"Open the gate."

"Hank! What does that mean? Is that you?"

"Open the gate," was his only reply. The words were a robotic murmur, and they conveyed a pain that sounded almost ancient.

Aaron flipped down Ellen's phone, ending the call, and

he jammed it into the pocket of his shorts before running out the front door. He didn't even bother trying to get Cooper's attention by shouting. Instead, he made a beeline for the dog. Cooper growled and snapped and snarled at the creature, the monster still frozen under the lights.

Aaron stumbled to the edge of the front yard and leashed Cooper, who bucked and pulled with the force of a stallion. If not for the rickety old fence, he would be out there mauling the thing — or dead from trying.

With the leash secure, Aaron twisted his neck towards the meadow and the monster within it.

It was all there. The shroud of flies, the bulky black body, the spindly fingers that could squeeze the life out of a lion.

The droning sound at the end of Aaron's dream was clearer in real life. It was a deep, monotone hum that could certainly not be made with any kind of vocal cords he was aware of. The creature hadn't moved at all and the dog was still going bonkers.

And the metallic smell, it was the same smell Cooper had brought back with him when he ran into the woods at Hank's. The same ashy taste from Aaron's dream.

Aaron stood locked in place, his shadow from the floodlights cast right upon the physical manifestation of his darkest nightmare in front of him. He tried to look away but couldn't. The more he stared at it, the more it burned itself into his psyche. Until—

Foooom.

The floodlights shut off and everything around him went black. His pupils weren't properly dilated for night vision because they'd adjusted to the bright lights. He gripped Cooper's leash as hard as he could and sprinted back to the house, dragging his berserk dog. Cooper had barked so hard for so long he couldn't bark anymore, and all that came out were cracked whimpers. Not for one second did the guardian of the household take his eyes off the creature, he wouldn't dream of it, even with his owner strangling him on the way to the house. Cooper wanted that thing's throat; its black, monstrous, impossibly thick throat.

Ellen stood silhouetted in the glow of the front door. Caleb was not with her. Even from down the hill, Aaron could see the unplugged extension cord at her feet.

"Ellen! Ellen! Did you see it? Did you see it?"

"Yes! Yes, I saw it!"

Aaron and Cooper ran inside, and Ellen slammed the door behind them. They bolted into the bedroom, and after Ellen grabbed a wailing Caleb, the entire family huddled together in a frightened puddle on the bed.

Aaron turned his head to look out the bedroom window one last time. The creature — the monster — had vanished.

• • •

The terrified family clung to each other. Aaron dug all ten of his fingers into the meat of his wife's shoulders, and she pressed her back firmly into his chest. With every inch of her arms, she wrapped herself around a hysterical Caleb, and she rocked back and forth, moving Aaron in the process, shushing and cooing to her only son. Despite having not seen any of it, he was more distraught than anyone. Cooper laid in a ball at Caleb's feet, his jaw flat against the bed and his eyes on the door. Only ever on the door.

"Hush. Hush, baby," Ellen said. Tears fell from her face

and onto his as she held him, covering him in a snotty, silvery film of sadness.

"Mommy! Daddy! I'm scared!"

"Baby, it's okay. Everyone's okay," Ellen said.

"But what happened? Why are you crying?"

Aaron reached a hand over to the back of Caleb's head. "It's nothing, chicken. We're sorry. We're gonna go back to sleep now. Okay?"

"But I—I don't—"

"Cooper got outside, baby," Ellen said. "That's all. Sometimes doggies like to sneak outside, and we were just worried about him. Your daddy heard him barking."

"But—but what was he barking at? Is Cooper okay? Cooper is my buddy and I love him!"

"Cooper's okay," Aaron said. "He's right here. He had a good run. He was just chasing a squirrel. Just doing dog stuff. You know how he loves chasing squirrels, right?"

"But he should be sleeping! We all should be sleeping!"

"Hush, hush. Hush, my little boy," Ellen whispered. "We're gonna sleep now."

After ten more minutes of indiscriminate sobs and groans and cries of misunderstanding, Caleb finally fell asleep in his mother's arms. Aaron didn't speak to his wife, but in between mental rabbit holes of existential dread, found moments in the pain and in the darkness to admire her. She clung to her son with an absolute ferocity, and in his hands, her entire body felt hard as stone. Here and there, as the minutes droned by, he would catch a glance at her eyes. They were ice cold, penetrating the door long after Cooper had shut his.

Neither had said a word since they'd rocked Caleb to sleep. There was nothing and everything to say at the same time. Ellen could have apologized for not believing her husband but they both knew there was no need. Aaron could have started down any number of paths about 'What are we gonna do?' but he didn't know where to start.

An hour passed in rigid silence, and at one point, Aaron traced the windowsill with his eyes. It had all started when he'd stood looking at the same meadow from downstairs and saw something he clearly shouldn't have. He fantasized about a different version of himself standing there, a vision of a timeline where he had left this whole thing alone. What if Cooper had not growled that night? Or what if he did and Aaron just chose to ignore it? Would his family be any safer? Would Hank be any less dead? Would Hank-back-from-the-dead or someone using Hank's voice be calling with cryptic messages?

Would Aaron be fast asleep in bed next to his wife, holding her softness instead of her steel, his perfect son dreaming up dragons in the next room and his best friend in the world guarding them all from nothing more than crickets and frogs?

In the faint glow of the moonlight, the streak of a white moth at the window caught Aaron's eye. He let go of Ellen and rose to face the window. The world slowed down, and the night descended into a depth of quiet, even past silence.

"Ellen. What did that patient say to you again?" he whispered.

"What?"

He turned around and stared at her for a long time before whispering in an even softer decibel.

In two soft steps, Aaron slipped back onto the bed. He brought his face close to hers, and a tear rolled down from his eye. "You know the one."

Ellen's glassy eyes reflected his question back at him. Caleb jostled but didn't wake. She looked down at her son, a tear of her own falling from her drooping and haggard face.

"He said, 'It's running in the back of my dreams.'"

"It was there. I saw that thing in my dream just now. I saw it exactly as it was. I'd never seen it before like that, but I saw it clear as day, as clear as I saw it in the meadow. I'd never seen it before like that. I'd never seen it before. How did that happen?"

"What do you mean?"

"I mean exactly that. I mean I saw it. I had this awful dream. Caleb was there. For some reason, we were at the pool I used to go to as a kid. Caleb was lying on the bottom of the pool and he was blue. But it was there. The massive body, the eyes. It had these terrible claws or long fingers, I'm not sure what. But it was there. It was all right there. And then it was real. I'm dead fucking serious."

In spite of everything, it felt so good to be talking about this with Ellen. For three days now, his terror and confusion were solely his own.

Ellen got out of bed with the grace of a gazelle and laid Caleb on her pillow. She went to the window. A strip of purple light had crept over the mountains. The beautiful Blue Ridge Mountains, under the descending and iridescent moon.

"God," she said. "What the fuck was that thing?"

"I—I have no idea at all."

"Was it running in your dream?"

"Running? No. It wasn't running. It just sort of came out of the pool."

"What?"

"I know. I have no idea. None of this makes any sense. I'm—I'm fucking terrified, Ellen."

She wrapped her arms around him and put her chin on his shoulder.

"Do you think anyone else knows about it?" she said.

"I mentioned that I'd seen something at night to the cop at Hank's and the detective who came by today. They both kind of blew me off. I think it probably comes out every night at the same time. This has to be the thing Cooper's been growling at. The only night it didn't come out was when I had the floodlights on." He stopped and sat back in shock. "What if the thing doesn't like the lights?"

"What do you mean?"

"Well, the only night out of the last three it didn't come out was when I left the lights on. Then tonight, it was moving, but it stopped when you turned the lights on. But when you turned them off, well, I didn't see it walk away but it was gone."

"What? Why?"

"I have no clue. Hank's dead. We need to find out if this thing killed Hank. Do you think it did? Wait. He wanted to talk to me. Man-to-man. Remember? You think it went after him?"

Aaron struggled to make out his wife's features in the darkness, but he could tell her mouth was hanging open and her eyes were glistening with tears.

"This is all so fucking weird, Aaron."

"Should we call her? The cop?"

Caleb lay snoring on the edge of the bed. The purple strip of light on the mountains had been nudged upward by a ribbon of blood orange below it.

Ellen scooped up her son. "She won't believe us," she said.

"What about that detective?"

"Will he believe us?"

"Probably not. He also didn't leave a card."

"Well," Ellen looked at Cooper, asleep on the floor. "What if we—"

"What?"

"I don't know. It's stupid."

"No, tell me. What should we do?"

DAY 4

A few minutes past seven in the morning, all four of the Dreyers were piled into Aaron's SUV, headed to downtown Bensalem.

After the chaos of last night, Ellen wanted to spend her much-needed day off anywhere but the house. She didn't feel as though she was running away, more that she was running towards something. Other people. The solitude of the house was a wonderful thing when it felt safe, and it always had done until last night. Now that it didn't, she couldn't bear the thought of no one being able to hear them if they screamed.

She stared vacantly at the landscape as it whisked by. Young pine trees, round slabs of rock, yellow wildflowers, a collapsed barn. The objects swirled together into a frothy stew of speed and color, nauseating to consume.

Ellen rolled her head from one end of the headrest to the other. It felt like a boulder on top of a toothpick.

"Can we eat something first?" she asked. "I'm starving. I feel like absolute shit."

Aaron kept his eyes forward and his shoulders hunched over the wheel. His messy hair and nervous body language made him look more like the vehicle's thief than its owner.

She put a hand on his knee.

"Hey."

He jumped to attention and shot a reflexive glance into the rear view at Caleb passed out in his car seat.

"Mama's starving. Can we get food, please? Aren't you hungry?"

"Sure," Aaron said.

The SUV rolled into the gravel parking lot of the Country Inn Diner and parked next to a white pickup truck, one of only two other vehicles in the lot. The diner had outdoor seating to accommodate the dog, and yesterday's rain had left the morning air immaculately cool.

Ellen peeled herself out of the passenger seat and cracked her back. Mourning doves cooed high above in the branches of a red maple as the early morning sunlight coated everything in a phosphorescent glow. Something about it annoyed her.

She unbuckled Caleb, thumb in mouth, and guided him out of the car. Cooper followed them. Little bags of fatigue had inflated under Caleb's eyes, and he moved slow, as if drugged. His hair, typically buoyant in his boyish excitement, seemed somehow still and subdued. He squinted in the sunlight.

Aaron went inside to see the hostess while the rest of the family made for the closest outdoor table.

"Mom, can I go in there with Daddy?" Caleb said sheepishly.

"Stay with Mommy, baby," Ellen said.

All of the other outdoor tables were empty. Not shocking for a day that would soon be blisteringly hot, but a little disappointing. The mindless chatter from folks she didn't know would have been nice. Regular people talking about regular things. Even strangers just sitting in silence would have done the trick, allowing her to marinate in the illusion of a normal life and let her forget, if only for a moment, that her husband had been right and that "creature" was real and it was indeed terrible. The thought of it was too surreal to address head-on. She shooed it away whenever it peeked over the barrier of whatever cognitive noise she could slap together, but it hung there like a helium balloon, ready to burst with the slightest pinprick.

Shuffling sideways to slide into the bench, her knees gave out under the weight of everything that had happened in the last five hours. The harsh contact of her butt against the iron wicker jostled her organs and left an ambiguous pain in her side.

Cooper stared up at her and cocked his head. He was trying to say something, but she didn't have the care or energy to try and interpret.

She shook her head and sighed. He started panting.

• • •

No one stood at the hostess stand inside the Country Inn Diner. Instead, a woman wearing a traditional diner uniform buzzed behind a long counter on the far side of the room. Besides her, the only other person in view was a burly-looking man sitting in a booth in the corner, probably a trucker tired of gas station coffee.

Roy Orbison played in the background, the volume turned down to facilitate conversations that weren't happening. Above the counter hung a row of non-uniform mugs that may as well have come from someone's kitchen cabinets. In fact, very little inside the diner matched. It felt less like a restaurant and more like a big kitchen, a place slowly cobbled together from small parts and big smells over the span of decades, not some boardroom concoction that fit together like a jigsaw puzzle and smelled like plastic.

Aaron took a seat at the counter to wait for service, and the waitress slapped down a laminated menu with pictures of the food. The name MARLA was stitched in red cursive below the left shoulder of her uniform.

"Hey there, Marla," Aaron said. "I've got my family outside. You mind if we eat out there?"

"Well, patio ain't open. Don't open 'til 11 'cause that's when we start servin' lunch. I ain't even cleaned it from last night yet."

She was incredibly busy behind the counter, pouring coffee, washing glasses, spinning around like some caffeinated bumble bee, even though the place was nearly empty.

"You can sit out there if you want, but I gotta serve ya in here."

"That's fine. I'll wait for it here and take it outside."

A plate crashed to the ground.

"Mother of fuckin' pearl!" she shouted.

Aaron peeked over the counter to observe the broken guts of an omelet and hash browns on the floor, and Marla, on her hands and knees, sweeping it with her bare palms into a more manageable mess.

"You need a hand with that?" Aaron asked.

"Matter of fact, yes, I do, but ain't your job. Thanks for askin'. I had to send my busboy home before his shift started 'cause he come in stankin' like reefer."

"Yikes."

Marla rose with a sign and clapped her hands together, ridding them of a surely small portion of the myriad germs and dirt they had just acquired. "Why don't y'all just come in here?"

"Well, we have our dog with us. I don—"

"Oh hell, I don't care. Ain't nobody cares here. Come inside and sit over in that booth in the front. It'll be easier for all of us."

"Okay. Thanks, Marla. We won't be any trouble. Cooper's very well behaved."

"Mm hm," she said, back on the ground and sweeping with her hands again.

· · ·

None of the Dreyers said a word to each other in the booth by the door. Its gaudy, red glitter formica table seemed to jeer at them in their solemnity. Even Caleb seemed to know this was no time to make a fuss. Cooper rested with his head on his paws under the table.

While they waited for service — for Marla — a middle-aged couple came in and sat down. Then a group of four elderly women came in. Marla greeted them with a cackle, the first time Aaron had witnessed any semblance of joy from the poor woman.

"Is Cooper in trouble?" Caleb asked in a soft voice that seemed to really be asking if he was the one in trouble.

"No, baby, he's not in any trouble. We just love him very much and want him to be safe inside. Don't you?" Ellen said.

"Yeah."

Marla, now in markedly better spirits since the plate incident, came by the booth.

"How is everything over here? Boy, you sure are a beautiful young family," Marla said. "Y'all don't talk much, I guess?"

Aaron and Ellen exchanged a miffed look.

"We've just had a really long night," Ellen said.

Caleb, on his knees in the booth, marched a plastic dinosaur along the windowsill next to them, paying no attention to Marla.

"What'ch'all havin?"

Ellen looked up at Marla, and for the first time that day, Aaron saw the faint glow of life on her face.

"I'll have the deluxe with scrambled eggs, hash browns and bacon, please," she said.

"Kay. You, sir?"

"I'll have the same actually, except sausage instead of bacon."

"Easy 'nuff."

"And, uh, mister dino man, you hungry over there?"

Ellen cut in. "Um, can we get him a half-stack of pancakes? Syrup on the side?"

"Sure thing, sweetheart. Anything else?"

"Yeah," said Aaron. "I want a vanilla milkshake."

"And I'll have a chocolate one, please," Ellen said.

"Good choice. I'm a chocolate kinda girl myself. Be right out."

She buzzed away to take orders from her new patrons.

As they ate, Aaron snuck Cooper the occasional scrap of human food. He deserved it. There were so many times Aaron wished Cooper could speak, but none more than right now.

Caleb locked eyes with one of the elderly women as he smeared syrup-covered pancake across his face. She laughed and waved, encouraging him to make more of a mess than he already had.

"Do you think we should ask the waitress? Marla?" Aaron muttered.

"I don't know. Maybe."

Just then, the burly man from the corner booth sauntered towards the door. He had a feather earring in his right ear and the heels of his cowboy boots smacked the linoleum floor as he passed by.

"How about you take the boys and I'll settle up and ask her?" Aaron said.

"What are you going to say?"

"I don't know. I'll think of something."

Ellen agreed, and Aaron strode up to the counter where Marla pecked at big plastic buttons on an old cash register.

"$32.45. And that's before tip."

"Thank you. It really hit the spot," Aaron said.

He retrieved his wallet and began wading through small bills.

"Hey, a quick question for you. My wife and I are new in town and we're curious about the town's history. My wife is a big horror movie buff, and we were going to see if there were any local bigfoot sightings or scary urban legends at the library or historical society. Any recommendations?"

Marla smacked a piece of Nicorette gum between her lips and gazed up at Aaron. "Don't know about no bigfoot."

Aaron chuckled dryly. "That's fine. Sort of a silly question."

He paid, tipping twenty percent.

"Come back anytime, now," Marla said as the last of the Dreyers departed the Country Inn Diner.

• • •

Most of the houses in Bensalem were half as old as the Dreyers' and about a quarter of the size. Cookie-cutter split levels from a post-war economy when rural hamlets were thriving.

But the promise of those days had been sapped out of the place decades ago. You could see it in the unkempt lawns, cluttered garages and mildew-stained doors on houses that hadn't yet been abandoned or collapsed altogether. Idiosyncratic garnishes set the properties apart from each other. The women's club members packed their gardens with tulips and chrysanthemums that blossomed in spring. Machine operators and mechanics erected lean-tos on the sides of their houses where they dumped heaps of metal and trash. Dogs and cats, sometimes with collars, sometimes without, roamed the streets at dawn.

It was the only version of Bensalem that Cheryl McNamara knew. A world in a snow globe where the snow had stopped falling.

The McNamaras lived in a prosaic little raised rancher on Willowbrook Lane, south of downtown. The cedar shake siding was painted a kind of puce color that made the house look either deep purple or hot pink depending on the light (or lack thereof).

Alan Vought had painted it as a joke for his wife on Valentine's Day more than two decades ago but the joke was on him when she remarked that it looked like 'Tinkerbell jizzed all over it'. That comment made him sell the place to Rick and a heavily pregnant Cheryl a year later. Lenny was born in May. Skylar came along four years later.

Cheryl missed Lenny desperately. In the background of every faded childhood photo that hung on the McNamaras' wood-paneled walls was the vague possibility that he might return and take care of the mother who had given so much to take care of him. Cheryl and Lenny had just clicked. It had been two-and-a-half years since he'd left for Virginia Tech, but the weight of his absence felt heavier every day. Weekend phone calls and spring breaks were never enough.

Cheryl had always assumed it was supposed to work the opposite way, that it would get easier with time, but the truth was that Lenny was the glue that held them together, and Skylar seemed unwilling to take up the mantle.

That morning, as the Dreyers finished up their American Deluxes, Rick McNamara stood over an ancient gas stovetop in his kitchen, a room just large enough for the necessary appliances, some cabinets, and a small round table in the corner. He huffed in the aroma of bacon cracking to perfection while steam from the stove billowed upward in white clouds and settled below the ceiling. Sunlight from the window poured through venetian blinds and cast white streaks onto the cabinets.

"Sweet Lord, that's nice," he whispered.

Rick was a State Farm agent who had represented the town for more than thirty years. "Auto, home, and life. If you don't have all three, you might as well have none," he'd say. He had a handful of similar canned lines that had kept his business as steady as it could be in a town like Bensalem. He even looked like an insurance agent: plump, plain, non-threatening.

Cheryl waltzed in and pecked him on the cheek.

"Mornin', bug," he said.

"Mornin'."

She looked down at the griddle and snatched a piece of bacon.

"Where you goin' with that? It ain't ready," Rick said.

"I'll say if it's ready."

She sat down at the table and unfolded the Washington Post. Hank's case wouldn't rise to national attention. Not if it was just a random act of violence. At least, that's what she hoped.

Rick interrupted her reading. She could barely hear him over the crackle of the bacon. "Do you know where your daughter was last night?" he asked. He had his back to her, too busy stirring and smelling to turn around.

Cheryl lowered the paper to look at him. "No. What now?"

With a frying pan in one hand and a spatula in the other, Rick came over and served his wife breakfast. Rick did breakfasts, Cheryl did dinners. Skylar didn't participate in either. She just snacked on crackers and gummy bears during the day and raided the fridge at night.

"Where was she? What time'd she get in?" Cheryl asked.

"Don't know," Rick said, sliding two pancakes and three strips of bacon onto Cheryl's plate. "You're gon' have to ask her."

"Oh, I'm askin'?"

"Well, she ain't been up yet."

"Good. Hope she stays sleepin' so you can ask her. I gotta roll soon."

Sixteen-year-old Skylar McNamara was about as different from her mother as she could be. Worse, she was the direct opposite of her brother. Skylar didn't have perfect grades. She wasn't athletic. The last time her mother had forced extra-curriculars onto her, she burst into tears and threw her ballet shoes at her instructor when she was nine. As Skylar became a teenager, the traits that worried her the most became all the more pronounced. She wore weird clothes, dark makeup, hung around with older kids, and smelled like pot.

The floorboards creaked above them in the kitchen. Skylar had risen. Rick chewed his pancakes while gazing off into space. He looked like a cow mashing its cud in slow, circular, motions, his eyes fixed on nothing.

Cheryl flipped to the Post's sports section and her eyes landed on a photo of a baseball player in the middle of a home run swing. Only when she read the words "third baseman" in the caption did her mind cast back to Scoot Hamilton for the first time in over a day.

Situations like his were the ones over which she felt at least some modicum of control. Maybe there was something she could say. Maybe a judge could give him a jail stint long enough to scare him but short enough to keep him sane.

Maybe if she could save a kid like Scoot, she could save her daughter.

• • •

The Dreyers waited outside of the Bensalem Library because it wasn't due to open for another twenty minutes. Like all the other businesses in Bensalem, it, too, was outdated. Either Bensalem kept them that way on purpose or the town simply didn't notice the neighboring towns beginning to modernize. Twenty miles to the north, Sperryville had installed a sprawling, kid-friendly, dog-friendly beer garden and farmers' market combo called Patagonia Dreamin'.

Aaron would drive up there every now and then just to soak in the atmosphere. Young people doing modern things, having conversations about politics, music, media. The place offered a connectedness that he couldn't replicate in Bensalem. Ellen's argument against the Patagonia Dreamin' model was that small towns had a responsibility to preserve their history and shouldn't be cheapened by "hipster establishments" to appeal to outsiders. Aaron didn't understand it.

Another thing he didn't understand was why there were no places of worship in Bensalem. Sperryville had Protestant and Catholic churches, and there was a synagogue a few miles to the west, but considering the way folks in Bensalem seemed to cling to nostalgia and the optics of tradition, the absence of all things religious seemed downright odd.

The sun was rapidly roasting the morning's coolness into oblivion, and the increasing humidity made everything feel soft and sticky. An analog thermometer on the wall of the library read 87°F.

Ellen basked in the sun while the rest of the family sat in the shade. Her eyes were closed and her chin was pointed towards the sky. Beads of sweat had formed on her upper lip and around her collarbones.

Across the street, an old man on a park bench rustled around and babbled incoherent words. Everything about the man was dirty and faded. He was dressed for a blizzard in a huge blue parka and long black pants. His scraggly beard was almost the same color as his skin — a sort of ruddy, graying orange. A brown paper bag and tattered backpack sat underneath the bench.

Just then, the doors of the library opened from the inside and a portly man stepped out. His cat-like smile and chin divot reminded Aaron vaguely of John Travolta.

"Y'all here for the Cyber Safety course? It don't start 'til eleven."

"No, sir, we're just here for the library," said Aaron.

"Oh, of course, come on in, get outta this heat. Sorry, we open a little late on Saturdays sometimes."

"Excuse me, sir," Aaron said, "I hate to ask this, but would you mind if we brought our dog inside with us? He's very well-behaved and we'll keep him close."

The question wasn't something Aaron and Ellen had discussed, but they hadn't let Cooper out of their sight since he'd barked himself hoarse last night.

John Travolta's shorter twin bit his bottom lip and looked at the dog. "Well," he peered back into the library. "Is he a service dog?"

"He is today," Ellen said with authority. "Just this once. We've all had a difficult night and we all just want to be close to each other this morning."

"Well, I can hardly argue with that. Y'all just keep him close and everything'll be fine, m'kay?"

"Yes, absolutely."

• • •

Immediately upon entering the library, Ellen made her move. She waited until the boys were inside and Caleb was dashing off to some brightly-colored section of the room.

"Hey," she said to the librarian, prompting him to turn around. "Sorry, I've got kind of an odd question for you. Are you familiar with any local urban legends? Or have there been any, um, like, mass murders in Bensalem's history?"

The librarian didn't take a physical step back, but he might as well have. His wide smile wilted into a befuddled sneer, and he eyed Ellen with cautious suspicion. "Uh, what did y'all say happened to you last night?"

"Nothing. Nothing happened to us. It's just, well, did you hear about that murder on the news?"

"Oh, yes, ma'am. I didn't know Hank Teakle but my father did, and, well, that sort of thing don't happen here much."

"Would you believe we, uh, we live right next door to him?"

"Oh my. You don't say?"

"Yeah. We're just a little spooked, so ..."

"Lord 'a'mercy! A little spooked? Well, I'd be just beside myself. Heck, nearly am now and I ain't even know him." He leaned in close and put a hand to his face to guard his words from non-existent onlookers and eavesdroppers. "You know, people in town are talkin'. This ain't never happen to us. Somethin' is wrong here."

"Really? What are they saying? What do you think happened?"

"All sorta hot garbage flyin' around. Some say he killed himself or OD'd on somethin'. Others think maybe some kinda animal in them woods wanted to tangle, and he got the raw end of some teeth or claws. Personally, I wouldn't put it past some hopped up meth head fixin' to steal his horses or raid the house and just leave him like that."

Ellen sighed. "Yeah. Could be any of those, honestly."

"Who's to say?"

Caleb's faint laugh, a welcome sound she hadn't heard yet this morning, drew her attention away from the librarian and towards a pile of books her son was stacking in the middle of the room. Cooper milled around unattended, his nose to the ground, his leash dragging behind him. Aaron stood staring out a window, ignoring them both.

A red wave of embarrassment washed over her. "Sorry, excuse me," she said, striding over to her husband. When she grabbed him by the arm and spun him to face her, the glassiness in his eyes shook her. She'd never seen those eyes before. He seemed to be looking through her, as though one or both of them weren't really there.

"Aaron? Hey. Look at me."

But he did not, and instead, opened his mouth as if to scream.

"Aaron. Aaron!"

"The gate," he said to no one, his slack jaw still not moving.

When he shifted his vacant gaze to meet hers, she suddenly felt she wasn't speaking with her husband anymore. His eyes dug into her with an intense focus that almost hurt.

"The gate is the light," he whispered.

Then, Aaron's eyes rolled back in his head, his body went limp, and he collapsed into a metal bookshelf, bringing down a heap of hardcovers with him. Some awful amalgamation of fear, shock and confusion wrapped its long fingers around Ellen's intestines. It squeezed, and it twisted.

Ellen's head began to spin, and the vision of her surroundings in the library swirled together into circular oblivion. For a split second, Ellen saw the face of the patient she had treated days earlier. He spoke to her from some hellish portal in her mind.

'Running in the back of your dreams.'

Ellen anchored herself to the bobbing jet-black head of her son jogging towards her. Focusing on her son, even if blurry, allowed her to regain her balance and fend off whatever dizziness spell had overcome her. But as she knelt to the ground to tend to her husband, her physical movements were slow, and her thoughts felt heavy, and she knew in the dark corner of her soul that whatever it was somehow connected to what just happened. It was connected to the patient, connected to Hank, connected to everything.

"Sir? Sir? Could you please bring water? And a towel?" she shouted.

Caleb stood there mystified, his ruffled little brow and his frown not hiding he was a hair trigger away from another meltdown. But Aaron suddenly jerked himself awake, just in time to prevent his son from going over the edge. Not more than a few seconds later, the librarian rushed over and knelt beside Ellen, who kneeled over her husband.

"Drink up," he said, offering Aaron a glass of water. "It's still cold and I got it from the Brita. Goodness, this heat is just beyond everything!"

"Oh. Yeah. Gosh. Aaron, it must have been the heat," she said.

"My mother says heat stroke ain't real, but heck if I ain't just been made a witness. You alright there, sir? Want me to call an ambulance?"

Ellen pulled Aaron to his feet. "Oh, no, that's okay, sir. Thank you for all your help. I'm actually a doctor, so he's in good hands."

The librarian began gathering the books Aaron had knocked down. "You know the heat index in Richmond is—"

"Oh, please, don't worry about those books. Let me clean up. I just need a minute with my husband. Caleb, will you start picking up the books so this nice man can get back to work?"

Caleb and the librarian traded skeptical glances.

"Sweetie? Can you help Mommy so the man who helped

Daddy can go back to work?"

The look of concern scrawled on the librarian's face over Aaron's welfare had reverted back to the same cautious suspicion he reflected back at Ellen when she asked him about urban legends. He placed the hardcovers on the now empty shelf and wiped his palms on his jeans as if they were dirty. "Well, I'll just, um, y'all just let me know if you need anything."

With Aaron's arm draped over her shoulders and Caleb's hand in hers, Ellen led her family out of the library and back to the SUV. Cooper followed, his leash still dragging behind him.

"What the fuck happened?" Ellen whispered.

"Where are we?" Aaron said.

"What? What are you talking about? We're at the library."

"I've never been here before."

"Do you not remember fainting? Aaron, you're scaring me, tell me what happened? Did you see something? You were talking about the gate and the light. You said the gate is the light."

"What? I did?"

"Yes. You were lost. What happened to you just now?"

"I—I have no idea."

"What's the last thing you remember?"

The question seemed to strike Aaron with great force, so much so that he recoiled as he tried to stand.

"Boots. I remember boots clicking on the floor. At the diner."

• • •

Ellen took over driving duties while her husband rested in the fully reclined passenger seat. Caleb and Cooper moped in the back together like two boys in self-imposed time-out. Sad because something was very wrong with their parents but confused because they thought it might be their fault. Ellen kept her hand on her husband's knee as they drove. Aaron put his hand over hers.

"I think I know why I fainted back there. I've been feeling funny all morning," Aaron said.

"Why?"

"I was so close to it. Last night. I felt something there. Like it was … I don't know. Telling me to … get away from it. Warding me off."

Ellen released a deep breath she'd been holding. The cold, industrial blow of the SUV's air conditioning provided her only modicum of physical comfort. She kept her eyes on the road.

Aaron craned his neck around to the back seat. "Cooper seems fine. He was closest to it the longest. Come to think of it, I felt really weird the first time I saw it. Are you feeling weird at all?"

"Define weird."

Downtown Bensalem was lifeless. It either hadn't woken up yet this morning or remained sedated in its more permanent existential slumber. A few parked cars dotted the shoulders of Main Street. Twiggy black poplar trees on the sidewalks scattered thin streaks of shade upon them.

"Can we stop for a Gatorade? Or three?" Aaron asked.

"Of course. That's a good idea," Ellen said.

Aaron pointed out the windshield. "That boutique sells drinks. The place I got your earrings."

Ellen parked across the street from M&J Fine Gifts and Aaron got out alone. She waited until he was out of sight and reached into her purse.

Deputy Cheryl McNamara's business card had brown and beige streaks on a white background. Every single character of the text was italicized. If Ellen didn't know any better, she might have thought it was advertising a race car driver.

She pulled her mobile phone out of her purse, and before she dialed, her ears heard for a split second the ghostly and hollow voice of Hank's ... something ... replaying in her mind.

"Hello, Deputy McNamara, this is Ellen Dreyer."

"Oh. Hello there, Mrs. Dreyer. What can I do for you?"

"I was just calling to see if you'd learned anything about Hank's cause of death? To be honest, my family and I are a bit worried about not having any sense of what's out there."

"Nothing yet, I'm afraid. I'm headed back up to Hank's later today, but VSP took over the case and frankly that's where we want it. I'm not exactly bursting at the seams down here with trained investigators."

Every police officer Ellen had ever dealt with had made her feel reassured and uneasy at the same time. Divulging enough info to be helpful, but always on guard. Always a little defensive, or at least ready to be, if a conversation were to go south.

"Okay, let us know if you do learn anything. We're really worried."

"Try not to fret, ma'am. Are y'all staying inside today?"

"Actually, no, we just hopped out of the house for a few minutes but we're on our way home now. Anything wrong?"

"Nothing at all, just want to make sure y'all stay close today. That's the best place you all can be. You haven't clicked on the news, have you? Media's startin' to get a hold of it."

"Believe it or not, we've avoided the news completely. We

were a bit ... tied up last night."

"Dealing with the attention might be the hardest part. Will be for me at least. Glad to hear it hasn't rubbed over to you yet. If the press knocks on your door, do me a favor and don't answer it. If you have to, invite 'em in for a drink but tell 'em you have no comment about the case."

"You got it. Thanks, Officer."

"Mommy ..." Caleb said softly.

Ellen's little boy looked so much like her. Her tired heart melted with love looking at those green eyes and knobby little knees in the back seat.

"Can we go play?" he said, pointing out at a playground to their left. No one was there. Its placement across from the stores on Main Street didn't quite fit, but then again, a lot of things in Bensalem didn't fit.

"Yep, let's go. Let Cooper out. He can come. Come on, chicken, I'll race ya!"

· · ·

Like most, Aaron was familiar with the old adage, "Humans only use ten percent of their brains," but he had never given it much thought. He certainly didn't preoccupy himself wondering what made up that other ninety percent. He just assumed it was reserved for mothers performing feats of superhuman strength to lift cars off of their children, or widowers who willed themselves to die just hours after their spouses of fifty years. Whenever he did consider that other ninety percent, he imagined it as some astonishing act of mortal accomplishment. A comic-book-like channeling of brain power amplified through the physical body.

He never thought it could be as nuanced as a pang of inexplicable dread that manifested while walking into a store he'd visited just days before. A simple room veneered in the trappings of a charming country shop but exposed to be something quite different when seen through the eyes of the soul.

The door was already propped open, relegating the bell on top of it obsolete. In one way, everything appeared to be exactly the same as last time. All the soaps, sweatshirts, jewelry and crafty little trinkets packed into their rightful places. But within seconds, Aaron's eyes were drawn to the negative spaces of the room that lurked behind the bombastic tourist traps.

Near the ceiling, a wallpaper border adorned with a pattern of budded crosses ran the entire perimeter of the room. The crosses were gold and had red roses in their centers. Below them, three yellow dots were painted on the wall behind the cash register. Just below the yellow dots sat a shelf brimming with garish, featureless, black figurines.

Aaron walked right by the mini fridge containing the cold drinks he had sought and took a closer look at the figurines.

"Hello! Good morning!" Jane said, intercepting him.

Out of nowhere, a heavy, invisible cloak of malaise wrapped itself around his shoulders. He moved slow and with great effort, as if walking through thick mud. The oddness of his physical state baffled him, and he screwed his face into a bewildered frown as he locked onto her eyes, just inches from his own. He consumed the sight of her. The laughter lines on her cheeks were as deep as canyons. Her eyes shone a radiant azure and the layers of tissue in her irises rippled in the morning light. They were two circular oceans, caving in on themselves, currents rushing from their outer rims into her pupils. Her pupils were dark, black portals through which Aaron thought he could see himself, a subconscious interloper watching this very interaction unfold from another dimension of reality.

"Aaron, right? Can I help ya find something?"

"I just came in for a drink. Gatorade."

"Well, ya look like ya could use one!"

Jane spun him around by the arm back towards the mini fridge at the front of the store. Through the front window, Aaron watched Caleb oscillate on the playground swing while Ellen stood behind him, pushing. Aaron's eyes locked onto the swing, watching it swish back and forth. A dense forest thicket backdropped the scene behind them.

"Will water work for ya? Afraid that's all we've got."

"I think the water will be fine."

"How 'bout ya take two? It's already so hot today. I can tell you've been out in the heat."

The part of Aaron's brain that processed reason and logic switched off and an energy existing outside his body entered him. His mind went completely blank.

"Yeah. It's already so hot today. You can tell I've been out in the heat," he said, his voice a dead monotone.

Almost in lockstep, as if he were being led by a string, Aaron followed Jane towards the counter.

"How'd she like those earrings, by the way?"

"Sorry?"

"Oh my, don't ya' remember those earrings? For the winter solstice babe?"

"Oh. Yes, the—" A slicing pain shot through his neck and up into his skull. A dense drum began pounding inside his head, and holding no agency over a means to protest, he surrendered himself to its beat. "—black ones."

Jane lowered her tone, and she narrowed her brow. Her eyes bored into him. "Yes. Yes. That's right. The black ones. Here, we love black things. Things born in the dirt and forged in the fire."

A dark haze settled over the room and over Jane. Only her deep blue eyes retained their saturation.

"Aaron. Is that your son out there?"

"Yes. That's my son."

Jane opened one of the water bottles and took a sip without blinking. "He reminds me of my own son."

Aaron said nothing. Instead, he dove into Jane's gaze, into those blue waves crashing over each other and into deep black holes. Wave after wave, forming and disappearing, rising and falling, spinning in circles.

The veins in Jane's neck began to poke out of their blanket of old, thin skin. Something tightened in her jaw. "I haven't seen my Mark in quite some time."

The waves in her eyes slowed down and began to clump together. They stacked on top of each other into one huge wall, taking their time and gathering strength.

"Of course, that's not entirely true. I do see him sometimes."

It was a tsunami now. It was so strong and so powerful it sucked the blueness out of the ocean and rose pure white up into the sky. The black holes shriveled to nothingness as the giant wave towered over them. The wave stopped and began to crest, and as it did, the gravity in the entire room deepened, pulling Aaron down, pulling his eyelids down. Finally, the wave began to collapse under its own massive weight, and it blended into mist as it readied for the crash. The mist rose up, and rose fast, and Aaron's heart pounded wildly in his chest. It raced towards him now. Its gravity pulled him in. It was going to crash into him. It was going to take him under and bury him alive.

It was going to take everything.

"I see him running in the back of my dreams. Trying to open the gate."

Clang!

At the front of the room, the aluminum door blasted open with such ferocity that the bell flew clean off its hinge.

"CALEB!"

Ellen burned in a smoldering aura of orange light, an aggressive contrast to Jane's blue. She sliced through the store like a streak of lightning, searing the cold and the darkness.

"CALEB! CALEB! Are you in here?! Aaron! Aaron, is Caleb with you? Did he come in here?"

Ellen grabbed Aaron by both arms and dug her fingers into his flesh. Aaron's vision of the room slowly returned and the tsunami that had been forming melted away as the fire around Ellen scorched all in its path. She even seemed to singe Jane, who now sat in a rust-colored repose behind the counter.

"Aaron! Is Caleb here? Caleb! Caleb! Caleb, sweetie?"

"Wh—What?" Aaron said. He blinked rapidly as if looking upon the world for the very first time.

"What the fuck is taking so long in here, Aaron? We have to go!"

Ellen darted through aisles and around end caps, thrashing her head in every direction and whipping her long black hair through the air.

Jane's grainy voice rose up from the counter. "Oh, dear. You lookin' for a little boy?"

Ellen charged towards her. "Yes. Caleb. Black hair. Green eyes. A little boy didn't just come in here, did he?"

"Haven't seen one if he did. I'm pretty sure I would have. No one's been in here except me and your husband."

Cooper's deep and rhythmic barks echoed through the walls from outside. Ellen put her hands to her head and squeezed her skull, almost as if she wanted to crush it. "Oh, Jesus fuck. Oh, fucking fuck, Aaron! Let's go! Come on! We have to find him!"

• • •

Cheryl readied herself to leave the house but paused when she heard Skylar's footsteps. Skylar wasn't being quiet about it either, plodding with the grace of an elephant, a posture far removed from her usual covert self. It was more typical for her to scurry around as covertly as possible, usually on a two-stop transit between her room and the kitchen. But as she trampled down the stairs earlier than normal, a pang of concern stiffened Cheryl's face. Skylar was fully dressed, which meant she had plans.

She wore a typical Skylar outfit. Dr. Martens, black jeans, a black tee big enough to be a dress, black eyeliner and tons of foundation. Only the color of her lipstick ever seemed to change. Today she'd chosen lime green.

Part of the problem with their relationship was that her mother never seemed to know what to say, especially if either of them were mad. Rick was no use, usually preferring to stay out of it.

"Mornin', young lady," Cheryl said.

Skylar brushed past her with a soft "Hey." The smell of marijuana followed her.

Now, Cheryl had to decide whether to go into the kitchen and ask her where she'd been the night before. Make it a thing. Should she be a mom or be a cop? In a situation like this, was there a difference? Rick was already in there with her. Would he say something? Probably not.

Cheryl charged into the kitchen. Rick was sitting at the table, his head buried in the paper. Skylar was standing with her back to her mother, hovering over the counter.

"Where were you last night, Skylar?" Cheryl said.

Skylar pretended she hadn't heard and filled a bowl with cereal.

"Skylar. Can you tell me where you were last night?"

Skylar ignored the question a second time. She drowned the cereal in milk and sat down at the table across from her father.

Rick put the paper down. "Skylar. Answer your mother. Where were you last night?"

"Out with friends," Skylar mumbled.

"You absolutely reek of pot," Cheryl snapped. "What time did you get home last night?"

All of the calmness in Skylar's face was suddenly replaced by an embarrassed rage. She looked up from her breakfast and shot daggers into her mother's eyes.

"Fuck you."

"Excuse me?" said Rick.

Cheryl stood calm and delivered. "Okay, you're grounded. For two months. And I'm searching your room. If I find—"

Just then, her cell buzzed in her back pocket. She looked at the number. Ellen Dreyer again, but she'd already called earlier that morning to ask about Hank's case. She let the phone vibrate in her hand. "Skylar, if I find pot in my house, you're grounded for the rest of the year. That's if I don't call the police."

Skylar scoffed. "You are the police."

The buzzing phone felt like a giant cockroach in her closed hand, trying to escape, hissing and gnawing at the edges of her fingers. "Do you know who this is? It's the next-door neighbor of the guy who was murdered yesterday. You know how he died?"

Red blotches formed on Cheryl's neck and her heart started pounding. The phone kept buzzing.

"A wild animal attacked him and ripped his body apart. His insides are all over the ground, and now this lady is scared, and I have to deal with her. And then I have to clean up the rest of Hank Teakle. The last thing I have time for today is you and your bullshit! Rick, search her room."

Cheryl stormed out of the house and slammed the door behind her, leaving her husband and daughter to gather the scraps of her rage. The claustrophobic humidity outside offered no quarter. She yanked the patrol car door open in white-hot anger and slammed herself inside.

She gritted her teeth, then closed her eyes. "Lord help me with that girl," she said.

On the passenger seat beside her sat a stack of papers from VSP regarding the Teakle case. She hadn't even begun to look through them, and the sight of the stack's height kicked her pulse up a notch.

"You're gonna have to wait," she said to the stack of papers. She pulled out her phone and called Ellen Dreyer back. The phone didn't even reach a full ring before Ellen picked up and started shouting.

"Officer! Come quick! My son is missing! Please come right now! Please send—"

"Whoa, whoa! Mrs. Dreyer? Calm down! What happened?"

"We're on Main Street! My son just went missing! I don't know where he—"

"Your son Caleb? The boy I saw with your husband yesterday?"

"Yes! I can't find him anywhere. He was right here. I was—"

"Okay. Where exactly are you?" Cheryl started the car.

"By the playground. We were on the playground. He was playing in the sandbox and I just looked up and he was gone! Officer, I swear—"

"Start lookin' for him if you haven't already. Look in the woods there. I know the spot. He's close. I'm on my way, okay? I'm coming."

• • •

Aaron and Ellen sprinted out the door of M&J Fine Gifts, across the street, and over to the playground where Ellen had last seen Caleb. Cooper was leashed to a picnic table, barking and tugging to the point of near strangulation.

"He was just in the sandbox. I swear I looked away for a minute and he was gone!" Ellen said. Her shoulders heaved up and down and her fingers were tensed and spread out, ready to grab him in an instant.

Although the dog struggled mightily, he managed to keep himself square to the woods behind the playground throughout his bucking. Ellen pointed at the trees. "Come on, come in here and help me look! Cooper thinks he's in there!"

Aaron followed her into the forest, and they began calling Caleb's name. As he ran through the woods, his head was a mess of bright colors and thoughts and fatigue.

"Let's split up! We can cover more ground!" she ordered, and she jogged off in the opposite direction.

Aaron ran every which way, yelling for his son. Cooper's barks from the playground grew fainter as he ran. Nothing in these woods was organized, the trees and the plants all looked the same. There were no trails, no markers. Caleb could have been anywhere — or nowhere.

His head started to spin again. The ground and the sky threatened to meet and the dense trees in front of him began to turn black. His center of gravity started zigging and zagging all over the place. The maniacal cackle of a woodpecker rained down on him from above.

Trying to round a corner too quickly, his body spun but his foot remained planted, twisting his ankle 90 degrees in the wrong direction. It released a sharp pop, and all the muscles around it deactivated at once.

An invisible hammer bashed the tendons in his ankle. The pain, the disbelief, the sheer confusion, and the last three days of hell all crashed into him in this sweltering maze of trees. He collapsed to the ground and cried to the heavens.

There in the dirt, the idea of losing his son started to sink in. Aaron's mind rifled through his mental rolodex of major moments in Caleb's young life. They played in rapid, quick-cut succession in his mind. The second he was born in the hospital in Charlotte. The first time he inhaled breath. He watched Caleb take his first steps in the backyard of their old house. He remembered how his mother had smiled when she cradled him as a newborn for the first time. He remembered his helpless family huddled together on the bed last night.

Even filtered through the trees, the heat of the noonday sun was unrelenting. Dirt and perspiration drenched him in a filmy, brown slime. It rolled down into his eyes, and it stung. Cooper's barks from the playground hadn't stopped. They were faint now, but they were as rhythmic as ever and seemed not to have lost any power.

Latching onto Cooper's calls as a lifeline to reality, Aaron pushed through the raging pain in his ankle, but after the third step on his bad foot he came crashing to the ground again. He crawled on the forest floor holding on to the faint hope of catching sight of an errant color in the dense thicket of green and brown, a clue of any kind to lead him to his son. But there wasn't a shred of human civilization here, just foliage and trash. These woods were as wild as the creatures that inhabited them. Aaron winced his eyes shut and breathed through the pain.

After crawling for some time in the direction of Cooper's barks, a police siren shrieked into earshot, and the colors of the playground peeked out through the foliage behind him. Cooper's barks ceased and were quickly replaced by Ellen's sobs.

"Oh God. Please be there, chicken. Please be with Mommy!"

Aaron crawled on, clutching to a pale glimmer of hope that his son might be waiting for him.

• • •

He found his wife in a broken heap, beet-red and drenched in sweat and tears. No words came. Just cries and heaves and moans from the pit of her stomach. She fell into his arms and wailed. Cooper sat panting on his haunches under the table to which he was still lashed.

Within minutes, a squad car pulled up, and Deputy Cheryl McNamara stepped out. She charged towards the couple, sunglasses down, face locked into solid stone, and already out of breath by the time she reached them. "Mrs. Dreyer, where did you last see your son?"

Aaron tried to shake Ellen to life. "Ellen. Look, Ellen, the cops are here. Can you talk to them?"

Ellen pointed to the sandbox, her hand shaking and her face a glistening tomato. "We were right there. He was in that sandbox one second and then, just gone."

"And that was what? About forty-five minutes ago now?"

Ellen nodded. "I have no idea what happened. I ... I just looked away for a second. I swear I'm not a bad mother. I just looked away for a second."

"Okay. He can't have gone too far in that time. Was there anyone else around? Did any vehicles stop by, or did you see anything suspicious?"

"No. I didn't see anyone. It was just us. Aaron went into the store over there."

"So, you believe your son entered these woods on his own and just got lost?"

"I don't really know. I thought he went into the store to find his dad, but he wasn't in there. I don't know how, he just disappeared. He was here one second and gone the next. If someone else was here, I would have ... I would have ... I ... I don't know, I don't know where he went, that's why I called you."

"Okay. If he really did go into the woods less than an hour ago, there's a very good chance we'll get him quickly. He couldn't have gone far. Hang tight."

Cheryl pulled a cartoonishly large walkie-talkie from her

belt and barked police codes. The talking box barked back.

Aaron kept his eyes glued to the trees, alert and ready to pounce on the sight of a little boy bumbling between them. Or maybe he'd see something else. These trees, after all, were part of the same forest in front of their house. A whole host of reservations held Aaron back from mentioning this to Ellen. Maybe she'd already put it together. Maybe she thought it already had him.

"Okay," Cheryl said. "I've got two officers coming to the south end of Main Street here. I've got a separate party headed to the northern perimeter of these woods on Route 45. If your son somehow travels out of the woods, that's the only road we would need to worry about. The east and west ends are bordered by farmland. My colleague is dispatching calls to those landowners right now. I'm gonna get a K-9 unit out here soon, too, but my hope is we find him before then."

Ellen peeled her damp and swollen face out of the crook of Aaron's shoulder, the same crook it had found itself in just hours earlier as a terrified family of four — now three — huddled together on the master bed.

"I'm not a bad mother. I—"

"Ma'am, this sort of thing happens. He couldn't have gone far. Once the K-9 gets here, it should be over fairly quickly. We're gonna get him back. You'll all be home in no time."

Ellen's head reeled. Her eyes squeezed shut and her lips curled back in agonizing emotional pain, and she burst into tears again as she sunk back into Aaron's shoulder.

"Officer, what can we do?" Aaron said. "Can we help? There has to be something we can do. We can't just sit here."

"Well, under normal circumstances, I'd ask you to go home and wait for us to clear this up. If you'd like to join the search, I'd ask that only one of you go so the other can stay on location with me in case your son comes back on his own. If it's okay with you, I'd like to send one of my officers down to your house, too, just in case he somehow winds up there. You never know."

All in a single motion, Ellen pulled herself off of her husband and sprang to her feet. The whites of her eyes were as red as her cheeks, and her top lip was covered in mucus which she promptly wiped away with a bare forearm.

"Yes," Ellen said. "I want to go. Where is the search party? When are we leaving? I want to go. I'm ready. Where are they?"

"Just a few minutes, ma'am. Once the other officers get here, I'll have you join them."

"Aaron, I'm going to go. Is that okay?"

Aaron tried to stand but his injured ankle buckled. "Ow! Of course. Go. I fucked up my ankle out there somehow. Officer, you said you need one of us to stay here, right?"

Cheryl snapped her head away from the giant walkie-talkie to face him. "That's right. With any luck, your son will wander back on up here on his own and you'll be home by lunchtime."

"This is all my fault," Ellen said.

"Sweetheart, please. Don't even start with that. We're gonna get him back."

Two more police cars pulled up. Cheryl had been barking orders into the walkie-talkie the entire time. She walked back over to the couple.

"Mrs. Dreyer, I want to introduce you to Officer Derek Brady. He'll be leading the party from the northern perimeter, the side of the woods that borders Route 45. You stick with him and he'll tell you what he needs. You alright taking orders from him?"

"Absolutely," Ellen said.

Brady had a poised, reassuring demeanor about him. "Morning, ma'am," he said, tipping his wide-brimmed hat. "I'm sorry to hear about your son. Like the deputy said, we'll get him back. Got a good charge on your cell phone?"

She checked it. "It's good enough."

Aaron gave her hand a squeeze before she whisked herself away from him. She turned around and reflected his soft gaze back at him.

"Hey," Aaron said. "I love you. I'll see you soon. I'll see you both soon. Okay?"

Ellen pursed her lips and nodded.

• • •

The inside of Cheryl's squad car smelled like old leather. Everything inside was beige. A timebomb-looking amalgamation of metal, wires, and buttons sat between her and Aaron in the center console.

The three of them — Cheryl and Aaron up front and Cooper in the back — sat in the unit with the windows down and the AC on.

Cheryl and the timebomb had been yapping at each other since they got in. Their game of police code tag both confused and comforted Aaron. Only in the last few minutes had the term 'K-9' been tossed around. That one, he knew.

He glanced up at the rear view to see his own K-9 looking like a sad little criminal through the wire mesh.

His ankle throbbed, but he decided not to say anything, instead twisting his foot in circles, and listening to it pop with every rotation.

"Mr. Dreyer, can you go over your timeline for me?" Cheryl said.

Aaron paused and closed his eyes.

"God. The last few days have been such a fucking nightmare. I can't even keep my thoughts straight. Where do you want me to start?"

"Tell me about your trip into town this morning. We can go back further if we need to, but let's start there. Everyone in the family was present, right?"

"Right. So, we came into town for some breakfast, and we ate at the Country Inn Diner. I think we got there around eight-thirty or nine. That was all fine. Then, we stopped at the library. We got there and it hadn't opened yet. So, I guess a little after ten. Oh, and—"

"What's that?"

"I had this, um, this weird fainting spell in the library."

"You fainted in the library?"

"Yeah."

"Why?"

Aaron looked down at his ankle. It was a grapefruit compared to his other one. "I think I was just hot. I—I don't know. We had a rough night last night and I haven't had much sleep lately."

Cheryl paused. "You get injured at all? Go to the hospital?"

"No, no, I came to pretty quickly. I'm fine. Anyway, uh, everyone was together when we left. Then, I asked Ellen to stop for a cold drink and we stopped here."

He pointed across the street to M&J Fine Gifts. All the lights were off, and a red-and-black SORRY, WE'RE CLOSED! sign hung in the door. It seemed to be taunting him.

"M&J?" Cheryl asked.

"Yeah, but ... I guess they're closed now?"

"Looks like it. You definitely went in there?"

"Yeah. I definitely went in there. That's ... so odd."

"That is odd. Don't know why they'd be closed at noon on a Friday."

Cheryl took a break to yell at the timebomb. She told someone to locate the owner of M&J Fine Gifts, and she seemed upset about someone named 'Bessie' taking too long. At times, she seemed to be talking to three people at once through the same machine.

"So, Mr. Dreyer, you went into M&J, then what?"

"Ellen came running in. She said Caleb was gone and she was ... hysterical."

"How long were you in there?"

"I don't know, no more than a few minutes."

"You sure about that?"

Aaron shrugged. "I guess I really don't know."

"What did your wife say when she came in? Did she say 'gone' or 'missing' or 'kidnapped'? Or somethin' else?"

Aaron turned his head to the left to look at her for the first time since entering the car. Cheryl looked formidable. Severe.

"Didn't she tell you what she said?" Aaron asked.

"She did, but I want to know what you think you heard."

"I, uh, don't quite remember what happened in the store at all. God, that's weird. I just remember Ellen coming in. That's it."

Cheryl fidgeted in her seat, the heavy leather rubbing loudly against her starchy uniform.

"What happened after Ellen came in?"

"Well, first she thought Caleb was in the store with me.

He wasn't, and so then we came out here and started looking in the woods. Ellen didn't really explain, she just said she lost sight of him and thought he might be in the woods."

Cheryl took off her hat and rubbed her fingertips across her brow. She looked at a rapidly panting Cooper in the rearview. "We should get you some water there, buddy."

"Officer, remember how I was telling you yesterday about seeing something strange in the meadow out by Wickham Road? By my house? I know how this sounds, but I saw it again last night. Ellen saw it, too. Except this time, I—we—we got a good look at it."

The radio kicked on after being silent for a while and a siren wailed from miles away. Aaron raised his voice to talk over the noise.

"I—I just think it's important for you to know that as you go forward here. There's something out there."

At least outwardly, Cheryl seemed to pay attention only to the radio. The name 'Duke' was mentioned repeatedly by whoever was on the other side, and after one such invocation, Cheryl's fingers clenched into fists.

"Son of a—" she muttered. "Excuse me, Mr. Dreyer, I need to make a phone call. I'll be right back."

She fumbled with her seatbelt and opened the car door.

• • •

One micro-frustration away from a full meltdown, Cheryl slammed the door behind her and walked far enough away from the unit so Aaron couldn't hear the call she was about to make. She had gone so far beyond standard protocol for a missing person that she almost felt guilty for having deployed so many resources.

Sure, she could have just mobilized her own department, called in a K-9, and asked Sperryville for an extra set of hands. No law enforcement or government official would fault her for stopping there. After all, how much ground could a little kid cover?

But the residue of Hank's death clung to her and she desperately wanted to wash it off. Although her job at Hank's was limited to securing the scene and calling in the bigwigs, there was no getting around the fact that a murder — a gruesome one, at that — had happened on her watch. Not Duke's.

She began to see this missing person case as a pitch she could knock out of the park. It was a chance to show she could take the lead, even under pressure.

So, she went all-out. The first call she made was to Officer Brady. He managed the Bensalem squad along with Officer Monica Nelson, and they covered the east and the south sides of the forest since they knew those backroads better than anyone else. Next, she called Sperryville and asked for two extra units. They were to join another unit from Martinsville and cover the north. Then, she called the captain of the unarmed volunteer auxiliary and asked them to send as many as they could down to Main Street to join the search party. As for the K-9, she wanted the big guns, and the Martinsville SAR had a bloodhound. Problem was, they needed authorization from Duke.

A good twenty yards away from her unit, Cheryl pulled her phone out of her back pocket. There was a text message from Rick. "No pot in her room."

She called Duke, and when he picked up, Cheryl didn't even give him a chance to say hello.

"Sheriff, listen, I'm sorry I don't have time to explain, but I need a big favor right this second. I need you to call Leo DeKeuster and verify a SAR over the phone. I'm trying to get him to release—"

"Okay, okay. I'll call him right now," Duke said over the hum of a car engine.

"And after that, I need you to call—"

"Mac—"

"Sheriff Kershaw and ask him for—"

"Mac. Slow down."

"Sir, I don't have time to—"

"I heard about it! Mac, I heard about it. I know about the kidnapping. I'm in the car now."

Cheryl had too many conflicting thoughts about Duke cutting his vacation short to come help her. Yesterday morning, she would have been embarrassed if he came back at the first whiff of trouble. By the afternoon, she felt the opposite, gladly willing to trade a little pride for help with VSP, the medical examiner, and every Tom, Dick, and Harry that rolled out to Hank's Horse Farm. But now that he was on his way, a blunting sense of disappointment clouded her vision of what the next day-and-a-half was supposed to look like.

She was supposed to find Caleb by herself and deliver a good, clean win. Now, it just looked like Daddy was coming to bail her out of trouble. In that moment, she didn't actually want Duke, just the access to the tools she needed to do her job.

"Alright, well," Cheryl paused and looked at Aaron back in the squad car. "Please call Leo on your way."

"Ten-four, Deputy."

• • •

Over the next two hours, a who's who of authority and non-authority characters alike arrived at the scene. The auxiliary came first. They were mostly retired folks who never usually got to do anything as exciting as this, and they all lived close by. They donned their water bottles and snacks, their yellow reflective fluorescent vests, and their official lanyards as if part of some mutinous army of traffic cops.

The unit from Martinsville pulled up a few minutes later. It was a hulking, black SUV with dark tinted windows. They had come to the wrong place. Brady needed them up his way, so Cheryl put them in touch.

About ten minutes later, just after 11am, the Channel 3 WNSP van rolled up to the Martinsville SUV's place.

"Motherfuck," Cheryl said under her breath. She jogged towards it, both hands clamped to her belt to keep its contents from jostling into her. She started yelling before she reached it. "Nope! This is an active crime scene, Rickey! Don't talk to anybody!"

A young man in the driver's seat of the van rolled down his window. "Can you give me anything, Deputy? Did they find him?" he said.

"Son of a bitch, Rickey, drive fifty yards away from my crime scene right now!" Cheryl said.

"Are the parents here? Can I have anybody?"

"Dammit, no! Get away from my crime scene. Do not fuck with me on this one, son!"

Rickey's face was rigid with the shock of Cheryl's rebuke. He scoffed and started rolling up his window. "Fine. Good luck, Deputy."

Cheryl strode back to a group of seven members of the auxiliary unit standing a circle waiting to find out what was going on.

"Sure is gettin' hot," one of them said.

"Done been hot! What'd ya' expect?" another replied.

A by-stander couple walking down Main Street gaped at the circus on the playground created. A few minutes later, a dusty yellow hatchback bumbled down the road a few hundred yards away. Cheryl squinted to get a closer look.

"Fucking finally," she said.

The hatchback, with a "Martinsville Search and Rescue" decal on the driver's side door, sputtered to a stop in front of her. Leo DeKeuster, an older, balding version of Mario from the Nintendo games, stepped out.

"I'm real sorry 'bout all this, Mac. It ain't nothin' personal, you know that?" he pleaded.

"I don't give a shit, Leo. This dickin' around might have cost a little boy his life. You wanna be the one to explain it to his mom and dad?"

"Sheesus, Mac! Come on! I came as fast as I could!"

"Well, come on, then!"

Cheryl spun towards her unit, a good thirty feet away, and beckoned an onlooking Aaron towards her. His dirty, sweaty, limping visage resembled something out of a zombie movie.

"You sure you don't want treatment for that?" she said to Aaron as he wandered into earshot.

"Who's this? Do you have any information? Are you here to help find my son? We just—" he said.

"Mr. Dreyer, this is Leo DeKeuster from Martinsville search and rescue."

Leo hopped around to the trunk, opened it, and out

jumped a bloodhound with a shimmering copper coat. "And this here's Bessie."

"Mr. Dreyer, do you have something in your car with your son's scent on it? Maybe an article of clothing?" Cheryl asked.

"Can it be a toy? His car seat, maybe? I don't know if I have clothing. Do you want me to go home and get clothing?"

Leo wiped the perspiration off his face with a handkerchief and squinted in the blistering sunlight. "Toy should be fine, sir. Has your son been in contact with it recently?"

"I'll go get one right now. I'm sure there's something in the car. Hey, does this really work? Will you find him with it?"

"Well, I won't, but Bessie here certainly may."

"Okay. Hold on. I'll be right back."

Aaron limped to his SUV and came back with a plastic dinosaur. "This is it. He loves this one. He was playing with it this morning. Is this good? Are you sure this will work?"

"Should be fine," Leo said, taking the dinosaur and bringing it down to the hound. He hushed and cooed to the elegant beast who wagged her tail with glee, signaling she was ready to go.

Cheryl did one of those old-school whistles with two fingers in her mouth and motioned for the auxiliary to come over. They ambled towards her, some faster than others, all of them sweating through whatever they had on. When all had arrived, Cheryl spoke to them. "Okay, everybody, sorry to keep you waiting. Wanted to make sure Bessie could join us and thanks to Leo, she's here. I'm not gonna waste any more time. We're looking for a boy named Caleb Dreyer. Caucasian. Four years old. Went into these woods a couple hours ago. About three-and-a-half feet tall. Wearing a white tee-shirt and olive-green shorts with blue sneakers. Dark hair in a bowl cut style, I guess you'd call it. Any questions?"

A middle-aged woman raised her hand. Her vest wouldn't close over her hulking body.

"Yes, ma'am?" Cheryl said.

"Um, yes, d'ya know 'bout how long we'll be out here? I'm s'posed to get my daughters from cheerleadin' camp and they usually wrap up 'round 5:30," said the volunteer.

Cheryl looked at her watch. It was just after 12 noon. "I'd see if they can hitch another ride, ma'am. With any luck we'll have found him, and you'll be home in time for supper, but you shouldn't plan on it."

"Okay, lemme call my husband."

"Any more questions?" Cheryl asked the group, only to be met with silence and head shakes.

Cheryl conducted the team with her arms in the sky. They formed a straight line and spread around ten feet apart, with Bessie and Leo in the center. The woman who spoke up earlier held the map and the walkie-talkie to report any findings. Cheryl wished them a final good luck and watched them evaporate into the forest.

She looked back at Aaron, his face failing to hide his inner panic, and then over to M&J Fine Gifts.

"Shit, where the hell is Jane?" she whispered.

• • •

Ellen trudged on through the forest with Brady and three other officers from the Bensalem Sheriff's Department. Her entire body both throbbed in pain and surged with adrenaline. As she marched, her eyes sliced through the chaos of the thicket with ruthless efficiency, scanning rapidly for any flash of color that might be out of place: a pale face, a white tee shirt. Or a ten-foot-tall pewter-colored monstrosity.

After an hour and a half of searching in the afternoon heat, she ranged back to Brady. His short-sleeved, brown uniform shirt was completely soaked. Sweat poured from his crimson face and so saturated the brim of his hat that a stain could be seen even on the outside. Nevertheless, his posture was strong and rigid, and his blue eyes burned with intent as he scanned the tree lines ahead of him.

"Hey," Ellen said, now walking by his side. "Don't you think we should have found him by now? He's been gone for more than three hours. He's just a four-year-old. He couldn't have gone that far, right?"

If Brady had lost any hope, his stony face didn't show it. "No. He could be in here. I just radioed Deputy McNamara, they sent a bloodhound and a search party through the south end of the woods by Main Street. They seem confident. They just left. The Martinsville folks canvassed the store fronts. We're gonna get him back, ma'am."

"But how do you know that? What if he's not here?"

Brady stopped walking and glnced at the trees behind his shoulder. They were deep into the woods now, far enough away from Route 45 that any sign of human life seemed a distant memory, save for the muted calls of "Caaa-leb" from the other officers in the party around them.

"Someone should have found him by now, Officer. He's not in here," Ellen said.

"Keep looking. Have faith. You've gotta keep faith in situations like these."

They walked on.

Ellen's brain had been scrambled ever since she realized her son was gone. Unlike her husband, she was used to operating at a high level with little sleep and sustenance. The ER demanded it. She pushed her brain to comb through every detail and allowed herself to consider any possibility. The most natural explanation — that he had just wandered off — was what she wanted to believe, but she was starting to doubt it. If he had just wandered off, they'd have found him by now. If he didn't just wander off, it meant someone took him, but Ellen didn't see or hear anyone near the playground. She was sure of it. Maybe there was someone in the woods waiting to snatch him if he got close, but that seemed incredibly unlikely.

There was one other explanation she didn't want to acknowledge. It hid behind a dark door in the basement of her mind, and whatever was in there when she opened that door would shake her to her core. It would make her question everything she'd ever known.

Her career had honed her mortal instincts into a razor-sharp weapon of truth, and everything in her was screaming that the hideous, towering mass she'd seen in the meadow had her son.

• • •

A chorus of afternoon cicadas rose around Cheryl's parked patrol car. Still sitting in the passenger seat, Aaron's eyes had been glued to the clock on the dashboard, watching the minutes tick by with excruciating sluggishness. Five minutes passed since Bessie had gone into the forest. Ten. Thirty. An hour. No one had found anything. Not a shoe, a scrap of clothing, not even a hair. Not a whiff. A fever of utter helplessness gnawed at his heart.

Cheryl had stepped out of the car to make a call and was taking a slow walk back. Something was different about her.

That hard-charging fervor he'd come to consider her defining
characteristic seemed to have slipped a notch into something
more tentative and fatigued.

She leaned down through the open window of the driver's side door. "Mr. Dreyer, it's my duty to keep you informed
every step of the way here. I just got off the phone with State.
We've reclassified this as a kidnapping."

The words rocked Aaron backwards. "What? What are
you talking about?"

"The thing is, the setup we have here with the bloodhound, the search party, your wife with Brady and the other
officers, officers from other jurisdictions ... I'm almost certain
that if he was in those woods, we'd have him by now. He simply
couldn't have gotten that far."

"What? Why? A kidnapping? How?"

"Well, neither you nor I were here when your son went
missing. I know your wife's as straight as they come but that
doesn't mean there wasn't another party involved. It's sort of a
process of elimination." She paused. "Can you think of anyone
who might have been motivated to take him?"

At certain points in time, every parent considers their
child falling foul of the most sinister and depraved elements
of the human world. Aaron had only ever danced around it in
his mind, convinced nothing like that could ever happen to
his kid. Yet here he was, listening to words that were so bizarre
he didn't believe them, and allowing his mind to flood with
thoughts of torture, abuse, his son crying for his life, crying
for his mommy and daddy, bleeding, hurting. Dying. His eyes
drifted into space.

"Mr. Dreyer. Hey. Look at me," she said, whipping off
her sunglasses. "I see in your face what you're doing. Don't go

there. We're not there, yet. It's only been a few hours. Think. Work with me and think. Can you think of anyone? Or any reason someone may want to hurt your son? Maybe as a way of hurting you or your wife? Anyone? Anything at all?"

"Listen, I know you think I'm crazy, but I saw something out there. We saw it again last night. Ellen and I both. I told you earlier. Ask her. I have no idea what this thing is, but I've seen it twice now, and the night we didn't see it, we got this completely fucked up phone call from someone or something that sounded like Hank Teakle. That was after he died, ok? I'm telling you, there is something in those woods that you don't know about and it's—I don't even know where to begin! It killed Hank! It took Caleb! I'm telling you, dammit!"

Cheryl was silent. She appeared to be chewing on it in her mind, grappling with it, but at least she was listening.

Aaron continued. "I don't know what you do about that but someone in this town has to know about this thing."

"Sir, I—I know there are animals—"

"It wasn't a fucking animal! Ask Ellen! I'm a fucking idiot, okay? Ask her! I don't fucking care what you think of me! Ask my wife! Do you know why we came out today at all? Because we were looking for someone who might know any goddamned thing about this ... this THING! But fucking no one knows anything! How do you not know about this? You don't know! How does no one know?"

"Mr. Dreyer, what you're saying might be true, but I have nothing to point me in that direction. It's far more probable that someone—a person, to be clear—has him. You don't know who, and I don't know who, but someone does. There are a lot of fucked up people in this world that don't need a motive. I hate to say it, Aaron, but it's true. This sort of thing happens, it really does, and there doesn't have to be a reason beyond 'wrong place at the wrong time.'"

"No. No one took him. No one would take my little boy."

"Listen, it's still very early. We still have time, but we need to use that time wisely. There are things we can do, right now, to escalate this and give your son the best chance of getting home safe and sound."

Aaron winced and gripped the bridge of his nose. He leaned back in the seat and began to heave.

"Mr. Dreyer, I know this is incredibly diffi—"

"You don't," he said, choking through tears. "You don't fucking know. You haven't listened to a goddamned thing I've been saying."

Cheryl leaned back from the window. "I just got off the phone with the Virginia State Police. They're on this. We are throwing every resource humanly possible at this. I promise you, Aaron. I goddamned promise you. And listen to me, there's another thing we can do."

Aaron struggled to listen. He struggled to stay sane. Cheryl opened the driver's side door and sat next to him.

She softened her tone. "I'm gonna go talk to the guy in that truck over there. You see him?" She pointed to the Channel 3 WNSP van still parked down the street. "I'd really love it if you'd be willing to join me to make a statement."

"What? Why?"

"If we give them an interview now, it'll be out in time for the 5pm news. And I'll tell you this, if whoever took your son happens to watch, a parent is way more compelling than a cop."

"I don't—"

"Think about it. Right now, it's about coverage. We're covering the forest. Now let's cover the media. Everyone in the state of Virginia will know about this by the time the sun's down."

"By the time the ... the sun's down?" Aaron's face winced and his chest heaved. He let out an agonizing moan, something between a cry and a scream that conveyed the despair or a father already in grief. An energy of fear and sadness poured out from him and reverberated in the cab of the patrol car as he sobbed in his hands.

Cheryl sniffled and put a hand on Aaron's shoulder. "I know. I know."

She let him cry for a good five minutes. She squeezed his shoulder and just kept repeating: "I know."

When his rawness weathered and his heaves came far enough apart for him to breathe, he whispered soft words from his wet and puffy lips. "This isn't happening. The monster. The dreams. Hank. None of it. This can't be real. Tomorrow I'll wake up and everything will be normal again. None of this is happening. None of this is real."

"Aaron," Cheryl whispered back. "Let's go talk to the news. Come on."

• • •

Ellen had spent the first hour of the search hopeful Caleb was just around this tree or hiding behind that bush. Scared, lonely, waiting for Mommy to come.

How many of the officers had kids? Brady had mentioned a young son on the way over here. What was he thinking about Ellen right now? About her ability to mother a child? Did these people think she was a failure? Because at that point, in the sticky summer heat under the oaks, Ellen certainly felt like one.

But unlike her husband, she wasn't ready to grieve. Instead, her mind raced through the details of her last moments with Caleb and played them on loop. Maybe by playing them twenty, thirty, forty times over, she'd uncover even the minutest clue that would indicate a next step.

But for some reason, every time she played the tape there was a gap, an irksome record skip that defied her typically photographic memory.

She remembered pushing Caleb on the swing. She remembered him finding a toy truck in the sandbox and obsessing over that for a good while. What time was that? Did she look away before, or after? And what was it that drew away her attention? It was Aaron, still in the store, and she'd hoped to see him coming out after being inside for so long. He'd been in there more than thirty minutes. Then, the gap, followed immediately by the realization that Caleb was gone. One moment, he was in the sandbox, the next he was simply ...

Gone.

She probed at the gap. It was a lapse that felt foreign, almost implanted, and she recognized it as such. It couldn't have been more than sixty seconds, but she remembered the sky collapsing down around her and the air feeling somehow heavy, like a daydream but deeper. What had caused it? The monster had affected Aaron's state. Had it done the same to her, just more subtly? Her memories of that lapse were blurry at best. Something in there was hiding from her and she knew it. She wanted to grab hold of it and claw its fucking eyes out and she wouldn't stop searching until she found it.

As she slogged around tree after tree, pretending to search for her son, she searched her heart instead. She forced herself to walk towards the direction of the truth.

The other half of her mind, the pure logician, was breaking down the options. She mapped it like a pie chart in her brain.

When this whole thing had started, the chart was a single color: deep blue, a hundred percent, because she believed for certain that Caleb had wandered off. Then, other possibilities and colors started filling in. A red section that represented abduction by a person she didn't see became about a quarter and it was where she correctly guessed the authorities ultimately would land. A yellow section representing the possibility that he wandered across the street trying to find his dad started as another quarter of the pie chart but evaporated after she really considered it. She even entertained absurdities like just being stuck in the sandbox or some kind of spontaneous dematerialization. Was there a 0.05 percent chance either of those things could actually happen? Probably not.

But as she let the possibilities marinate, as the various colors of the pie chart in her mind waxed and waned and she worked her way through it, a new idea began to take shape. It started as a fraction of a percent, a thin black line originating from the same section of her brain that had been erased during those sixty seconds of blackout, as if whatever was responsible for the erasing had left a trail of breadcrumbs.

The afternoon sun rained down unforgiving heat through the cracks of the trees. The hollow and surreal calls of "Caleb!" from Brady and his crew perforated the natural heavy hums of the forest around her.

And as her body began to break down from fatigue, from thirst, from sadness, the thin black line in that pie chart started to expand. As it did, she saw it wasn't exactly black, but a murky, pewter gray.

That thing. That monster.

That heinous presence that moved through the meadow. That inexplicable being with gnarled, elongated fingers and legs thicker than tree trunks.

That thing was out there. It was right here in this forest. And it had her little boy. She would navigate the maze of her memories towards the truth, and she would crystalize snapshots of those last moments into an album she could study for years if that's what it took.

Without even knowing, she touched a phantom overalls pocket on her chest to feel for the cold, viscous remains of a baby bird that wasn't there.

By the time Brady shut down the search a little after 4pm, she had already formulated a plan.

• • •

After Aaron had made his tearful plea to the press, Cheryl drove him back to Wickham Road where two officers greeted him with a "Sorry, sir", having just searched his home. None of their efforts that day — the search parties, the K-9, the media hit — turned up a trace of Caleb.

The first thing Aaron did when he got home was take some pills for his ankle, hoping to at least knock out the swelling. He watched a clip of himself on the news and saw a person he didn't recognize. He saw a zombie, a sunken-eyed shell of a human. His arms looked frail, and all the color was gone from his face.

Brady dropped off Ellen an hour later. She gave her husband a long hug and she felt so brittle in his arms that he thought her limbs might just snap off. Without a word, she sulked upstairs to shower off the sweat, the dirt, the emotion of the day.

Aaron was too tired to shower. Too numb to eat. Too sad to cry. Too confused to think. Too paralyzed by the sheer fatigue of the last eighteen hours. Even if he did have energy, he would've had no idea what to do with it. Cheryl had asked him to stay home in the event that the perpetrator had a change of heart and returned their boy.

So, he curled up with Cooper on the living room couch while the sun set behind them. It slipped behind the outline of the mountains without fanfare, as if ashamed to be there. He could hear Ellen upstairs on the phone. It sounded like she was calling her mother.

Time moved at an erratic pace. Ten minutes seemed to take forever while an hour flew by. Aaron kept thinking he should do something, anything, but he'd been explicitly told to do nothing.

It was dark now and Ellen was cooking something in the kitchen. Cooper crunched kibble beside her. Aaron watched them the way one watches animals at a zoo. Proximally close, but spiritually miles apart. The sight of Ellen and Cooper doing mundane things almost tricked Aaron's brain into thinking everything was normal.

Minutes later, Ellen walked into the living room with two steaming bowls of pasta.

"Eat up," she said.

He did. Even after just a few bites, he began to feel more awake.

"Hey, do you have anything stronger than ibuprofen? My ankle is killing me."

"Did you ice it? R. I. C. E." Ellen said, barely pausing between huge spoonfuls.

"No."

"I have a bunch of samples in the closet upstairs. Look in the wicker basket, but come back down, I wanna talk about what we do next."

The wicker basket was indeed full of sample packs of pharmaceuticals. Big ones, little ones, colorful ones, some completely unmarked, almost none of them opened. He dug down to the bottom and found some old prescription bottles. One of the labels jumped out at him.

OXYCODONE.

Ellen had been prescribed the opioid after back surgery two years earlier and he had forgotten. Looking at the bottle, he remembered her saying she wouldn't take them no matter how much pain she was in. She must have kept her word because the bottle was packed to the brim.

TAKE 1-2 WITH FOOD EVERY 4-6 HOURS AS NEEDED.

He gave the bottle a slight tilt, only wanting one, but he went too far and a good third of the pills scattered onto the carpet. It was as if they'd flown out of the bottle, yearning to wield their addictive power over the first sucker dumb enough to release them.

Ellen wouldn't touch the things and she was a doctor. That alone should have stopped him. But as he picked one up and examined it in the light, he succumbed to the same repression of instinct that had gotten him into trouble so many times before.

He sighed and put it into his mouth.

The acidic taste of the pill on his tongue triggered

thoughts of Caleb out in the woods, in whatever world of pain he might be in, whether it be physical or emotional or something otherworldly and indescribable, and Aaron spit the pill out onto the ground.

"What the fuck are you doing?" he said to himself. "What the fuck is happening to my family? Where the fuck is my son?" He slammed his fist into the closet wall beside him, laid back, and cried. He left the closet sometime later, having taken nothing.

Downstairs, Ellen was stroking Cooper's weary head in her lap. Although she had showered and eaten, the skin on her face clung to her cheekbones. Her eyes were pained and exhausted, yet somehow eager.

"How you doing?" she asked.

Aaron shrugged. "Awful."

"Did you find anything up there?"

"No. I'm fine."

"We have to find him, Aaron. I feel like this is a bad dream. Everything that's happened in the last however long. None of this feels real."

"This is my fault. It all started three nights ago. I know this is all related, I just know it. If I had just left this whole thing alone, the creature out there, the lights, Hank, all of it. If I'd just left it the fuck alone—"

"You didn't lose him. I lost him."

"Don't say that. We wouldn't have even been out this morning if I hadn't—"

"It's not on you, Aaron. He was with me and then he was gone. That's on me."

"Let it at least be on us. It's not on you. It's on both of us. It would kill me to know you're taking it all on your shoulders.

We're a team, Ellen. We were both there. I was, what, twenty feet away?"

Cooper stirred and hopped off the couch.

"Do you really think he's gone?" Aaron asked.

"You're not gonna believe what I think."

The irony of hearing his wife say something like that wasn't lost on him. After days of begging her to even pretend to take him seriously, now she was the one about to say something crazy. Just another wrinkle in the utterly backwards universe they had found themselves in, where the craziest and worst outcomes became the new normal. If Hank's reanimated corpse had hopped off the slab and knocked on Aaron's door, he wouldn't have been surprised. "Well, hey there, Aaron! I missed ya' for dinner last night!"

"Try me," Aaron said, still hearing Hank's voice echoing from the void.

"I actually agree with you. I totally agree with you. I think Caleb has something to do with that thing we saw last night. You've been reacting to this thing, whatever it is. Today at the playground, I had a mental lapse that I just can't explain. Cooper and I were sitting at the picnic table and Caleb was playing in the sandbox. I turned my head towards the store you were in, and then my memory just went blank. Something happened when I looked at the store. I don't know what or why, but it felt like something was inside my head. And then Caleb was just gone. It was almost like he had never been there at all."

Aaron's jaw was in his lap.

Ellen continued. "And listen, I think I know how to find him. The problem is, I don't think we can do it alone."

"Ellen. Yes. Fucking yes, Ellen. I tried to tell that cop! She wouldn't listen! I fucking knew it! So, what's your plan?"

"What do we know about it? How it behaves? What it wants?"

"Not much. It's a total mystery to me. All I know is it looks like something out of a nightmare."

"We know a lot more than that. We know it comes out around the same time every night. We know it has some kind of reaction when we shine those lights. We know it starts in one place and ends up in another. If it behaves the same way as last night, I think we should turn on the lights when it's visible and try to trap it again. Then, we fabricate a crime happening here, like let's say the house is on fire, something that will get the police to move fast."

"Wow. I can't believe I'm hearing you say this. Just yesterday I thought you thought I was crazy, now you've figured the damn thing out. Okay, so, once they get here, they what? Go after it?"

"Yes. They get here, we release it, and we follow it back into the woods. We'll want the cops in case it's dangerous."

"Yeah. Yeah, okay. I like it. Let's do it. See, Ellen? This isn't your fault. It's not my fault. It's that fucking thing's fault. It all started, all this weird shit, it all started when I first saw it. Hank, Caleb, the phone calls. It's been so clear to me this whole time and now it's clear to you."

He got up and grabbed Ellen's face and kissed her. Her lips were dry and cracked.

"I fucking love you, Ellen. I fucking love you so much."

"Well, don't get your hopes up. It's a long shot."

"Hey, one question. Why do we have to make up a crime? Why don't we just tell them we finally have proof of this thing?"

"Because they'll never believe us."

• • •

The front door was unlocked when Cheryl got home. Examining the peeling purple paint around its edges unearthed a deeply receded memory of the first time she ever saw that paint, all those years ago. How different her life was back then. Hell, her life was quite different just sixteen hours ago when she'd stormed out of the same door with what seemed like an insurmountable set of problems at the time. Somehow, she now had even more shit on her plate.

Discordant voices of fast-talking women fighting with each other echoed from the TV. Skylar must have been watching one of her reality TV shows where the women do little more than drink and yell.

She wrenched off her boots, and the hot, stale smell of suffocated feet shot up into her nostrils. Bypassing ceasefire negotiations with Skylar, she trudged upstairs and filled the tub with cold water. She let out a sigh as she placed her feet in the icy water. The shock was soothing medicine for her rocky, molten bare feet. Her toenails were yellowing with age and the edges of her feet looked almost translucent through the water.

Although she'd barely eaten all day, when she snuck back downstairs and peered into the fridge, her pure exhaustion sapped any lingering motivation she had for nourishment. She considered a glass container filled with old lasagna before caving to a bowl of cold cereal.

She plopped the empty bowl in the sink, and ventured over to the living room to say goodnight to her daughter. Skylar was hunched in Rick's recliner with an oversized tee pulled over her knees. Two women fought about lunch plans on the TV.

"Skylar?" Cheryl said.

Skylar didn't move. She clung to herself in the darkness. The synthetic light of the TV gave the living room a bluish hue.

"Skylar? You okay?"

"Yes. Goodnight." Skylar said, her monotone voice muffled by the tee.

"What's wrong, princess?"

Skylar pulled her face out from between her knees to reveal black tear streaks on either side of her face. Suddenly, Cheryl didn't see the defensive, petulant teenager who most days she wanted to strangle, but her little baby girl, a tiny, precious thing she loved so much that she didn't know how to express it. She saw an ultimately gentle, curious soul who was just learning about the world, and the pain and the horrors within it.

"Baby girl, I know you're going through changes."

"Ugh, no, mom."

"You have to realize that in a town like this, it's so easy to make one mistake and—"

"Mom, stop. I'm over it. I know you're just trying to be a good mom. That's not the problem."

"What is it, then?"

"Just stuff with friends. I don't want to talk about it."

Cheryl often got the impression that Skylar antagonized her more out of boredom than actual disdain. She certainly couldn't remember the last time she'd made her daughter cry. Everything real in her life revolved around her friends. Cheryl had memorized most of their names and even looked them up in the crime databases. Most of them were kids with no records of any kind, too young to have done anything significant, especially in a town like Bensalem. A couple had warnings, one had a bunch of speeding tickets, but that was it.

"I want you to understand that I care a lot about the way you and I treat each other. I don't want you to hate me and I'm only trying to protect you. I need you to show me a little more love and respect. Can we keep the f-bombs out of the house, please?"

"Yeah. I'm sorry."

"You and your friends aren't in any sort of trouble, are you?"

"No! Mom, I said I don't want to talk about it."

Now the TV women were all on some kind of boat cruise. They weren't fighting but their voices still sounded more aggressive than the setting called for.

"And I'm not as dumb as you think I am. I'm smart. Yes, I have smoked pot before but I'm not a pothead and my friends aren't potheads. We don't do meth or anything like that. We think meth heads are losers. I'm tougher than you think."

"I know, sweetheart. I know you're smart. You've always been smart."

It appeared that one of the TV women had had way more to drink than she was supposed to. None of the others were drunk, or at least they claimed not to be, but they were gathered around their incoherent pal like a bunch of vultures huddled over fresh prey.

Cheryl tip-toed to the couch and sat down. "What's this you got on?"

"It's just a dumb show."

"Why do you watch it?"

Now, the drunk woman was crying and screaming. This threw the others into a frenzy.

"I heard a boy went missing. Is that true?" Skylar said.

"Yeah. Still haven't found the poor kid. Between this and Hank's death, I don't—"

"How did Hank die?"

"Well, luckily, that's not my job to figure out."

"I heard it was kinda nasty."

Cheryl shook her head. "Guess I know who told you that. If I hear that damn phrase one more time ..."

"Is that why those people called you this morning?" Skylar said.

"Yeah. They live next door to Hank's place. They're new around here and they're scared. It's their son who's been reported missing, on top of it all."

"Really? Do you think they're connected?"

There was an enthusiasm in Skylar's voice that Cheryl found odd but somehow encouraging. Never had she shown this kind of interest in her mother's work. Of course, Bensalem had never seen these kinds of crimes before. Not in her lifetime, at least.

"I don't see how there could be any connection. I'm half expecting those parents to say they just forgot the kid somewhere in that huge house of theirs."

"Really?"

"I don't know. All I know is Duke's coming back tonight, and that'll be good for everybody. Me, especially. When I called him today, somebody'd already told him about the kidnapping."

Skylar shuffled in the recliner. "Kidnapping?"

"Mm hmm. I think so, unfortunately."

"When did you call him?"

"Who? Duke?"

"Yeah. Are you sure he used the word kidnapped? Not missing?"

Cheryl wasn't much older than her daughter when she fully realized the concept of a blind spot. It came to her the hard way on speeding down a desolate stretch of Vermont in mother's 1980 Ford Taurus. How could there exist a vortex of literal blindness amongst a menagerie of mirrors that so clearly illuminated everything in her wake? They'd presented no evidence of vehicles for miles, so Cheryl didn't even bother to twist her head around and actually look when she merged straight into the side of the pickup truck that had been lingering beside her.

The accident that night triggered a unique and confusing mix of shock, anger, and embarrassment. She had sworn there was no one there. She looked in every mirror — twice — and there wasn't a hint of another vehicle in sight. But a vehicle was there, a big one in fact, and it was in the one place she didn't look, the place closest to her the whole time.

That same concoction of emotion returned to her in the company of her daughter on an equally desolate night in Bensalem, watching bad reality TV and realizing her blind spot had been exposed.

"Son of a bitch," she said, "Duke knew."

• • •

At 3:52am, Ellen stood tall behind the living room windows, her eyes burning lasers of vengeance across the meadow. Clouds had rolled in during the night, quelling the glow of the moon and blurring the contours of the terrain.

She did well to hide the nerves raging inside her and she kept her heart rate down through sheer force of will. Her hand had created a slippery film of sweat around the hilt of a flashlight. Her husband was a wreck beside her, but she couldn't think of anything comforting to say. The meadow was vacant. The house was silent.

Until it stepped out of the darkness, right on cue.

As if he had seen it too, Cooper's brisk click-clack on the hardwood floor broke the stiffening silence. He joined them at the window, this time not barking, but calm and ready to strike at a moment's notice.

"Okay?" Aaron asked.

"Yeah, go."

He plugged in the extension cord and light gushed into the meadow. The monster stopped, and within seconds, all the phones in the house started ringing. The raucous noise ripping through the house forced Cooper to start barking.

They ignored their mobile phones, both buzzing on the side table by the couch, as well as the landline in the office.

Ellen couldn't stop gawking at the thing's fingers, those long and knotty tentacles, hanging there, drumming ever so slightly in some otherworldly coded pattern, communicating with God knows what. She lost focus of the foliage and the grass around the monster and studied it. It drew her in like a tractor beam, demanding every fiber of her attention.

When the mobile phone calls had gone long enough to go to voicemail, Aaron went over to the table and grabbed his, but it started buzzing again in his hand.

"Shit. I can't decline the call. How are we gonna contact the police?" Aaron said.

At once, Ellen gasped and buckled to the ground. She tried to stand, but instead collapsed again and started hyperventilating on the floor.

Cooper moved on her, snapping and growling with a rage

so powerful and so pure it predated the history of man. Not once in six years had he shown his teeth to anyone, yet here he was, bearing down on Ellen as if she were the very incarnation of evil itself and he was the agent to deliver it.

The growling yanked Aaron's attention away from the phones, and he jumped down to intervene.

"Ellen! Ellen! What happened? Cooper! Hush! HUSH!"

Ellen leaned her back against the windowsill and clawed her way to her knees. She had an overwhelming desire to gaze at the monster again, but she fought the urge violently within her mind. Instead, she stayed focused on Cooper, still snarling but somehow holding back from attacking.

"Ellen! Stay there! Don't look at it. Don't look! Hold on!"

Moments later, Ellen shrieked as an overwhelming, icy shock of cold smacked the life back into her body. Her limbs flailed and she dug her nails into Aaron's outstretched arms. An empty plastic pitcher of water clattered to the ground as they embraced. Aaron gripped both sides of her soaking wet face and forced her to look into his eyes.

"Ellen! Look at me! Ellen!"

The splash was a strong enough to surge to her system to fully rebuke whatever had tried to get inside. Cooper backed away from Ellen and started barking at the monster through the window. The timing of his barks against the rings from the landline created a deafening rhythm of auditory chaos. Foam dripped from his mouth.

"Oh my God! Aaron, you can't look at it! It's fucking with our heads. It tried to get in my head!"

The two sat staring at each other, but Cooper's wild barks and snarls didn't let them forget the thing was still standing out there, still frozen in suspended animation.

"I'm gonna go get them," she said, rising, nearly slipping in the puddle of ice water that now coated the floor.

"Get who?"

"The police. Stay here. Just stay here and I'll get them. I'll fucking show them!"

She yanked her keys from her purse and slammed the door behind her.

• • •

The Dreyers had never really explored the forest on the other side of Wickham Road. They'd gone on hikes with Caleb around the edges and they let Cooper run through the meadow. He chased squirrels that scurried up pine trees, but he never strayed away from them.

They knew the forest wasn't part of a state park or overseen by any government entity. They knew you could get to Hank's if you walked a mile through one edge of it, and that you could reach Route 45 if you continued about ten miles west.

Ellen saw a new piece of the forest during the search for Caleb, but those old, wise trees stretched on quite a bit further. The Dreyers had no real knowledge of the forest's nature, its history, or its inhabitants.

But now they'd seen a monster, night after night, stalking the outskirts of this forest, just outside their home. The home where their child slept, or had slept, up until last night.

And certainly, never in their wildest dreams did they imagine the thing connecting the strings between those harrowing events over the last few days could be so much worse.

When Ellen sped away from the house to fetch the police, she didn't even notice the white pickup truck parked on the shoulder of Wickham Road by Hank's.

The driver of the truck carried a burlap sack over his shoulder, and he had a shovel in one hand and a battery-powered camping lamp in the other. He marched into the trees with his cargo, and although the contents of his sack were heavy, its weight bore no comparison to that of Bensalem's history and truth, which at this moment, also rested firmly on the man's shoulders.

The lumpy sack made the walk difficult, especially at this hour. He stopped when he reached the part of the forest that felt more black than green, where sunlight barely broke through the towering oaks and where it always seemed cold, even in the summer.

He went where the cleric had told him to go.

The ground there was a sort of damp, muddy sludge that smelled like wet metal. Around him, the dirt expanded into an almost perfectly oval shaped glade with more thick black pines lining its perimeter. It was so quiet here. Insects from other parts of the forest could only be heard distantly, and not even the faintest of animal tracks could be found impressed upon the soft earth.

The man's body ached from the dig and the anxiety of his assignment. He was not a young man anymore, at least by human standards, but he took up the mantle of the task tonight with pride and honor. He did what he was told because he believed in the cause. He believed in the ritual, and he believed in the cleric.

Before rolling the sack in the hole, he sat down on a rusty folding chair at the edge of the glade that had been there for

God knows how long.

A tiny part of him had hoped to catch a glimpse of the sentinel, the great protector of the forest. "Hey Mark. It's me, your brother Ron. Remember?" he would have whispered to the titanic creature in the night, knowing full well that he — it, now — wouldn't be able to understand him anymore.

Tiny orbs of sweat had broken out on his forehead but the chilly air in the canopy kept him cool. The man wiped his brow, and when he moved his arm away, he saw something staring at him. The shock of it almost knocked him right off the chair.

There it stood: the earthly manifestation of a thing that should only exist in nightmares, casting a thin silhouette of black chaos mere steps away from him. It stood a foot outside the light of the lamp, perfectly shrouded and still in the trees, its bold, red eyes boring into him from the darkness. Only then did it occur to the man why this part of the forest was so quiet: it had been right here watching him the whole time.

"Oh ... God ..."

Something must have gone terribly wrong. It shouldn't have been here, couldn't have been here, but it was. If he had been engaged by anything else, any creature of this world, he might have tried to fight. Instead, beginning to know the unknowable, his body held him in a state of prone functional extinction on the folding chair. It wasn't the red eyes from another dimension or the great, twisted silhouette it cast upon the ground that scared him the most. Rather, it was the sheer calm and stillness, the lack of sound and movement, that ravished him with a creeping terror. All the man could hear was the sound of his own breath. It had consumed all other sounds and sights around it.

The elders had spoken of the pestilence a handful of times since his induction into the Order. Whenever they discussed it, the topic seemed to cause great consternation, and they didn't tell anyone who didn't need to know. They spoke the ancient tongue to name it, the Nothus Noctis — the Night Bastard. The man's mother, the cleric of the Order and the sage who hated it more than anyone, so much so that her heart turned black, simply called it the Nothus.

The man had read about the Nothus in the Grimoire and he knew what was going to happen next. He was going to lose his mind. The Grimoire said it fed on feeble and broken minds, and when it found a mind that was still healthy, it would swiftly facilitate the breaking.

With a whoosh so thick and cosmic it seemed to pull on the very gravity around it, the Nothus stepped into the glade, into the light of the lantern.

Thick, twisted antlers sprouted from what looked like a hideously massive deer or elk skull. The head wasn't white like a normal skull but black, conveying an otherworldly alloy of bone and flesh. Its eyes were stark, blood-red balls. No pupils or irises, just radiant, vermillion orbs set deep into their sockets, glowing in the light.

The Nothus' arms were rail-thin and covered in a sort of fur, but its hands were constructed from the same black bony substance as the head. Stemming from its hands were fingers ten times longer than they should have been, daggers of obsidian dangling at its sides, twitching in a rapid pattern, communicating with something in this world or the next through a demonic sign language. It drew breath through a narrow snout, and its hefty torso heaved upon animalistic legs that ended in shiny, cloven hooves.

The Nothus was already in the man's brain, cutting the tissue apart. The man's dreams and visions and fears and memories collapsed into themselves one-by-one and fell into the void. It methodically severed every synapse and sinew of the man's brain matter until all that was left was a chunky, bloody stew. And it stood there, perfectly silent and perfectly still, save for its horrible finger twitching.

On the surface, the man appeared placid, but only because the Nothus had started with the nerves that controlled the muscles in his face. Underneath, he was aware of every searing little slice. The cuts started off with excruciating pain, but as his nerve centers gradually disconnected, the pain subsided and instead the man just heard scratches inside his head, like the sound of a dull knife being dragged across rock.

The Nothus opened its mouth and emitted a high-pitched, rhythmic sound. It was not unpleasant, and it soothed the man into a feigned sense of comfort, as if persuading him it was okay to let go.

Just before it ended, the man gained an out-of-body moment of capacity. He spent it wondering whether anyone had ever witnessed the Nothus in its earthly form and lived to tell the tale.

It was all over before he arrived at an answer. The man's mind melted into nothingness, and a quiet stream of blood poured out of his left ear.

The sound stopped. The night was still. All the creatures of the woods: the deer, the raccoons, the squirrels, the warblers, the crows, the frogs, the salamanders, even the ants and the peepers; they all knew the Nothus in a way that humans never could. They lived with it. They survived despite it.

The Nothus hoisted a hulking hand of black bone upward

and thrust it into the man's chest cavity. With a wet crack, its long fingers sliced through muscle, tissue, fat and bone as if the man's body were merely vapor.

It drew back its hand, dripping blood and entrails. It thrust the hand back in, back out, back in, until the area from the man's neck to his crotch was completely hollow. What was left of the man's mortal coil was strewn all over the ground. Red, pink and white clumps dripped with bodily fluids under the light of the camping lantern, here, where moonlight dare not enter.

In a single movement, the Nothus got down on all fours — two hideous bone hands in front and two hooves in back — and began eating the man's organs. It made rasping, slurping, crunching sounds, moans of demonic pleasure. A long, spindly tongue extended from its skull and licked up whatever blood it could. It stopped briefly over a feather earring that had been ripped from the man's body during the carnage, but after touching it with its tongue and determining it was not food, moved on.

The man's gallbladder and half of his left lung were flung the furthest, landing several yards next to the burlap sack the man had meant to bury. The Nothus scampered on its mad appendages to the spot and sniffed.

It sensed life inside the sack. It knew the smell of a fresh human, still alive, but relaxed and devoid of fear. After feasting on the soul of an old horse farmer and the man now strewn about the glade, the Nothus craved that smell of fear above all else because it tasted so, so good.

Only a thin layer of burlap separated the monster from the boy inside. It placed a single fingertip of black bone upon an indentation in the center of sack, and it stopped pressing when the soft part of the boy's cheek would cave no further without force. The Nothus lowered its head, and its burning red eyes shot light through the holes in the loosely braided cloth. Its nose crept closer now, just inches away from the finger it held to the sack, still touching the drugged and unconscious boy, waiting for the smell of fear to flood its nostrils.

But that smell never came.

It held its finger this way for hours until the first glint of sun began to break through the trees. Sensing the oncoming day, the Nothus rose. It peered into the blackness of the forest and carried itself away as silently as it had arrived.

PART III

DAY 5

Aaron's life split in two the moment he first saw the creature, when it rattled his body and left him grasping for breath and for sanity on the floor of his own living room.

Ellen's moment of painful clarity came as she sat on the living room floor, the life sucked out of her, her mind taken over by an invisible conqueror. The mechanics of that moment were not unlike those of her husband, but the results couldn't have been more different.

Unlike Aaron, Ellen knew exactly what was happening while it was happening. She got a taste of the creature's power. She understood what it was doing to her in a way that Aaron did not.

No longer would she be duped into a false sense of security just because the creature was hundreds of yards away from the house and could be trapped in place by light. No longer would she have to be persuaded that supernatural forces could hold quarter in the material world. The realist in her would not die, it would expand to include the new reality.

Because for those few minutes on the floor, it was in her brain. She was certain of it. She felt it moving around and sorting through her memories like files in a cabinet.

Only in hindsight, as she sped towards the Bensalem Sheriff's Department with all ten of her fingernails dug into the vinyl steering wheel cover, did she view it as a missed opportunity. Ellen raged. Not at the monster, but at herself. That moment of contact, disorienting as it may have been, could have been her chance to find her son. If the creature could get into her thoughts, maybe there was a way she could get into the creature's. Was the answer hidden somewhere in the chaos of those moments?

She couldn't keep her thoughts together as she sped down State Road 639, a fragment of sunrise behind her. They crashed and cascaded over each other; salmon swimming upstream.

She recalled families of decades-long missing children she'd seen on the news who'd kept the faith that their children were still alive, still out there, just waiting for the right moment to simply knock on the door and ask what was for dinner. What a sick joke of an existence. What a cosmic con-job. Thinking about how pitiful those people sounded made her skin crawl.

Ellen knew she wouldn't be like them. She was never a woman of faith; she was a woman of science, and women of science do not hide from the truth. At some point, she'd stop thinking about other lame duck parents and start thinking about the thing that would haunt her for the rest of her time on this earth: she was a bad mother. No, she wouldn't just be a bad mother, she would be the worst mother. Ellen Dreyer would be the woman whose perfectly happy and healthy kid simply vanished from right under her nose for no good reason.

All it took was a sixty second gap in her memory caused

by ... something ... for the well-manicured world she'd fought for tooth and nail her entire life to be well and truly shattered. The millions of hours in class. The thousands of cups of coffee to stay sharp as a tack on the ER floor. The crippling aches she burdened carrying Caleb, the tearing of what felt like every capillary in her lower body to birth him, the biting pain and numbness of feeding him in the middle of cold and sleepless nights. All of it for nothing, for less than nothing, because at one point she had the payoff but now it was gone. Caleb was gone.

She mashed her molars and her lungs burned with the thought of it. For Christ's sake, there wasn't even anyone else around. It was just her and her son.

"Right?" A whisper of the word barely slipped out of her mouth.

And how much had she poured into a career supposed to literally prevent people from dying? Wasn't she supposed to know a thing or two about keeping people safe? The sheer irony of the situation made her consider jerking the wheel thirty degrees to the left and into the next tractor trailer that whizzed by.

Would that be the easiest way? Or would it be better to take a bottle of pills? No, that might not work.

The wrists would be the way. Quick, unstoppable, painless. She knew exactly how to make the cuts, too. It wasn't anything she hadn't seen dozens of times before.

• • •

Back inside the Dreyers' house, the landline was still ringing.

The monster was still standing there, frozen. The hour Ellen had been gone felt like days, and a hazy blue layer of sun had begun to peek over the mountains. Songbirds warbled in the trees, seemingly unaware of the chaotic presence still lingering in the meadow, still shrouded in weird mist and emanating that faint, buzzing sound.

On the porch, Cooper rested on his haunches next to his master, calm but staring at the monster. His eyes were glassy and drifted shut every few seconds, but his eyelids sprang back open each time sleep tried to take him.

Aaron's ankle throbbed, but he distracted himself from the pain by trying to remember where they had put their digital camera. So many things remained unpacked, and Aaron had rifled through the boxes in the office at least a half dozen times looking for it. He didn't look at the meadow. He didn't need to use his eyes to know it was still there.

Suddenly, the phone stopped, and Aaron darted his eyes back out towards the meadow. As he did, his jaw fell wide open as the monster began sinking into the earth. Its tree trunk like legs didn't move an inch as they descended, and neither did its hulking gray body or long arms with fingers that could crush a man lifeless. It sank further and further until all that was left above ground was its odd nub of a head and those three yellow eyes, eyes that simply lost their color before also going underground, as if someone had turned off a light switch inside it. Like that, it was gone, leaving behind an unremarkable patch of loose dirt and a cloud of mist that dissipated with the early morning breeze.

"What? What the fuck?" he said.

Either it had found a way to burrow underground without moving its limbs or the dirt had somehow sucked it down into itself. It didn't run, it didn't scream, it didn't evaporate. It didn't do anything. It just sank, and in a moment's notice, was gone.

It now lay dormant under the ground somewhere, or so Aaron was left to assume as Ellen's sedan appeared on Wickham Road, trailed closely by a police cruiser. Both cars stopped, and Aaron heard his wife yell something before continuing up the driveway. To his surprise, it wasn't Deputy McNamara that stepped out, but Officer Derek Brady.

Aaron hobbled over to them. Cooper followed. "Ellen! It just vanished! It vanished when the sun came up! It was right here! It just sank into the ground! Officer, I swear to God we're not making this up! Officer! Ellen! I swear it was ri—"

"Wait, what?" Ellen said.

"Honest! It was here just a few minutes ago! It was there and then it just somehow went underground! You see that brown patch of dirt out there? It's under there!"

Ellen sighed. "Officer Brady, he's right. It was here. I saw it, too. It was standing right where that patch of dirt is now a little more than an hour ago. I believe my husband. I swear he's telling the truth. I know this sounds ridiculous, but there is something living out in these woods that is terrifying us."

Brady gave the couple a baffled glance. "I'm sorry, ma'am, I just see a patch of dirt."

"Look," Ellen said, "I know we're new here, but my husband and I are not crazy people. We have good jobs. We have no criminal records. My husband has been seeing this thing for days. I saw it up close last night and our little boy is ... he's out there!"

Brady cocked his head towards the meadow and squinted. "Well. I don't quite know what to tell you, ma'am. I hunt these woods regular, and ain't seen nothing outta the ordinary. There's lotsa deer, that's about it. I have to say that I can't fathom an animal harming your son. We're fairly sure it's a kidnapping at this point, and VSP's involved."

An awkward silence passed.

"They're the best in the state on this stuff. Promise. If a little boy gone missin', it'll be a real high priority."

Brady took a step towards them. He was young, and Aaron couldn't help but wonder what a kid like this could possibly do to find a kidnapped toddler. Bless him for trying, but this clearly wasn't his area of expertise.

"Guys, this isn't over," Brady said. "Not by a long shot."

Aaron sat down right where he'd been standing in the driveway. The gravel grated at his weary sit bones. His peeled his eyes off Brady and gazed out into space.

"If it makes y'all feel any better, I've never seen the deputy more determined," Brady said. "I know y'all don't know her, but I'd be takin' some comfort in that."

• • •

Cheryl sat on the edge of the bed as the sun crested over the eastern basin. Her hands looked old, frailer than they used to be. The cracks in her palms and the spaces behind her knuckles were black canyons in the early morning light.

A familiar tranquility filled the bedroom at this hour. An open window by the dresser pulled in crisp summer air, still cool from the night and the dewy ground. Birds outside the window greeted the day.

Alone with her thoughts, and with Rick sound asleep next to her, Cheryl thought about her children.

Lenny would be sleeping right now. Maybe in his bed,

maybe in someone else's. Likely sleeping off a Saturday night of hard drinking on campus. She knew he was a drinker but tried to convince herself it was normal for kids in college to drink. He was almost of age anyway. Skylar was asleep in a room not ten feet away. Safe under mama bear's roof. At least for now.

The events of the last two days ached in Cheryl's chest. When she put her hands on her knees and took a deep breath through her nose, it felt like there was a brick between her lungs. The stiffness from the stress had burrowed deep into her muscles, still hard as concrete even after a good night's sleep.

The way she saw it, the safety of the town had been entrusted to her in Duke's absence, and she'd failed. She'd failed Hank, the Dreyers, poor little Caleb. There had to be something she wasn't seeing, something she'd missed. There had to be a reason for the two most serious crimes in the last decade to happen one right after the other.

And Duke knew something. Had he definitely said 'kidnapping'? How could he have known? A missing person case is quite different from a kidnapping. It's not some slip of the tongue a veteran law enforcement officer would make. Of course, Duke was getting up there in age.

A hand touched the small of her back. She looked over her shoulder to see Rick smiling.

"What's on your mind, bug?" he said.

A diesel engine down the street interrupted the songbirds' morning serenade. This thin stretch of the morning belonged to those birds. Blissfully melodic, they woke before first light and announced themselves to the world in symphonic splendor, all soloing together. They only had a few more minutes of tranquility before the world of man awoke from its slumber.

Rick sat up in bed and swung his legs around to her side. "You don't wanna talk about it?" he said.

"Not particularly."

"Might make you feel better. Know you've got a lot on your mind."

A series of dry cracks burst out of her neck as she rolled her head from side-to-side. "The murder. Now this kidnapping," she said.

Rick began massaging the skin on the back of her neck with his thumb and index finger. "Yeah. I seen both on the news. Not gettin' anywhere?"

"Not just not gettin' anywhere, seems to be gettin' worse by the hour."

"Duke back yet?"

"Shit, I don't know. He's part of the problem."

"What do you mean?"

"Don't quite know yet. Maybe nothin'. I don't know. I don't know anything anymore. I'm losing control."

"You considered maybe you ain't s'posed to have control?"

Cheryl rubbed three hours of sleep out of her eyes.

"It's my job to have control," she whispered.

"Ain't none of this your fault, bug. Whoever did this shit didn't wait for Duke to leave town to make you look dumb. I hate to say it, but this ain't all about you. How can you have control over somethin' like this?"

The most stressful part of her morning routine was checking the voicemail on her mobile phone. She stared long and hard at the little gray Nokia monolith lodged upright in its charging station on her dresser. With two major active crimes, VSP embroiled in both, and a sheriff just back from a vacation he'd cut short, there would certainly be a deluge waiting for her.

"It's not your job to have control. It's your job to be honest with people when you don't, and just do what you can to make 'em feel better. That's all anyone can do. It's okay to ask for help."

Cheryl chuckled. "You sound like an insurance salesman," she said, and pecked him on the lips, "and I already got a guy for that."

"Guess I'm doin' somethin' right, then."

. . .

Aaron spent the morning ambling through the house in a lethargic stupor while Ellen finally slept. She had gone upstairs without saying a word and cried muffled sobs into her pillow for maybe thirty minutes before sleep took her.

Never in his life had Aaron experienced such a state of existential meandering. His son was gone. His rock of a wife was one more crack away from breaking, if not already broken. Not only did the police not believe him, they didn't even really care to listen. The minutes and the hours blended into abstraction, and when he didn't want to go back to sleep, he wanted to scream. The house felt disturbingly vacant without Caleb, and every time his eyes grazed one of his son's toys or articles of clothing, it was another dagger of rage and confusion in his heart.

Aaron opened the front door simply to remind himself that a world existed outside. Sunlight blasted his irritated eyes, and he breathed in the cruel summer air, already thick with humidity. He squinted at a pair of deer grazing in the meadow. The doe stood to attention while her fawn munched quietly behind her, its nascent head hidden in the golden grass. A swallow dipped through Aaron's sightline, rose, and dipped again.

For a moment, Aaron saw himself with Caleb out there.

He scanned the front yard, the floodlights, and the spot of dirt where the monster had foiled him in a way he never could have dreamt possible.

"What in the fuck were you thinking?" he said to himself, fixated on the black extension cords lying in his yard like a sloppy network of veins surging with poison.

Aaron's head throbbed with the painful thought of that day. He considered what he might be willing to sacrifice in the making of some backroom pact with the cosmos for a chance to go back to that moment, with his son by his side and his life still intact. But that day, those lights, they ruined everything. Why didn't he listen to his instinct and leave it alone? What aggrandized sense of purpose did the pursuit of this thing provide him that wasn't right there the whole time? What kind of shit father doesn't recognize that until well after it's too late?

"FUCK!"

Aaron found his right fist a millimeter into the vinyl siding by his front door and a scalding pain building up through his fingers.

The sound of Cooper's heavy panting behind him told Aaron he had forgotten to close the door. The dog stepped outside and rested at his feet with a resigned chuff.

When Aaron returned his gaze to the meadow, the deer were gone, and a gray sedan was rolling north up Wickham Road toward the house. Cooper yanked his head up and began to pant again as the sedan edged into the driveway. Out stepped the detective from two days ago.

"Mr. Dreyer, remember me? Detective Pierce."

"Yes! Oh my God. Thank God you're here! Did you hear about my son? Did you hear Caleb is gone? That's why you're here, right? Do you have any news? Did you find him?"

"That is why I'm here. It's rare I talk with the same folks in a week about two separate crimes."

"Two crimes? What?"

"Remember we spoke about Hank Teakle? Now your son? Two crimes?"

"Jesus. That felt like a year ago. Yeah, I—I remember. I've just been a little preoccupied. Listen, did you find him, or what? You have any leads? Anything? We've gotten nowhere with the police. We—"

Two bulbous beads of sweat rolled down Pierce's brow, and one settled along the rim of his glasses. He had on the same tweed blazer and pants he had worn the other day, either uncaring or unaware of the suffocating climate. "No news, I'm sorry to say we don't have any updates. I came over to get your accounting of the day and see if we can't find something. Do you have a few minutes to talk?"

"Uh—I, yeah, sure. There's nothing? Like no trace or anything? No clothing, no nothing?"

Pierce sighed and slid the tweed blazer off his narrow shoulders. "I'm sorry, sir. Nothing."

Aaron paused long enough for the warbler tweeting in the tree between them to catch Cooper's attention, the dog flicking his ears back as he searched for the sound.

"Well, in your professional opinion, what do you think the chances are at this point? I mean, it's been almost 24 hours. What—"

"Mr. Dreyer, I'm terribly sorry to hear about your son. I don't want to jerk you around here but getting into things like the chances is a dangerous mind game. I'd urge you to not to play it. How about we go inside for a few minutes and get out of this heat? Your account of the day might hold something that unlocks the whole thing."

Inside, the two men sat down in the same seats they had occupied two days ago. Cooper pranced upstairs.

Pierce flipped open his steno pad. "Can you start by telling me in your own words exactly what happened?"

"Well, I guess the first thing is that I wasn't there when he went missing. I was in a store and he was with his mother, Ellen. She's asleep." Aaron said.

"M&J Fine Gifts?"

"Yeah, that's the one."

"So how did you know he was gone?"

"Ellen ran into the store. She was super upset, screaming that Caleb was gone. I can probably wake her up if—"

"Won't be necessary. I've got her police statement and the search reports. Local did a good job. If I have any follow-up questions for your wife, I can contact her. I'm sure she's quite tired."

"Are you sure? I mean, her point of view is pretty important here, don't you think?"

Pierce flipped a page. "Can you go back and tell me what happened in the store? Anything notable?"

"We'd stopped there to get a drink. I wanted a Gatorade. I went in, got one, and—"

A troubling silence filled the room. The detective looked up from his pad.

"And then what?"

Aaron fidgeted in his seat, searching his mind for the next event. He couldn't find it. "This might sound silly, but I actually don't remember."

"Don't remember what?"

"It's like there's a part of my memory missing. I walked in

the store, I got the drink, and then ... I think ... Ellen barged in."

"Are you saying something else happened in the store?"

"I'm sorry. I'm not sure what I'm saying."

"Was anyone else in the store with you?"

"Yes. The woman who runs it. Jane, I believe."

"Jane. Yes, that's her name. Are you saying you don't remember what happened in the store? It seemed like a fairly normal interaction, no?"

"With Jane?"

"With Jane."

"I mean, I wasn't in there for more than a couple of minutes. Why? Is something wrong?"

"We spoke with her, too. She remembers you coming in, getting a drink, your wife entering soon after. Never saw Caleb that day. Her story sounds a lot like yours."

"Huh, okay," Aaron said, recalling the CLOSED sign hanging in the door as he'd recounted his story to Cheryl. "I guess nothing happened in there besides that."

"And then what happened when Ellen came in?"

"Um, well, I didn't fully realize what was happening. But she asked if Caleb had come into the store. Then she suggested we start looking for him in the forest across the street. We ran around the playground area and the woods back there for maybe ten minutes, I don't know. We didn't find anything. I came back to the road soon after that, Ellen had already called the cops and they got there pretty quickly."

"And the cops took over from there?"

"Pretty much."

"Deputy McNamara?"

"Yeah."

"We were in the same class in the academy."

"No shit?"

The detective looked up at Aaron. "No shit." He went back to his pad. "Anything else you think is worth noting?"

"What do you mean? That's all you want to know? That's it?"

Pierce leaned forward, resting his elbows on his knees. He took a handkerchief out of his pocket and started cleaning his glasses. "You tell me. Is that it?"

"I, uh," Aaron drew his bottom lip between his teeth and stared into Pierce, sizing him up for his appetite for the fantastic. "I ... I guess not. No. Nothing else. I don't know of anyone who would have a reason to take him."

"Is that your belief?"

"Cheryl said it was a kidnapping. I guess someone took him. I mean, what do you think? Is he still out there?"

"We're still confident. An associate of mine might be by later to give a more detailed update. I'm mostly here to gather information. As I'm sure you've heard before, these first couple days are the most important. If it gives you any comfort, so far, everything has been done completely by the book. If your son's out there, we will get him."

"If?"

Pierce closed his pad and stood up. "Give my best to Mrs. Dreyer. We'll be in touch."

Two jarring sensations collided as Aaron opened the front door to let the detective out. The first was the heat, only this time, ratcheted up even higher. It was a hundred degrees outside, easy. The sort of heat that forced everything to slow down and made Aaron want to claw the next living thing he saw. It wrapped itself around him the instant he opened the door, as if it had been waiting just for him.

The second was a downright nauseating sense of déjà vu. The doe and her fawn were back in the meadow. The feeling was so disorienting and so acute that Aaron felt his center of balance sink down and then come back up again.

The last week had been a level of hell like nothing he had ever imagined possible. The India trip didn't even feel like a distant memory anymore, it felt like someone else's life completely. That old version of Aaron was an inter-dimensional facsimile, or a life played out on a different timeline. As he watched the detective's sedan roll down Wickham Road, like watching a video backwards, he envied the person he used to be.

• • •

Having spent the better part of the day roaming the county roads in her patrol car, Cheryl found herself behaving like Skylar moving around different parts of the house to avoid her parents: scurrying, looking over her shoulder, waiting for some higher power or authority to chastise her. She hadn't spoken with Duke since yesterday afternoon.

How did he know? Did he really know, or did he just say something — anything — to shut her up?

Cheryl gulped down the rest of her lunch alone in the unit. Condensation dripped from the plastic air vents with the AC on its highest setting. Her phone buzzed, and when she flipped it open, she recognized the number of the Coroner's Office.

"Hey Reuven, what'cha got?" she said.

"Not much in the way of news. Pretty straightforward autopsy, all told. You know most of it. Cause of death is impossible to determine due to the absence of organs. I guess you could say it was blood loss. Mass evisceration, you could call it. To be honest, I've never seen anything like it."

"You got any idea what coulda done somethin' like that?"

"Hard to say. Guess it's possible a mountain lion went to town on him. Could be man-made, but the cuts are quite clean. Whatever — or whoever — did it had some serious technology or firepower. Maybe somebody with a giant ice cream scoop?"

"Yeah, beats me, too. You tell State yet?"

"They're my next call."

"Better you tell 'em than me."

"Hey, when's Duke getting back? He's on vacation, right?"

"Yeah, he's on his way back or back already. I'm not sure. We haven't spoken since yesterday, but I'm sure we'll have words quite soon."

"Well, good luck to you, Deputy."

"Thanks, Reuven. Holler if anything comes up."

With VSP more or less handling both cases, she finally had the space to start gaining some perspective, but every time she opened a door of possibility, it seemed to close three others. Nothing added up. But despite the facts, there existed within her a growing and nagging sense that maybe, even if the chances were slim, something beyond the realm of normal understanding was at work. Maybe this whole thing — Hank, Caleb, all of it — extended beyond the plain and obvious.

• • •

Ellen woke up in bed with her head pointed towards the bedroom window. A blurry panorama of purple, orange, and yellow layers blended together through the evening horizon. The tranquility in her body at that moment was so thorough that it took a few seconds for her physical sensations to return to her.

Then she remembered her son was gone, and a slow and creeping ache worked its way through her head, her neck, and all the way through her body.

Hours had passed. Maybe six, maybe eight. Outside, cicadas screeched at the waning of the day. One clung to the screen and ripped a cry right through the window and into the bedroom.

For as much as she loved the outdoors, she knew little about the habits of some of its most populous creatures. Did cicadas have any concept of time? They had the uncanny ability to coordinate decade-long hibernations, so they had to understand something.

Did they think about their offspring? Did they love them? Probably not. Maybe that was a better existence.

The sound of the doorbell cut through the big bug's mating call, and one-by-one, Ellen shook life into her limbs and found enough strength to get out of bed.

Downstairs, Aaron was seated at the kitchen table with a man shaped like a refrigerator. The man got up and extended his hand.

"Detective Salim Williams with the Virginia State Police," he said, with a tight smile. "Please call me Salim".

Salim was tall, at least six inches taller than Ellen, and his muscular arms bulged from the tucked-in navy blue polo pulled tightly over his broad shoulders. At his waist, a platinum buckler-shaped badge glinted in Ellen's eye, almost as if to say, "Wake up, Ellen, time to get down to business." The air of retired military was undeniable.

He reached out a great hook of a hand, but when Ellen

shook it, it was surprisingly gentle. "Dr. Dreyer, I'm the lead detective on Caleb's case. I've been a Missing Persons Investigator with the Virginia State Police for the last twenty-three years and we're going to do everything we can to get Caleb back. I already thanked your husband, but let me thank you as well, Dr. Dreyer, for allowing me into your home to discuss Caleb's case."

"Of—of course," Ellen said in a way that came out more bashful than she had intended.

"Now, I've already been brought up to speed on the accounts from Deputy Cheryl McNamara, and your husband was gracious enough to relay his own account, but I'd very much like to get a detailed account from you. I've already noticed a few discrepancies that I would like to discuss with you and your husband. Would you mind joining us for a few minutes?"

Ellen felt herself blushing at the candor and focus of Salim's delivery. VSP had sent the top brass, and for the first time since Caleb had gone missing, she felt comforted, almost inspired.

"Thank you, Salim. What did you mean by discrepancies? Have you found anything? Is there any movement or any sign of Caleb at all?"

"No major updates, I'm sorry to report. But I'll get to that in just a second. First, though, would you mind giving me your account of the last few hours before you lost sight of Caleb? What did you do and what did you experience that morning?"

"Well, we were all together that morning. We had gone to breakfast and then to the library. Even Cooper, our dog, came along. Aaron had a little fainting spell in the library. We've had a kind of, I don't know, touch-and-go last couple days. Not sure if Aaron told you that. Oh, and the heat was awful. But anyway, before heading home, we went to get a Gatorade. Aaron found a store from the road and went in."

"Do you remember the name of the store?"

She looked at Aaron and squinted. "M&J, right?"

Aaron nodded.

Salim squirmed in his seat. "And before Aaron went into the store, did you notice anything off about your surroundings? Was anyone else walking around? Was there traffic?"

"No. It was dead. I'm sure of it. It was pretty early, and no one was out. If there were any people or cars, nothing seemed odd. I've racked my brain a few times over that and I really don't think there was anyone."

"Understood. What time did Aaron go into the store?"

"Let's see. We went to the library right at 10. I think the librarian let us in a few minutes early. So, I guess he went into the store around 10:30?" Ellen said.

"Does that sound right to you, Mr. Dreyer? About 10:30?" Salim said.

Aaron looked up for a second and then nodded. "Yeah, I think that's probably about right."

Salim pulled back the page on a yellow legal pad and looked down at it. "Right. So, something's not adding up here."

The Dreyers exchanged puzzled looks and Ellen swallowed a lump of anxiety that had formed in her throat.

"Dr. Dreyer, you placed two phone calls to Deputy McNamara that morning. One at," Salim flipped another page in his pad, "10:44, where you spoke for two minutes, and one at 11:22 which she didn't answer. She then called you at 11:27 and you two spoke for one minute." Salim glanced up from his pad and cast his iron gaze upon her. "Is that consistent with your understanding? Do you remember the content of those phone calls, Dr. Dreyer?"

"Yeah, that sounds right. I'm happy to show you my phone records. The first was actually to talk about the Hank Teakle case. I just wanted to know if she'd found anything. She said she hadn't. The second call was me trying to tell her Caleb was missing. But then she called back like you said, and that's when I informed her."

"And did you place the phone call at 11:22 before or after you went to get your husband?"

"After. My first thought was that Caleb went in the store to see Aaron. When he wasn't in there, I ... I guess I panicked and called the police."

"How much time did you spend in the store with your husband?"

"The store? I don't know. Two or three minutes, tops? Certainly not more than five. I just dashed through the store really quickly and then grabbed Aaron and we ran."

Salim sighed and looked at his pad again. He flipped a page and then flipped it back. "This timeline is not adding up to me. Mr. Dreyer, you said you were in M&J for a total of what you described as 'a few minutes.'"

"Wait, what?" Ellen said, shooting her eyes towards her husband. "You were in there for like forty minutes."

Aaron's face wilted with exasperation. "W—What?"

"Aaron, you were in there for a long time. That's the whole reason I took Caleb out of the car and went to the playground in the first place. Remember?"

Aaron's mouth hung open and his lips quivered as if to form words, but nothing came out for some time. "I ... no. To be honest, I don't remember. I honestly don't. Was I in there for forty minutes? I have no recollection of that. I even said that to Deputy McNamara, and I said the same to Detective Pierce today. All I remember was Ellen coming in and—"

"Sorry," Salim said, "Detective Pierce?"

"Yeah, your colleague? He was here earlier today. He came by and asked a lot of the same questions. He asked us about Hank's murder a couple days ago, too."

The profile of Salim's face reminded Ellen of a rock wall. His dark eyes, chiseled features and half-frown all bore down on Aaron. Something was happening that she didn't understand.

"What department did he say he was with?" Salim said.

"Um, he didn't," Aaron mumbled.

"He didn't what?"

"He didn't say what department he was with. Ellen, it was the same guy who came by a couple days ago. You remember him, right?"

"No, actually," Ellen said. "I didn't meet him. I was sleeping off a night shift."

"Oh, that's—that's right," Aaron said.

"The same guy came back?" Ellen asked.

"Yeah. He was here a few hours ago. He said he was working both cases. Skinny guy, tweed jacket. Sweating his face off in the heat. He came by and asked me questions about Caleb. He said he was going to call you later if he had questions."

"Both cases? What other case?" Salim said.

"The Hank Teakle case. Hank's our neighbor and he died. It was a murder or a homicide or something like that. We don't know the details yet."

Salim swung his arms forward and rested his elbows on the table as gently as a man of that size possibly could. "Mr. Dreyer, I don't have a colleague named Pierce. I'm the lead detective on your son Caleb's case. VSP has completely separate Homicide and Missing Persons divisions. They're two different fields of expertise. They wouldn't send the same detective out for those two kinds of incidents."

The room went silent again. No one knew what to say but a grimace of panic had worked its way onto Aaron's face. The last time Ellen saw that look, he was warning her about the monster in the meadow. Then she remembered how she'd brushed him off, and she felt a chilly pang of shame creep into her stomach.

"Did he leave a card?" Salim asked.

"Actually, no, he didn't."

"Did he show you a badge? Any identification? He didn't say anything about where he was from?"

"Come to think of it, I don't think he did."

Salim turned his gaze to Ellen. She felt like she was looking at her father. She felt like a bad mother all over again.

"I—I don't know, Detective," she said. "I never saw the guy, but I believe my husband. If he says he was here, he was here."

"I'm certainly not saying he's lying. I'm saying you let a man into your house who didn't properly identify himself. Twice in the span of a week. And once with your son in the house, correct? Did this man meet your son?"

Aaron's face when gravestone cold. "Oh fuck. You ... you don't think?"

"Can you describe this man for me, Mr. Dreyer?"

"Oh God. He was just here. Brown hair. Parted to the side. Wore glasses. Like, real thick ones. Thin guy. White. Wore that jacket like I told you about. He didn't seem like he was from around here. Said his name was Roland Pierce. That's honestly kind of it."

Ellen put her hands on her head. Salim wrote feverishly while Aaron spoke. "Describe his vehicle for me. Did you get a plate number?"

"Gray sedan. Old. I didn't look at the plate. Oh, fuck, Detective. Oh fuck. Do you think he took Caleb? Wait. If he did, why would he come back to visit us after the fact?"

Salim shook his head. "You know, the folks that do these things have a very different worldview than we do. Some people look at the world as if it's their plaything and they get pleasure out of pain and torture. Sometimes it's physical, sometimes it's mental or emotional. Sometimes there's no discernable reason at all. I've certainly seen cases of criminals taunting their victims in ways that are truly disgusting. Now, I'm not saying that's what happened here, but I think this is a valuable lead."

Ellen subconsciously touched her chest. There was no baby bird there, but she did feel something pulling her to the ground when she realized where Salim was going with this. His was a logical conclusion, but it didn't feel right to her. She could only move in one direction. The direction of the truth.

"Detective," she whispered. Both men turned and looked at her. Ellen felt her jaw stiffen and her heart begin to beat faster. Harder. "There's something you should know. Something that might seem a bit hard to believe."

• • •

Cheryl couldn't shake her husband's words as she drove. He was right. This wasn't about her, and the thought that she had done anything over the last three days for anyone other than

Hank Teakle or Caleb Dreyer made her sick to her stomach. She wished she could have explained to Rick that really, she was just tired of feeling alone. Brady, Nelson, and the rest of the Department were great cops, but they were young and didn't take the initiative the way she had in the face of all this. They deferred to Cheryl to lead them, and she truly did feel responsible for everyone beneath her. With Duke around, the burden of leadership had never fallen on her shoulders quite so hard. Whatever fantastic assumptions of higher law enforcement glory she'd had before all this happened were gone and left no trace in her mind.

She came to a stop light and looked up at the mountains blanketed under the thin light of the evening sky. A squirrel bounded happily across a telephone wire. Above it, a half dozen bats flitted in chaotic circles. The smell of healthy soil and pine crept into her nostrils.

Her phone buzzed. Skylar. Cheryl couldn't remember the last time her daughter had called her.

"Hey, princess, what's up?"

Skylar didn't answer, and already Cheryl could tell something was wrong.

"Skylar? You there?"

"Yeah. Yeah, I'm here."

"What's wrong? You okay?"

"Um, yeah, I—"

Cheryl's throat caught on something and a fire from the depths of her womb instantly ignited. "Baby. Skylar. Sweetheart, what's wrong? Where are you?"

Skylar's voice cracked and she let out a soft sob. "Everything's wrong. I'm sorry. I love you, Mom. I just wanted you to know that. I'm just going through some stuff right now. I don't want to talk about it, but I just wanted you to know."

The fire inside Cheryl turned into a volcano of affection for her daughter. It erupted in her chest and forced fast tears from her eyes. She didn't even notice that she had grabbed the fabric of her starched uniform pants above the knee with her other hand and balled it in a tight fist. "Baby, did someone hurt you? What happened, Skylar?"

"Mom, I don't want to talk about it."

The register of Cheryl's voice heightened under the weight of her tears and sudden emotion, and she tried but failed to mask her sniffles with words. "My Skylar Mary. Whatever you're goin' through, I've been there. I have been there. I have been there. I know how hard and awful this age is. It's the worst one there is, baby. It only gets better from here. I promise you that. Do you need me to come home, sweetheart?"

"No," Skylar said, choking back tears of her own now. "I'm just gonna go to sleep and I'll see you in the morning."

"Skylar Mary, I love you so goddamned much. If someone hurt you, so help me. Where's your father?"

"He's here. He's watching NASCAR."

"You stay there and watch it with him. I'll be home in morning. Dad'll make us pancakes and bacon, okay?"

"Okay. That sounds good."

Cheryl kept the phone to her ear as she watched a second squirrel frolic across the wire. The hard plastic in her hand slipped around on the sweaty skin of her cheek, and she pressed the phone harder into her ear in some ineffectual effort to hear more of her daughter's pain. But Skylar didn't speak, and Cheryl only heard muffled stock car engines zip up and back down again in the background of the world she wanted to be in.

For the world in which she currently resided, a world of isolation and confusion and darkness, was a prison to her now. The thought of calling Duke and resigning on the spot flashed in her mind before evaporating. But Skylar's breathing through the phone, still thin like a child's, pulled her thoughts again towards Caleb Dreyer. She took a deep breath and closed her eyes, forcing the last of the tears down her face. "Okay, baby. I love you. Call me if you need anything, okay?"

"I'll just send a text."

"That's my girl. Just send a text."

"Okay. Bye, Mom."

"I love you, sweet girl."

Cheryl closed the phone in her hand. "Oh God," she whispered.

Up ahead, the traffic light was now green, and Cheryl wondered how long it had been that way.

• • •

"Go ahead," Salim said. "I'm listening." He wrote in big, sweeping print and filled the pages in his pad quickly.

Aaron watched his wife with cautious optimism, and he hoped the look on his face was one that encouraged her.

She began. "I'm not a particularly religious or spiritual person. I've been a lover of the natural world and a student of medicine and science all my life. I'm a Doctor of Emergency Medicine, and while I've seen some fantastic things, I've never seen anything in my life that I couldn't explain. That is, until a few nights ago. My husband and I, and our dog for what it's worth, we've all witnessed activity around our property that we can't explain. We've seen things that if I were to describe them to you, I don't think you'd believe. The cops here don't believe us. I didn't believe it myself until I saw it with my own eyes."

Salim stopped writing, put his pen down, and closed his pad. He slowly craned his boulder of a head up to meet Ellen's gaze and folded his hands. Aaron saw something flash inside the hulking, military man, an awareness and a focus he hadn't seen on the face or in the heart of anyone he'd dealt with all week.

"With all due respect, try me. You may not be religions, but I am, and I've seen some things I definitely can't explain. Doesn't mean they didn't happen. Just means I can't explain them. What have you been seeing?"

Ellen took a deep breath, as if preparing to deliver incredibly difficult news to a patient. She stared into her lap, unable to look the detective in the eye. "Right outside, across from that road you came in on, there's a meadow. And every night, well, morning, I suppose, around 4:00am, a ... a creature of some kind has been walking through it and roaming around. We have no idea what it is. It's massive. I mean, it's just huge. Unlike anything we've ever seen before. It's not a bear or a horse or an elephant or ... I mean, we have no idea. But it's so large, and it's so dark, and it has these hands that we've seen. Its fingers are like, this long." Ellen extended her arms out to her sides to denote the size. "I know how this sounds, but this thing comes out of one side of the forest, walks through the meadow, and walks to the other side of the forest. It takes the same route at the same time every night. We only just noticed it, but we think our dog's known about it for some time. It, um—"

She glanced at Aaron, a look that seemed to seek permission to keep going. Although Salim had given no indication to think otherwise, Aaron could see Ellen's confidence waning.

He knew better than anyone that saying it out loud to another person made it real in a way that was deeply disconcerting.

"She's right, Detective," Aaron said. "I've seen it, and we've observed a number of things about it. It has an aversion to light. It seems to come out at the same time every night, except if our yard is lit. You certainly saw those floodlights in our front yard. I set those up to try and get a better look, but it won't come out if the lights are on."

Not a single fiber or tendon of Salim's body moved. He sat like a statue staring at Ellen. He didn't blink.

Ellen continued. "We're still learning about this thing, but we know it lives in the woods out there. The same woods that Caleb went into that day. The same woods that connect to Hank Teakle's property. We've told the local authorities about all this and they don't believe us. I can certainly understand why."

She paused, giving Salim a chance to speak. He passed.

"Detective, I'm guessing you rely heavily on instinct in your line of work. I know I do. I understand why you would be drawn to a man like Aaron is describing, but if I'm being totally honest, every motherly—"

The utterance of that word caused the muscles in Ellen's face to tense and for her throat to catch on the emotion it had conjured. "Every instinct I have is screaming to me that the thing we are seeing took—"

Her eyes slammed closed, and she could only choke out the rest of her sentence through tears. "—took Caleb. It ... has ... it has him. I ... I know it. I just ... I just know it does."

Aaron swooped around the table to his wife and wrapped his arms around her shoulders. She heaved as the tears poured from her. Her body was scalding hot. He looked at Salim and spoke softly, holding back his own overwhelming grief long enough to finish Ellen's thought. "No one believes us, Sir. No one believes us. No one fucking believes us."

Salim's face softened, and then he gazed down at Cooper who had strutted over to the detective. Salim stuck a hand down and rubbed between the dog's ears. He kept his eyes on Cooper as he spoke. "When I was a kid growing up in South Carolina, my father used to go to this prayer group. It was way out in the sticks, this place called Wadmalaw Island. He went every month for years, and he never, ever talked about it. All I knew at the time was they'd meet at this little old lady's house. My father would come back from this lady's house, well, I can't think of another word for it besides just plain happy. As I got older, I became more curious about what they were doing at that prayer group, and one night, after years of going alone, my father asked me if I wanted to join him."

Cooper released himself from Salim's grip and collapsed at his feet in satisfaction.

"He told me something on the ride out there that I'll never forget. He said—" Salim paused and looked upward, taking himself back in time. "He said, 'Sometimes I think we're ants that got hold of a fresh pie. Most of us go through life, we walk on the crust of this earth, we take a piece of it, and then we go back home. But for the few of us that are willing to put the work in, there's so much more to this world. There's so much more that lies below the surface if we look for it.' I didn't know what he was talking about, but we arrived at this little old lady's house. Her name was Mabel Clyne. I'll never forget that, either. There were maybe about a dozen people in this swampy little shack, and we all started praying to God. To the Christian God.

"But then, Mabel Clyne got up out of her chair, walked into the middle of the circle, put her arms out, and lifted her chin to the sky. And I swear on my father's grave, her eyes went completely white, and she started chanting in a language I had never heard before. She was sweating and she was shouting, and she was rattling off these ancient words that, well, trust me when I say Mabel Clyne was not fluent in any other languages. She was so old she was barely literate at all."

Both Ellen and Aaron were transfixed on the detective. Aaron stood behind his wife, leaning down on her back and holding her shoulders in his arms. Ellen remained seated and her fingers clutched Aaron's arms with a Herculean strength.

"Something entered that woman. Something I couldn't see. Something none of us could see, but it was there. Somehow. Everybody else in the group just kept on praying like it wasn't a big deal. They'd probably seen this hundreds of times before, but since it was my first time witnessing it, I had to stop and just watch. I couldn't believe what was happening. After about, I don't know, ten minutes or so, Mabel stopped and walked back to her chair, and that was it. The prayer group went on praying. When we were done, we all went out on the back porch and had lemonade and talked about the Atlanta Braves like nothing had happened."

Ellen opened her mouth to speak but all that came out was a fractured whisper. "Do you believe us?"

"It doesn't matter if I believe you. I'm not going to sit here, in the house you invited me into, and tell you you're wrong. I'm not going to tell you that you're crazy, or that you're digging in the wrong place, or that some unknown outsider hasn't crossed into the world. And as a father of three, my youngest also being four years old, I'm absolutely not going to tell you how you should feel about your missing son. Your son, Caleb."

Salim stood. Ellen's face broke again, and her head collapsed into her chest.

"Now you may not want to hear this next part, but I've been doing this a long time. A very long time. And ninety-nine times out of a hundred, these cases end with men just like your husband described. If you'll please excuse me, I'd like to make a couple of calls. We'll be in touch." He took two steps towards the door and turned around. "But off the record, Dr. Dreyer, I do believe you."

• • •

Detective Salim Williams swooped his frame into his state-issue police cruiser and peered out the windshield towards the bottom of the Dreyers' driveway. He picked up the radio.

"A.P.B. Squad 50 to all squads, wanted in connection with a child abduction of Caleb Dreyer that occurred on Saturday, July 17, at about 10:45am in Bensalem, is a Roland Pierce, approximately 40 years old, male, white, slim build, about 6-feet tall, short hair, short mustache. Last seen driving a gray sedan, unknown make and model, southbound on Wickham Road in Bensalem, Virginia. Unknown if the subject is armed. Over."

It squawked back at him. "Copy, Detective."

As he drove on towards the main road, something bright shimmered briefly on the shoulder of the road in front of him. He stopped and glared at the white pickup truck sitting there vacant, its headlights and front grill plastered in a sinister chrome grimace.

"One more thing," he said. "Need you to run a plate for me."

• • •

Cheryl saw a beige lump in the middle of the road. She was on the service road south of State Road 639 heading to the station. No one would be there at this hour, except maybe Duke. The terrain out here was flat and wooded. Empty. Her high beams were the only source of light for miles.

She parked on the shoulder, got out, and pulled a compact LED from her belt. There in the road was a young doe. The skin that had once held its belly together had been ripped open and slimy pink tissue glistened under the deputy's light. Blood pooled by its nose and mouth. Cheryl leaned in and heard rapid, labored breathing.

The sight brought her back to Hank's Horse Farm and its owner's butchered corpse. His last moments of life probably weren't all that different. Earthly vessel shredded, not dead but not alive, contemplating whatever it was the brain could still contemplate at that point. He probably thought about his daughters and how sorry he was for being stubborn. Maybe he tried to trade his soul for five more minutes with them or even just a glance or a smile. She wondered whether he'd asked God or the devil for that. Or both. She wondered if it hurt. It probably hurt a lot, a pain she couldn't fathom. Either that, or he bled out quick enough to skip all that.

Cheryl sighed and wiped her brow. The day's unrelenting heat lingered and was settling in the valley. Kneeling beside the doe, she listened as it inhaled blood and exhaled life. She placed a delicate hand on the top of the animal's head and caressed it. She looked up at the sky. Somehow, it looked bigger than it did a minute ago.

She closed her eyes and recited an Our Father. Not because she wanted to talk to God, she didn't believe in one, but because it would calm her nerves before she had to do the hard part.

She traded her LED for her service weapon and fired a single round. The shot rang out, and its clang bounced off the cut of the mountain and echoed through the basin. By the time the echo had stopped, so had the gurgling.

Cheryl gripped two of the doe's hooves, and the back leg made a gravelly snap when she began to pull. The broken bone hung flaccid in its container of muscle. There was blood all over the pavement.

She hauled the animal into a shallow ditch several paces away from the road. The soil was rocky and crunched under her boots.

"Take good care of her," she said. "She deserves it."

She stood with the gun in her hand for a good while, collecting herself, listening to the sounds of the forest. She wanted to cry again but she couldn't. She was too tired. She didn't want to get back in the car, but she had to. She just wanted to stay here, to rest, to stop, to do anything but get back in and press on, but that's exactly what she did.

• • •

Ellen poured herself a glass of straight bourbon and shot it back to calm her nerves. The liquid flame scorched her throat on the way down and settled like a lighted torch in the pit of her stomach.

She had spent the last three hours sorting through Detective Salim Williams' words. When everything had been cleared away — the stories, the leads, the times, the details of the case

— Ellen gravitated towards with the one thing he didn't actually say. While it was clear he wasn't going to directly encourage her, neither would he discourage her from doing whatever she deemed necessary to get Caleb back. As fantastic as it may be.

The only time she could remember feeling this anxious was before taking the Medical College Admission Test nearly fifteen years earlier. In a way, every trauma patient she dealt with was their own little fight, but they weren't situations that triggered her base survival instincts. Instincts that raged inside her right at this moment. Going into the MCAT, every fiber of her being knew the test would define her. It would either give life or kill her.

What this detective or that detective knew or did or said didn't matter in the long run. Ellen had been contacted by the monster in the meadow. It had selected her, targeted her. It had stared her down and put its hands on her, and it said, "If you want your son, you have to go through me."

It was dark inside the shed in the back yard and Ellen hadn't brought a light. Her skin tingled at the idea of a snake jumping out at her for disturbing its slumber, but she was not to be deterred. Its haggard door creaked open, and smells of stale earth and rust seeped out.

She stuck her hand out into the black until it contacted the wall of the shed. The brittle old wood was coarse from decades of neglect. She pawed the wall until the tip of her finger landed on a cold, raised metal object. The frail wooden walls creaked in the summer wind and the metal object rocked slightly away from her.

With a clawing motion, Ellen wrapped her hand around the whole of the twin cylinders and lifted them off the hook.

She held her father's pump-action shotgun up to the

moonlight. He had shot their family's first dog with that gun back when Ellen was a baby. He had taught his daughter to shoot it, and although she wasn't exactly a sniper, she knew how it worked. She wasn't planning to shoot from a distance anyway.

No, she wanted to be right next to it when it died. She wanted to hear it scream, if it was capable of screaming. She wanted to latch on to the thing's pain the way it had latched onto hers.

She pulled a handful of cartridges from a frayed cardboard box, loaded two in the tube, a third into the chamber, and stuffed a couple more in the back pocket of her jeans.

• • •

Aaron wasn't surprised to see his wife come in from the patio with a shotgun in her hands. She seemed calm, almost reverent. "So, that's the plan, huh?" he said, with what could have been misinterpreted as a twinge of encouragement.

"That's the plan."

"Have you considered that you might not like what you find?"

Ellen went back outside and slid down into one of the Adirondack chairs. "I've considered a lot," she said with her eyes closed, hugging the gun close as if it were Caleb himself. "I just want it to end. I need closure."

They sat there for a long while as the crickets chirped, and the wind blew, and the stars shone.

"I'm gonna get some rest before we go," Aaron said.

"We?"

"Yeah. Of course. I want it dead, too. Meet you down

here at 3:50? Wake me if you see anything before then?"

Ellen nodded. She kept her eyes closed and her fingers wrapped tightly around the barrel of the shotgun.

Inside, Aaron went to the living room where Caleb's toys had remained just as he'd left them. Dinosaurs, blocks, crayons. He crouched beside a pile of pictures his little boy had drawn in recent weeks and sorted through them. Looking at the simple images warmed his heart and broke it at the same time.

He shuffled a picture of dilapidated stegosaurus to the bottom of the pile, and then one of Cooper that was for some reason red and pink. The next one he saw nearly knocked the wind out of him. There on the page was a crudely sketched but unmistakably accurate representation of the monster. Caleb had used his black and gray crayons to swing wide, circular strokes forming the body. He'd drawn long, angry-looking arms and fingers with brown, as if they were tree branches. He'd even captured the three yellow eyes.

"Oh my God. Ellen. ELLEN!"

Aaron sprinted out to the back patio despite the jolts of pain searing through his ankle, finding his wife exactly as he had left her.

"Ellen! Look at this! Look!"

She took the paper and studied it for a moment before her face made a horrible shape. "What the fuck?"

"What the fuck is this? Did you see him do this? Did you know he did this?"

"No, of course not!"

"What the fuck is this, then?"

Ellen loosened her grip on the shotgun. The tightness in her hands and arms seemed to transport itself into her face and neck, and her eyes darted around the edges of the paper, digging madly at its contents to excavate any further meaning from the ghastly scribble.

"Caleb knew about this thing. He somehow knew. It must have been in his dreams, too. He had a nightmare a couple nights ago, the same night you were gone, and I got that terrible phone call in the middle of the night. Do you think that's what it was? He wouldn't tell me what he dreamt about!"

She ran her thumb along the long arm of the monster, and it was clear from her vacant face that her mouth was unable to form words.

"Ellen, there's something bigger going on here. I just know it. Hank knew it. That's what he wanted to talk about. I'm sure of it. People do know about this. They're either just giving us the run-around or we've been talking to the wrong ones. I'm gonna call that detective. Salim, I'm gonna call him."

"Yeah. Call him." Ellen's words were soft and distant, her eye still glued to the picture.

• • •

Back on the road, Cheryl felt her entire body enter a state of calm. The muscles in her neck loosened, her eyelids lightened, and she could barely feel the heavy boots strapped to her feet. It didn't feel natural, as though her brain had simply ordered her body to relax against its will, but the sudden relaxation offered her a clarity of mind she hadn't experienced in days.

She combed over the two crimes in her mind, clawing in the dark for an explanation, searching for even the faintest of similarities between them.

For starters, the locations were, in a way, related. Hank

was murdered on his own property, and a boy who lived right next door was kidnapped. Plus, the timing was too close to be coincidental. These were crimes that didn't happen twice inside of ten years in Bensalem, much less within the space of two days.

But the crimes themselves were so different and bizarre. Hank Teakle. Caleb Dreyer. What connected the two?

The moon hovered between rows pines sandwiching the shoulders of State Road 639. She gazed up at the two-toned, gray orb.

The green flash of a street sign came into view on her left. Its retroreflective coating sucked up the headlights and appeared incandescent in the night.

WICKHAM RD.

She pulled her gaze back down to the open road ahead of her. The Hank part of this didn't make any earthly sense. No creature known to man does that to a human body. There had to be something else. Someone had to have missed something.

"That poor, damn deer," she whispered.

Cheryl jerked the wheel hard to the left and barely made the turn. If it was desolate before, Wickham Road was even more so now, being that its number of residences had been effectively halved. The Dreyers were the only ones left. Cheryl took the road carefully, letting the tires roll along the gravel so they wouldn't kick up dust. Up ahead, a banner of yellow police tape blocking Hank's driveway flickered in the breeze.

She parked, and as she stepped out into the darkness, adrenaline surged through her, flooding away any lingering physical calm. Her forehead pounded under the tight pressure of the sweatband of her wide-brimmed hat. The mating calls of millions of frogs and crickets saturated the night sky, muffling the sound of her footsteps and the movements of anyone or anything else that might be out there.

Everything around her was black. Darker and deeper than black. Her flashlight provided only a narrow window of light that made her feel exposed no matter where she pointed it. She held it high above her head like an ancient warrior holding a spear, and she pointed her service weapon straight out into the darkness. It was not lost on her that whatever had attacked Hank had done so with such remarkable force and brutality that a 9mm might not do any good.

With her hearing and vision limited, her other senses became heightened. The air had an alien feeling to it and tasted vaguely metallic. She sensed Hank's pain in the trees. It was as though his soul had been reincarnated into a sad spider that drenched the branches in an invisible cobweb of panic and fear. The flashlight wobbled in her hand.

Halfway up the driveway, the crickets began to hush, as if some invisible hand had dialed down their collective volume. Something rustled in the foliage to her right, and she spun the light and the gun around to meet the sound. Nothing was there, but vines and creepers swayed back and forth signaling that something just had been. Long, knotty branches from dead trees hung listlessly in the background of her tiny spotlight, partially obscuring the quivering shadows of distributed foliage. The taste of metal in her mouth intensified and her throat began to close. A faint rumbling sound began to build, deep and gradual.

Then the rumbling stopped, and the crickets, as if compelled by some force of nature, all went totally silent. Every single one. The only sound remaining in that driveway was that of Cheryl's panicked breathing.

She cocked her head slightly towards the road, and the corner of her eye caught a glint of chrome from the unit, much further away than she thought it had been. Running towards it, or running anywhere, may have meant running into the arms of a dealer of Hank-like death. Memories from the last fifty years flashed in rapid succession. Lenny's fifth birthday party, Skylar's birth, her own wedding day, a sycamore tree in the backyard of her childhood home.

The rumbling resumed and got closer and closer and closer still until it came right up beside her and stopped. And when it did, a soft gust of cold air plucked her left ear, and it imparted her with a single word, whispered in a voice both shrill and deep.

"LEAVE."

Cheryl released a roaring scream, swatted wildly at her ear, and fired three rounds in the direction of the whisper. Her legs churned towards the unit before the third bullet had even left the chamber. A wake of dusty gravel billowed up from the driveway as she sprinted, clouding whatever else might have been standing there.

Inside the unit, her chest heaved, and her hands shook as she pawed for the headlights. She threw the car into reverse and floored it, and as she sped away, the only sight out of the ordinary was her wide-brimmed hat lying upside down in the dust.

· · ·

Aaron's eyes sprang open, and not from his volition. It was as if some invisible presence had stuck its fingers in his sockets and pried the eyelids apart. The crispness in the air on his skin told him his body was lying on top of a perfectly made bed in his bedroom. The moon outside draped the room in a paling blue light, and elongated shadows of small objects on nightstands streaked the walls in curling, black marks. Ellen wasn't next to him.

He scanned the room to look for her but stopped when his eyes landed on a large shadow in the far corner of the room, by the door. It appeared to quiver, almost vibrate, and as the pieces of it came together, Aaron realized it was the shadow of a man. A man right there in the room with him, obscured by darkness. It stood still for some time in silence, breathing, heaving its shoulders up and down and permeating the room with its silent, creeping energy. Then, it moved slightly forward, not carried by the legs it clearly had, but in a smooth, hovering motion. Aaron tried to speak but his throat had closed, and his jaw was jacked open in shock.

As the figure moved into the dim light of the room, it revealed its identity: Hank Teakle. His head was down and there was a giant, dripping crater in the middle of his chest. His beating heart reflected in the moonlight, and thick drops of blood fell from his chest and pooled at his feet. The corner was too dark to make out Hank's face, but Aaron knew it was him.

The room was completely silent. No sound at all, not a single cricket's cry wafted in from outside. Aaron couldn't even hear himself breathe. His feet were cold and exposed, and he couldn't move them. He couldn't move anything except his head.

And then, soft and strained, sounding very much like it had on the phone, Hank's voice echoed through the room. "One is good ..."

But the voice wasn't coming from the corner where the

ghastly husk of Hank Teakle stood dripping. It came from the other side of the room by the fireplace. Aaron turned his head in that direction and saw Caleb, defying the laws of gravity, sitting cross-legged about seven feet high on the wall. His body was parallel with the ground, and his head was craned upward at a painful angle so he could look his father in the eye. The sight of his son's spider-like presence sent a torrent of dread gushing into his mind and through every nerve ending in his body. He remained glued to the bed, unable to muster the faintest of flinches from his muscles, helpless in watching whatever bedlam was unfolding.

Caleb's face was dry and clear, and he stared at Aaron with sunken eyes. His mouth hung open, slack-jawed, looking as though he had been drugged. There was some kind of dark spot, maybe a black bead, in the middle of his forehead. The spot shone slightly in the same light that illuminated Hank's dripping torso on the other side of the room. Caleb opened his mouth further, and Hank's voice came out of it. "One is good ..."

From Hank's direction, a harrowing version of Caleb's soft voice echoed forth. It sounded mostly like him, but the tone was severely distorted and muffled with static. "One is bad ..."

Silence ensued for at least a minute. Dead silence. Aaron still couldn't move or speak. He remained cruelly aware of his physical state through the slamming of his heart in his chest and the cold sweat filling his armpits and covering his face.

"One is bad ..." Caleb said again in Hank's voice. "One is bad ..."

Then, they spoke at the same time, a twisted harmony of discordant voices that pinched Aaron in between them. "One is good, one is bad ..."

It was as if their voices had been looking for each other and had finally found their counterpart. They spoke together in a pattern that sounded choppy and unnatural, and far from human. "One is good, one is bad ... one is good, one is bad ..."

Hank took two steps forward out of the darkness, revealing a face completely devoid of features. A slimy lump fell out of his gurgling, open chest and landed on the floor with a splat.

Clusters of slender shadows at Hank's sides drew Aaron's eyes towards the long, thin sticks hanging at his wrists. Hank had fingers like the monster in the meadow, except they were so long they dragged on the floor and left streaks of blood behind as he moved forward. His arms were loose, weighed down by the burden of his impossibly long fingers. Whatever this being was, it was not Hank, as much as it tried to be. Which could only mean—

When Aaron turned his head to Caleb, the boy was suddenly just inches from his father's face, his jaw hanging open further than it should have. But that wasn't the worst of it. The spot Aaron had noticed in the middle of Caleb's forehead wasn't a smudge or a bead at all. It was a third eye. The beady little eye wasn't slanted one way or the other, but perfectly symmetrical, set slightly higher than the other two.

Caleb's head turned towards Hank, making tight clicking sounds as it moved, as if it were some wind-up toy about to violently snap back and shriek in Aaron's face.

A dull groan began to rise from the very back of the room by the hall, not from either of the specters, but from something else, a third ghastly but as of yet unseen presence. The groan built upward, and soon it was accompanied by soft footsteps on the staircase. Peering through the bedroom door and out

into the hall, Aaron watched a dark cloud ascending the staircase. It gradually began to take form when—

—Aaron's physical senses abandoned him. If he had been
able to process what he saw next, he would have simply called
it darkness, a featureless sea of black stretching on for miles.
Wherever he was, it did not feel like a physical place. More like
a motion.

He was dropping. Sinking. Going down, somewhere.

The darkness began to lighten through periodic pulses of
smoky clouds that seemed to emanate from Aaron's very being.
One-by-one, in perfect rhythm, the clouds pushed out from
him and dissipated. One would form, hang in the air, vanish,
and moments later another would arrive.

There was no sound. No touch. His brain had ceased
thinking, and the very few thoughts it carried did not feel like
his own. That urge to panic, to lash out, to yell for help, wrestled for some minute degree of control. It fought for a single
moment to release itself but the force holding it down was
stronger. It wrestled him down and it didn't let go.

His sense of touch returned to inform him he was very
cold, which indirectly reminded him he had a body and that
he was in a seated position. Although he could not see them,
his forearms and the bottoms of his feet yelped at their lack of
protection from the cold.

On an otherwise black canvass surrounding him, three
pale streaks of blue light formed in the top field of his vision.
He felt the vague presence of new objects close to him, but his
clouds of breath cloaked whatever they were.

The silence was broken by a low rumble, not unlike the
deep groaning he had heard in his room just minutes earlier,
and the memory of the sound brought him back to that room.

Hank's inhuman form. The eerie orb of blank flesh that should have been his head. Those fingers, the blood, the organ that had flopped onto the floor. Caleb. That gaping jaw. That awful third eye.

As the rumble grew louder, the three blue streaks of light in the distance jostled. Somehow, in their frantic movement, Aaron recognized them for what they were: three silhouettes of windows, pulling in moonlight and splashing it on a dark wall behind them.

His windows.

His wall.

And he was in his chair, in his living room.

The room snapped and creaked into place as the moonlight settled on the walls.

Whatever had been holding his emotions down jumped away, lifting the lid on his adrenaline and sending his breath racing to keep up with his blood pressure. Then, the room began to warm, and as the temperature rose, each successive cloud of breath faded, slowly revealing what was in that room with him.

The objects started as circles, pale and empty. Long shapes stood beneath them, all shades of white and blue and gray in the moonlight.

A hot cloak of horror wrapped itself around his heart and his lungs when he realized they were people, all firm and rigid, dozens of them, and not even the slightest movement from a single one. They stood in rows facing him, grimly gazing through the windows and out into the meadow like stone statues that could have been there for centuries. The weight of their presence sucked the barometric pressure out of the room and the air coursed with a powerful and ancient kinetic energy.

It took Aaron a few seconds to identify one of the faces as one of the four elderly women that had come into the diner the other morning. Standing next to her was another woman from the same party.

Some wore clothes from different time periods. One man wore long stockings and a powdered wig, and a large, gold cross with a red rose in the center hung from his neck. Another woman wore a dress and bonnet from centuries ago. Her bottom jaw jutted upward, and the flesh in her cheeks hung loose, telltale jowls of a toothless mouth.

Hank Teakle stood perfectly intact in the back row, his face as healthy as the last time Aaron had seen him alive.

After scanning nearly every one of the ominous figures, all of them well on in years, all of them cold and vacant, Aaron's eyes settled on a woman seated in front of the first row — the only eyes that were looking at him.

Jane Harcourt's.

They raged at him, not their usual blue, but a wicked yellow saturated in fire from another world. Here in some version of Aaron's living room, she sat on the same stool from her shop and held a naked boy in her arms. Aaron could only see the back of the boy's head and the mangled fingers of Jane's left hand behind it, leafing softly through strands of smooth, black hair.

When he saw that hair, Aaron tried to throw every particle of his being up to pull the boy away from Jane, but his body remained completely paralyzed. Only a suppressed, two-syllable whimper escaped from his slack jaw, a whimper that sounded something like, "Caleb."

Jane smiled and turned slightly to show Aaron the boy was latched onto her left breast. "My milk has soured," she hissed in a voice that was a bastardized version of her own, thin and high and alien.

An irritating silence filled the room, so dense it made the boy's tiny suckles sound like screams.

"You've disturbed the order of things," Jane said. "Your meddling prevented our sentinel from performing its duties. You have cost us the lives of two of our own. There are forces at play so far beyond your comprehension, forces my Order has been fighting for centuries."

The boy unlatched and nuzzled his head into Jane's elbow. It wasn't Caleb, but a boy who looked very much like him. Two drops of black liquid fell from Jane's decrepit breast, and the smell of damp metal rose into Aaron's nostrils. Stomach bile lurched up into his esophagus.

The boy bucked and turned further towards Aaron. He had three eyes and his jaw was wrenched open, two features that caused Aaron to reconsider whether this was indeed Jane's son and not his own.

Limp in Jane's arms, the boy hung from her with a face that seemed to be permanently screaming. Another black drop fell from her downturned nipple and dropped onto the boy's cheek. He didn't seem to notice.

"My family and my Order made the ultimate sacrifice to protect this world from the pestilence. I gave my son to the forest. For forty-two years, my son has served us."

The boy emitted a weak groan as if he were in some great pain but unable to properly convey it.

"And last night, you and your bitch wife allowed the evil ... the pestilence ... to take my other son. Now, I have nothing."

The yellow glow evaporated from Jane's eyes. She suddenly resembled the sweet lady who had given him a hometown discount on a pair of blue topaz earrings, save for her nudity and the boy at her breast.

"Caleb will serve our Order for many years, and through him, you will pay for your transgressions. He will be the one to subdue the Nothus. He will subdue the pestilence. He will protect our Bensalem. Our New Atlantis."

In an instant, everything in the room shot upward and out of sight, as though Aaron had fallen through the floor. He kept falling, not floating like last time, but plummeting.

Down, down, faster, down into the deepest, scariest dimension of his mind. The part where the truth was hiding.

He rocketed down, and he fell and fell until—

—He found himself in a space of utter void. No light. No sound. No points of physical reference to give him any sense of scale. At least the last place provided him with a sense of color, of blackness. This place, if it even was one, provided him with nothing.

Aaron's body was gone, his world was gone, and all that remained was a plane of pure and utter vacancy. Even his thoughts, feelings and memories had been stripped away from him, as if locked away in some time capsule of the material world.

A speck of an object appeared far down the empty black plane, and a force Aaron did not control or understand began pushing him slowly towards it. The object was blurry from this far away, and oh, how far away it was. A single, solitary object existing alone in its own dimension of space and time.

As he traveled closer, his basic cognitive function returned. Memory of color told him the object was red. Spatial recognition told him the object was thin and vertical. And when the only physical inhabitant of this place was nearly upon him, the veil over his earthly perceptions lifted and Aaron saw his son.

Caleb stood before him coated in dark, arterial blood from head-to-toe. Only the blinding whites of his eyes stood out against the blood and the blackness that engulfed him. Various dripping, squishing, and sloshing sounds accompanied him, and as Aaron's vision focused further, he observed drops and clumps of redness peeling away and dripping off him into a vast chasm of nothingness below.

"Daddy," Caleb said, in a voice as clean and soft and true as Aaron remembered it. His real voice.

But Aaron couldn't respond. He had no mouth, he had no person, he had no means whatsoever to speak, nor any agent of this hell with whom to negotiate.

"Where were you?" Caleb said.

Aaron did, however, feel the cut of those words slice open his heart and spill its contents into the chasm below, the same chasm bits and drops of his son were peeling and plopping into.

"Where were you? Where were you when they took me?"

Far in the distance behind Caleb, another object began moving towards Aaron. Another person. A man. A man with completely white eyes.

"You disturbed it. They TOOK me because of you. Where were you when they took me? You let them take me away!"

Caleb opened his eyes wider, peeling the eyelids back nearly over the entire round of the ball, and his voice morphed from his own into a deep, demonic roar.

"YOU KILLED ME!"

Aaron fell. He shot down through the chasm below and plummeted with incredible speed further, deeper, darker. As he fell, every fear, anxiety, insecurity, and regret he'd ever had coagulated into a dense, sadistic force that tried to pry open the door to his soul and crush it into oblivion.

And part of him wanted to let it.

Down here, he met his demons. The voice that told him in the middle of the night that he had never done anything good. The seed of doubt that whispered in his ear insecurities about never being worthy of a woman like Ellen. It was the nagging, visceral knife of truth that stabbed his heart and cut him open, and told him he was a bad father, and for that there would be no sympathy, only a punishment befitting the fires of hell.

There was a faint light that Aaron wanted to go towards. It was the light of the other man's white eyes—

• • •

"CALEB! CALEB! NO! CA—"

Aaron screamed himself awake but stopped when he heard the trill of the landline phone in the office downstairs. He was in his bed, drenched in sweat, and everything ached. He frantically scanned the room for Caleb, for Hank, for Jane, or any of the people that were standing in his living room. None were there.

In the front yard, the floodlights were on and Ellen was marching forward with the shotgun.

"Ellen! No!"

Aaron bolted down the stairs, his ankle stinging with every step. Cooper had his front paws clamped to the windowsill and barked feverishly at the monster — the sentinel. It stood still, trapped in the floodlights, just as it had the night before.

Aaron yanked out the cord that supplied the lights with power, grabbed the flashlight by the door and ran out, barely remembering to close it. The thought of putting on shoes didn't even cross his mind.

"Ellen! Wait!" he yelled, chasing after her down the slope of the front yard.

An unlit battlefield didn't deter her. She didn't even turn around. The sentinel, meanwhile, free of the light that bound it, resumed its own march.

"Ellen! That thing is good!" Aaron panted between gasps for air. "Don't ask me how I know, I just do. I saw it all! It's protecting us!"

"Protecting us? Aaron, that monster has Caleb! You know it does!" Ellen said.

"No! Trust me! Caleb ... he's somewhere else. There's something else in the forest that's killing everyone. This thing is good! Trust me! It protects us from the real problem! She called it the pestilence. The ... the Noth-something."

"The what?"

Aaron loped down the rest of the hill and tumbled over the fence. As he approached Wickham Road, he spun around to check on his wife. She hadn't moved from where he had found her, frozen in place and time.

"Ellen! Caleb's out here! Come on, let's go!"

• • •

The Bensalem Sheriff's Department sat nestled in a grove of maple trees behind Main Street that kept out the light. Not that there was any at this hour.

Cheryl trudged up the concrete steps. For so many nights, her desk had felt like a prison cell, but tonight it would have been freedom. What she wouldn't give to be mired in paperwork and boredom. The last three days had ravaged her.

The room was quiet besides for the clicking of a ceiling fan on its highest setting.

"Zat you, Mac?" a familiar voice called out.

Cheryl sighed, and she steeled her nerves before standing to meet him. Her quads turned to jelly as she trudged into the sheriff's office.

Everything in the room was yellow, beige, or brown. The musty office hadn't been redecorated since the seventies. A desk sign reading THE BUCK STOPS HERE welcomed new visitors as they entered. Hunting rifles and faded photos of the sheriff in Vietnam littered the walls. He had been a dashing young man with a strong jaw and a full head of hair, and an even fuller life ahead of him.

Darryl "Duke" Quinlan was old now. His jaw was still strong, but his hair was gone, and his face and hands had cracked open with the passing of time.

"What're you doin' here at this hour?" she whispered, leaning against the door jamb, staring down at him like a lioness stares down its prey.

Seated in the chair behind his desk, he placed his aviator-framed eyeglasses on the desk and gazed up at the drop panel ceiling. The once-white squares had turned yellow like the rest of the room.

"Well, I'm a bit discombobulated, you might say. S'pose I should be sleepin'." A smile crept across his face, deepening the cracks below his eyes.

"S'pose we both should be."

"How's all this?" Duke gestured broadly with his hands.

"Not too good, Sheriff."

"How you holdin' up?"

Cheryl took a seat in one of the two nylon-covered chairs

across from his mammoth desk. Duke tapped the heel of his boot against the linoleum floor.

"Found Hank slashed up in his driveway and a little boy went missing in the span of twenty-four hours. You left and it all went to shit. I tried to take care of it."

Duke leaned back in his chair, its steel frame squealing with age. The clicking of the ceiling fan and the lateness of the hour heightened their moments of silence.

"Mac, you ever hear what happened to Mark Harcourt?"

The randomness of the question disoriented her. She shot him a quizzical look.

"What? The one from way back? The boy?"

"That's the one."

She stopped to think before continuing. "Well, he died, didn't he? What in the hell's that got to do with this? Listen, I'm sorry about Nags Head."

"Don't worry 'bout the vacation. I don't count how many days I spend in this chair versus another. It's all just sittin'. Any day above ground suits me."

She didn't respond. She was still afraid to call him out, so she tried to let the silence do the talking. It appeared to be working, as his smile began to morph into a tight frown.

"I came back because I realized I'd made a mistake with you. I didn't realize 'til you called me."

"What're you talkin' about?"

"You're not from here, Mac. You've been with me some twenty-odd years now. I can't do this job much longer. I can barely do it now. We both know that. Reckon it'll be you in this chair soon enough. I'd like that, anyway."

"What do you need to tell me?"

"I was gonna tell you years ago. Tell you about this place.

It's um, well, it ain't right. I wanted to protect you from it for as long as I could."

Cheryl leaned forward. "Sheriff, you knew about that little boy, didn't you?"

Duke's right hand began to tremble. Beads of sweat formed on his forehead. "Okay, now this might be hard to hear. That boy was what you might call a sacrifice. For a greater good. He had a higher calling. There's something out there in them woods, Mac, and it's been there for centuries. We ain't had to deal with it for a long time. Reckon just us old folks know about it now, and the other towns don't want nothin' to do with it. I guess it ain't really their problem. It's our problem. It's always been our problem. It's been here as long as my family, and it was here long before them. The reason I bring up Mark Harcourt is because what happened to him is ..." Duke's eyes narrowed. "It's what happenin' to that little boy now."

Cheryl was astonished to realize, for the first time in two decades of staring at the sheriff from this exact angle, that his trophy moose antlers lined up perfectly behind his head as he sat there. He was wearing them, almost ceremonially. The sight unnerved her. Her breath quickened and she dug her fingers into the chewy old foam of her armrests.

"Mark Harcourt is the product of a kind of ritual. He was the last one, must be forty years ago now, but they need to do it again. Mark, if you wanna call him that, is the thing that family's been seeing out their window. I know this all sounds, well, a bit odd. That's because it is."

The warm room became cold on the deputy's skin. Hair stood up on her forearms and pricked the back of her neck. What little strength was left in her muscles evaporated and she sank deeper into the chair. She couldn't look the sheriff in the eye. Not after seeing his head in a crown of antlers or hearing what he'd just said.

The last thing Cheryl expected from Duke was a possible corroboration of Aaron Dreyer's garbled ghost story, and it wasn't lost on her how quickly she had dismissed it. Twice.

"So, wait, you sayin' Mark Harcourt killed Hank?" Cheryl said.

"No, no, that ain't it. Mark is the thing that was protectin' Hank. Protectin' all of us, for all these years."

"Protectin' us from what?"

Duke cleared his throat. "A, uh … a very evil thing. A thing no one should have to know."

Cheryl could barely hear him now, his voice diminished to a focused whisper.

"They call it Nothus Noctis. The night bastard." Duke paused to let this sink in. It didn't. Cheryl sat there dumbfounded and painfully bewildered about the state of her world. A tear formed in Duke's eye. She'd never in her life known him to be a man of fairy tales, and certainly not a man of tears. If he said it was real, it was real.

"It moves at night, and if you ain't got somethin' in place to deal with it—" Duke ran his thumb and index finger across the thin wire frame of his glasses. With a sudden motion, he cracked the frames in half. "—you get what Hank got."

"You. You knew about Caleb Dreyer? How did you know? For Christ's sake, his parents are worried sick. Where is he? Why are you tellin' me all this? Where is he?"

"I wanted to tell you all this so you wouldn't have to see it. I shoulda told you a long time ago. To be honest, it hasn't been an issue until now. When Ethel Thomasin lived in that house, she knew well enough to leave it alone. But that Dreyer boy, the husband—"

"Aaron. His name is Aaron. Sheriff Quinlan, where is Caleb Dreyer?"

"Aaron fucked up, Mac. He seen that creature Mark become and put light on it. Can't do that. Can't do its job in the light."

"What do you mean he fucked up?"

"Before Mark, some other boy did the same. Before him, another boy, and so on all the way back through the generations. Every night the Nothus comes up, and every night, Mark walks through that forest and stops it. That's the way it's been. It's how we survive here."

"Survive here? What? What the hell are you saying? Where is Caleb? What do you mean Aaron fucked up? You're not makin' any damn sense. You're sayin' he saw this? He saw Mark? And because of that his son is gone? Did you take Caleb Dreyer?"

"Dammit! I didn't take his son!" The old stone man shook off decades of lethargy and slammed down an open fist into the desk, chattering the trinkets strewn about it.

"But you knew about it. How did you know? Is he still alive?"

Cheryl shot up out of her chair with such force that it skidded loudly across the linoleum. She now stood towering over an out-of-breath Sheriff Duke Quinlan.

"Where the hell is he, Duke?"

"I don't know! I don't know where he is. I didn't take him. But I'm almost positive I know who did. And I reckon I know where to find 'em."

• • •

In the murky light of the summer moon, under the watchful eye of the mountains, Aaron and Ellen Dreyer paced several yards behind the sentinel as it strode towards the forest, the object of so much fear and morbid curiosity over the last week finally confronted.

A putrid miasma of wet metal breezed through in the air. Shrouded in mist, the sheer bulk of the thing seemed to reverberate with its every movement, but it left a surprisingly light footprint on the wheat grass.

Two of its more mysterious features, the humming noise and the mist, were both explained in a single, sickening moment. Flies, millions of them, swarmed the Sentinel from top to bottom, and their train extended so far behind the beast that Aaron routinely had to swat them away from his face.

The sentinel's long, terrible hands swung back and forth as it lumbered. A single one of those fingers could have effortlessly impaled Aaron if he came too close. Ellen, who seemed to already have realized this, followed a few feet behind him with the shotgun.

It wasn't lost on him that the sentinel had not yet attempted to invade his mind tonight, nor his wife's. That led him to believe there must be some decision-making component inside of that pewter mountain of mystery, whether it was a human brain, another kind of brain, or some other incomprehensible force. He wanted to believe it somehow knew they no longer intended to hurt or expose it. Maybe it even knew they were hoping it would lead them to their son.

He so badly wanted to explain his dream to Ellen, but he dared not speak. The sentinel wasn't bothering them right now, but any assumption of safety seemed like a foolish one. Instead, he glanced back at Ellen, her jaw hard as steel and her hands wrapped tightly around both barrels.

They walked on. The forest floor brought them over dead leaves, scrubby plants, and thickets of god-knows-what. Every now and then, Aaron's bare feet would scrape a thorn or land on a sharp twig, but trivial pains, including the pain in his ankle, barely registered as he watched this unbelievable creature lumber through the trees. Aaron kept expecting a creature of its height and size to knock the forest around to make way, but it traversed an invisible path that was somehow clear of major obstacles.

Yet through all his fasciation, fear and wonder, there was one thought he couldn't shake: Caleb. Aaron was convinced Caleb was here, somewhere, connected to this sentinel and lost out here in these woods. Tears streamed down his face as the white orb of the flashlight danced on the leaves ahead and he considered the possibilities, earthly and unearthly alike.

Eventually, the ground smoothed out and became moist. The smell of metal seemed to emanate not just from the sentinel now, but from all around them. The air was thin, and the crickets and other creatures around them quieted, heightening the scree of millions of flies buzzing around the sentinel.

Without warning, the flies scattered into the air. Hundreds, maybe thousands, whipped through the flashlight beam and pelted Aaron's face. Several swooped into his open mouth and one or two went down his throat. Ellen started coughing. Aaron swung his arms — and the flashlight's beam — in all directions around his head to shoo them.

Once most of the flies had dissipated, the contours of the sentinel's body became plainly visible. Aaron's flashlight reflected brightly off its skin, but he was careful not to hold it too long, fearing that any prolonged exposure to light might harm it. All Aaron could make out was that the surface of its body appeared to be more like some grainy mineral paste that had been rubbed on, not necessarily organic matter.

The world was still for a brief moment until something shuffled in the distance. Aaron jerked the light towards the direction of the disturbance, and it fell upon a thicket of tightly-packed dead branches, a gnarled conglomeration of trunks and sticks that looked almost deliberate, constructed. Whatever was over there, the sentinel was walking straight towards it.

The sight of that twisted and wholly unnatural looking thicket gripped him. Aaron ground his teeth together and blinked away the tears blurring his vision. The light shook in his hands, and he wrestled his nerves for control enough to guide it towards two pale, red dots hanging in the air.

"OH—OH GOD!"

Another being stood there, just yards away from the sentinel. It was several feet taller than any human, and it had an animal skull for a head, tall antlers, and glowing red eyes. It heaved its giant barrel of a chest, a chest matted in heavy fur.

Aaron's light wasn't on the Nothus long enough to view the rest of its body, but that split-second vision put a vice grip of celestial power on his mind that broke him. White-hot pain radiated through every inch of his body and his world fell away from him.

• • •

Garland Road wasn't just asleep at this hour, it was dead. Cheryl's unit rolled slowly down over the loose pavement. She squinted to see house numbers. Some homes had them, some didn't. All of them had front porches that sagged, siding that was stained, and yards with more dirt than grass. Not a single light was on in any of the houses.

For a long time, Cheryl stared at Jane Harcourt's house, soaking in a sense of dread that had nothing to do with the darkness.

"She ain't here, Duke," Cheryl said into the radio.

"Ten-four."

She waited for him to speak again but he didn't. A stiffness from being up so late had invaded her body, and as she released a cathartic crack from her neck, she couldn't help but wonder how Duke must have felt.

"I'm gonna swing by her store," she said.

"Ten-four. I gave her a call and she ain't picked up."

"You call the store, too?"

"That's where I called. It's the only phone she's got."

At the end of the street, a sliver of orange light poked through the trees.

· · ·

Ellen saw two bright, red orbs when Aaron shifted the flashlight, but he dropped it too quickly for her to see what they were. The pained grunt his body squeezed out sucked her attention down to the ground with him, and a millisecond-long miserable vision of a life without Caleb or Aaron flashed through her mind.

A great, booming shriek reverberated from the depths of the forest: a huge sound, already wrapped in layers of its own echo by the time it reached Ellen's ears. It blew her hair back and shot out through the trees.

Unable to see anything, she leapt in Aaron's direction, determined to guard him from whatever had made that terrible cry. Surging with labored breaths, gasping through tears, she sheltered him with her body.

"Ellen ... don't ... don't look at it!" Aaron's voice was a strained and broken whisper. His body felt lifeless in her arms and she had to bring her ear to his mouth to make out his words.

"What happened to you? Don't you leave me! Don't you leave me, Aaron!" She clutched him closer. Her fingers, charged with the wild desperation of a woman on the verge of losing everything, dug into the flesh of his back. "Aaron! Stay with me! I can't! I can't, Aaron! I can't lose you. Are you okay? Are you?"

"Don't ... don't ..."

"What? What? Don't what?"

"Don't look at it, Ellen."

"What? Don't look at what?"

"The pestilence ... it ..."

A thundering crash followed by a series of brutal grunts, slams, scrapes, and cracks bludgeoned Ellen's eardrums. Metal on bone. Power against power. Two titans from a medium beyond her comprehension bashing each other with the force of planets.

Keeping one arm wrapped around Aaron, Ellen patted the ground around her for the flashlight. Her pinky finger grazed a cold metal object — the shotgun — and she kept on stabbing in the dark. When she finally found it, she mashed the power button only to realize the bulb had shattered.

Sounds from beings born in hell surrounded them. There was no recourse but to hunker down and cower on the cold ground, deep in the forest. Here, in the wake of a melee between two entities clearly able to crush the life out of a human with a misstep.

Clinging on to each other, Aaron and Ellen sobbed as one, waiting for one of them to strike, waiting to die.

• • •

The sun hadn't risen on Main Street yet, but its scarcity of trees ushered wide swaths of light from the moonlit sky. Cheryl took cautious paces towards M&J Fine Gifts. She winced as her boot crunched over a shard of broken glass on the sidewalk.

Suddenly, a very out-of-place and far off shriek, a sound not quite human, yanked Cheryl's ear towards the forest that the Dreyers claimed their son had lost himself in.

"Shit. Duke, come in," she said into her walkie.

"Yeah?"

"You hear that loud sound over your way? That scream?"

"Scream?"

"Yeah, I heard somethin' like a scream."

"Where?"

"I dunno, where would there be screamin' at this hour?"

Duke went silent for a moment. "Mac, what if it's the Dreyers and those lights? He can't do that, Mac. He can't do that!"

"What can't he do? I don't understand."

"He can't turn on those lights!"

"Copy. I'm on my way over." Cheryl shook her head and deposited the walkie back into her belt.

• • •

The clashing sounds had become more one-sided, narrowing from a requiem of madness into a singular series of hammering thuds. Ellen gripped down on Aaron, and it seemed at one point that the sounds were moving further away. The light of a nascent dawn allowed the slightest tint of green to penetrate an endless void of black.

Some distance down a small hill, a large being hoisted itself up and then slammed down out of view, in time with the thuds.

Ellen strained to get a better look. The sentinel had wrapped its long fingers into colossal fists the size of boulders and was pounding them into the ground.

Aaron remained in a catatonic ball under her, where he had been since he'd fallen. "Don't look at it," he whispered again.

"I'm not! It's gone! I—I think it might be over!"

Her words seemed to have little impact. She scanned the trees around them. "Aaron, stay right here. I'll be right back."

She crawled to the top of the hill, pulling herself through slimy puddles of metallic sludge. The sentinel was submerged in the ground from what looked like the waist down. For the first time ever, it was facing her. The shape of its head, if one could even call it a head, was rough and inhuman, just a mound sticking out of a broad pair of shoulders. In the middle of the mound were three hollow, yellow eyes.

She tried to peer through the haze of the dawn and into those eyes to see just how human they were. Without it making a sound or a motion, she felt the sentinel deliver a gentle knock to her consciousness, which she took as a warning not to observe it further. She scampered back to Aaron, who was now sitting cross-legged with his head in a slump.

A whippoorwill cooed from far away. The forest was waking. It cooed again, and this time Ellen was compelled by an unknown hand to lift her head towards it. As she did, that same invisible hand guided her to a rectangular object further down the ridge. A folding metal chair.

Leaving Aaron behind, she darted down the hill, kicking up leaves and barreling through shrubs and vines until she found herself in a grove of black-barked pine trees. The body of a man whose torso had been ripped apart stopped her dead in her tracks.

"Oh, Jesus! Fuck!"

The dead man's eyes, wide open in horror, were set above a gaping mouth locked in a plea for help, all on a face of bloodless gray. The man's body was completely eviscerated and saturated in flies. Beside him, a camping lantern emitted a fading white light. No stranger to corpses, even the bad ones, Ellen pressed on to the small grove that seemed utterly carved out of these massive woods from another place entirely.

The ground under the scaly black pines was hard-packed dirt, unlike any other ground in the forest. At the far edge of the grove, a small burlap sack rested on dirt.

Ellen flew across the grove screaming her son's name into the dawn. She loosened the opening of the sack, and landed her hand on two tiny human feet, bound together by a dirty string.

"OH MY BABY!! NO!!"

She yanked off the rest of the sack off to reveal a lifeless Caleb.

"NO! NO! CALEB! CALEB!"

His naked body was covered in a pewter-colored paste that was warm to the touch and smelled of metal, just like the sentinel. A green bandana was tied around his forehead, and in the center of it, a garish, white, hand-drawn third eye leered up at her. A shimmering black rock was stuffed into Caleb's mouth and Ellen noticed bruising around his jawline.

Aaron shouted his son's name from the other side of the grove, and he staggered towards them, still weak from whatever had crushed him earlier.

Ellen's ER training took over, scanning Caleb for injuries, assessing him for damage. She gently pried away the rock in his mouth and tossed it to the ground. She put her ear down to his open mouth and took his fragile wrist in her hand. She closed her eyes and listened. She begged. She called to him from her womb.

"BABY! Baby boy! CALEB! Please come back to me! Come back to Mommy, baby. Mommy's here. Mommy's here, baby. Come back to Mommy."

The gentlest of little pulses grazed across her index finger. His breathing was soft, but it was there.

"OH CALEB! Yes, baby! Caleb, can you hear me, baby? Caleb? Caleb! Caleb?"

Aaron clattered to the ground next to her. "Is he okay? Is he still here?"

"He's here! He's here. We have to get him out of here, but he's alive! His jaw is dislocated."

"What else? How else is he hurt?"

"I don't know yet. I have to get him to the hospital!"

Aaron pulled off the bandana to expose what looked like a pebble placed in the center of Caleb's forehead. He tweezed the pebble with his fingers — a shiny, silver orb no larger than a pea — and tossed it into the dirt.

"Wake up, baby. Caleb! Caleb!" Ellen cried.

Just as she was about to place a thumb on her son's eyelid to pull them open, he did so on his own.

"Oh, my sweet boy!" She scooped him into her arms, careful not to hug too hard, not knowing what else was dislocated or broken.

While Ellen held him, Aaron worked to smear the black sludge off of Caleb's back and his legs. "What is this shit? Is this the sentinel shit?" he said.

But he didn't stop. He swept his son's body down until it was gone, and then he untied the strings that bound Caleb's little wrists and feet together. Then, he wrapped his arms over both of them.

The young family huddled close and cried together on the ground. The sounds of waking birds and the shade from the black pines surrounded them.

DAY 6

The founders of Bensalem first arrived in a then-treeless valley on the east bank of the mountains on a warm summer dawn not unlike this one. They came upon a clearing, looked up to the sky and stared in awe as the morning sun bounced a beam of white light off the mountain and into the sky.

Many generations of Bensalem had come and gone since then, but the geometry of the landscape still offered the same resplendence for a few minutes on a day when the sun was exactly right.

The Dreyers hadn't yet felt the warmth of the day but it would be waiting for them when they reached the meadow.

At the same time, another sunbeam filtered through the boughs of a tree in front of the Bensalem Library and onto the closed eyelids of an old man sleeping on a bench. Maurice Bacon reluctantly peeled open his eyes and propped himself upright. His matted hair burned hot under his skull cap and his skin crawled with dried sweat under his blue parka. The spot on his forehead itched where the third eye had been.

Before it all happened, he remembered the long days that dripped with gold as he and his sister ran barefoot through the meadow. He remembered the fresh smell of pine sap on winter mornings. He remembered the faces of dread his parents wore as they tried to explain to him that he'd be going away for a while, that they were proud of him, and that they loved him.

He could still feel the chemical paste, the scalding pain of his mutating body and the lonely despair of a tortured child. He remembered physical forces that were not his own, compelling him to wake up in the dead of the night. He remembered that, for as long as he was out there, he never got used to waking up in a cold ditch in the ground in the middle of the forest, instead of in a warm bed next to his family and under a roof.

And he remembered It.

The pestilence. The bastard. The Nothus. The cosmic transgressor brought to physical life that he, in this painful and awkward suit of armor, was charged with subduing each and every single day as it woke. On good days, he would arrive at the spot where the Nothus rose before it had fully risen. Those days were easy.

On bad days, the Nothus would be out of the ground already. It could have been feasting on a deer somewhere, or a raccoon, its shiny little tongue sucking and slurping up whatever was still left. Or, it could have been standing there, waiting for him, boring into him with those bright red eyes and eating away at his brain bit-by-bit. Sure, the armor and the third eye helped, but they were not impenetrable.

Then, he remembered waking up in a small, dark room one day and being told that his job had come to an end. Someone else would be taking over and he was now free to live his life, with whatever was left of his world.

Who knows how many years had gone by or how much damage had been done? There was no prize, no parade, no article in the paper. It was the town's secret and its sanctity his reward.

All Maurice Bacon got for decades of forced torture and repeated exposure to the fear-eating demon of hell was a world he didn't know what to do with, and an invitation to the Order of the Old Roses. A young deaconess named Jane, a girl he vaguely remembered from grade school and the mother of the new sentinel, would weep in his arms late at night and beg for some reassurance that her son would be alright. But Maurice, unable to see the world or understand it, could offer her none. His time in the ground had stripped him of his abilities to feel, to reason, or even to think in a complex manner. It was a wonder his body had survived.

Unable to ingest the light on his corneas any longer, the scraggly old man closed his eyes.

"I have seen a New Atlantis," he whispered to himself.

He sighed, and his jaw clicked back into place.

• • •

Aaron had no sense of time when he finally stepped out of the forest and back into the meadow across Wickham Road, a sleeping Caleb draped around him. The boy hadn't said a word. He had only cried and effused a level of exhaustion the likes of which his parents had never seen. Ellen followed Aaron with her head down and the shotgun hanging low in her hands.

Suddenly, Ellen's soft footsteps whisking through the dewy grass stopped. "Aaron. Look."

In the middle of their front yard, just past the row of unlit floodlights, a figure in a hooded brown robe stood between the battered family and their home. It appeared to be something out of a fairy tale, unaware of the time or the place or certainly the weather. The figure was perfectly still, save for the periodic flapping of dark fabric in the morning breeze. Nothing could be seen under the hood besides blackness, a blackness whose depth seemed to stretch on for miles when Aaron gazed upon it, but the direction of the hood told him that whoever or whatever was inside was staring right at them. Aaron tightened his grip on his son.

"Who is that? Ellen, do you have your cell phone on you? Who the fuck is that?" Aaron said.

Ellen responded not with words but with two sharp clicks of the shotgun. The wail of a distant police siren entered Aaron's ears, but he didn't process it. The entirety of his senses focused on the robed trespasser who was now moving towards them. The thickness of the robe cloaked the movement of its feet, if it was moving them at all, but it was indeed closer than it had been just a moment ago.

Not moving his eyes, Aaron scampered backwards to get closer to Ellen, to the gun. "In my dream, I saw them. They mentioned something about an Order. Some crazy fucking cult right here in Bensalem. That's what this is all about. They want Caleb. They want him to be the sentinel. They're the ones who took him and—"

"I don't care who they are," Ellen said.

A brisk morning wind picked up, and it swept the hood clean off the figure's head. A twisted wisp of long gray hair unfurled, and a pair of deep blue eyes wrapped in wickedness radiated in the sunlight.

"Jane!" Aaron yelled.

Jane moved faster now, rapidly descending upon the family. The color of her eyes seemed to expand beyond their anatomy and formed an orb of bottomless cerulean blue around her head. As Aaron gazed into them, they once began to spin, just as they had in her store. She moved like a woman forty years her junior. Aaron clutched Caleb tight against his body and sensed Ellen ranging in front of him, her steps calm and even in the midst of all this.

Some cosmic aura seemed to draw the two women towards each other, like two comets set on a collision course millions of years prior, but Jane kept her eyes on Aaron. Neither woman spoke. Neither of them needed to. In this moment, theirs was a language much older and more powerful than the spoken word.

The blue orb of light around Jane's head widened, and the backdrop of the front yard and the house receded into a vast sea. Aaron's grip on Caleb loosened. The boy slid through his arms, and for a moment, only a weak hand glued to Caleb's chin kept the boy from crashing to the ground.

When Jane spoke, each word reverberated off the atmosphere. "Give him to me!"

Ellen stepped in front of Aaron, her aura a blood-red cauldron of lava against the sea of blue projecting forth from her opponent.

Aaron's body reacted before his ears did. The jolt came on so hard it triggered the pain in his ankle and caused him to drop Caleb all in one motion. Only a second later did the sound follow, a deafening blast that sucked all sound out of the meadow. Flaps and caws of errant birds filled the negative spaces of the blast and a cloud of gray smoke rose up in front of him.

Jane's spell came to an abrupt halt and Aaron regained his bearings. Ellen lost her red color but none of the rigid poise in her legs and her back as she reached into her pocket and reloaded her father's gun. She kept walking towards Jane, her gait mind-bogglingly calm. Jane's eyes were wide, burning with shock but stripped of their power, and her astonished mouth discharged a breathless sigh. Down towards the middle of her body, just above her long-barren womb, the smooth brown canvas of her robe was reddening.

Jane's knees buckled and smacked the ground in front of her, briefly holding her teetering frame erect. She slowly craned her neck to the sky and lifted her arms, and she began reciting something in a language that sizzled with hard consonants, long vowels, and odd clicking sounds she made by snapping her tongue in her mouth.

"Ellen! Stop! Don't!" Aaron cried.

But she didn't, she strode on towards an utterly frenzied Jane still entreating some dark force through this demonic tongue. Aaron dropped to his knees to crouch over Caleb, lashing his arms and fingers over him so there was no way the boy could see what was happening.

Ellen now stood mere feet before of a catatonic Jane, still kneeling, still chanting, still gazing into the sky. She did not look upon the old woman with fear, but with pity, and she sneered her upper lip into a curl of revenge.

Then, Jane stopped her mad language and met Ellen's gaze. Her eyes went completely white, leaving not even the faintest of capillaries visible upon her ivory orbs.

When she rose to her feet, she released a wail with the strength of the heavens. The wail was so loud and so dark it shoved Ellen a half step backward, and before she recovered,

Jane's bony hands were clenched around her neck.

But Ellen didn't flinch. She ignored the hands on her neck, regained her footing, and lodged the end of barrel under Jane's chin. An instant before Jane was set to let out another terrible scream, Ellen squeezed the trigger. A booming rocket of sound blasted the meadow, shocking Aaron's nerves into a full body spasm.

The shot rocked Jane's body up off the ground, and she landed a yard away in the billowing grass, not far from the patch of dirt the sentinel had wormed into 24 hours prior. Ellen stood over the body but didn't look at it. Her skin and clothes had miraculously avoided the ropes of blood that jettisoned out of Jane's annihilated skull.

The siren was louder now. Aaron peeked out from under his son. "Ellen? Are you okay?" he said.

But Ellen kept her back to her husband and her eyes fixed on the house. Aaron waited for his wife to do or say something — anything — but she stood like a statue in the grass. A brisk wind rippled the flowers and wheat grass around her, but somehow, as if held in place by the hand of God herself, not a single long, black hair draped over her back wavered.

• • •

A wicked wave of déjà vu hit Cheryl as she sped down State Road 639 and made the turn onto Wickham Road, but it was altogether replaced with panic and dread when the shots rang out.

The old police cruiser didn't take well to high speeds on rough roads. It clunked and pushed along as best it could, leaving massive dust clouds in its wake. She blew past the police tape still strewn across Hank's driveway and a white pickup truck on the side of the road.

As she came around the bend to the Dreyer house, she saw Aaron and Ellen standing in the meadow, and for a minute, was relieved to see Caleb in his father's arms. That relief quickly subsided when she saw another person lying on the ground beside them and a shotgun in Ellen's hands. She slammed on the brakes and the car skidded to a dusty halt.

Cheryl got out slowly, and although she didn't draw her weapon, she kept a hand on it to show she meant business.

"Mrs. Dreyer, drop your weapon!"

Ellen's face remained vacant as she placed the shotgun at her feet. Jane Harcourt's face, however, lay in thousands of little red and white pieces strewn about the canvas of golden grass. The entire front half of her head had been shorn clean off. What remained was a frothy purple-and-white amalgamation of blood, bone, and rendered motherly rage.

"My God, Ellen. My God! What the hell happened here?" Cheryl said.

"Take him," Aaron said softly to his wife. He handed Caleb to Ellen, got down on the ground, and started rubbing down the shotgun with the outside of his shirt.

"Aaron! Put down that gun!" Cheryl said.

He did not obey, but instead looked her dead in the eye as he rubbed his hands up and down the barrel and over the trigger.

"I did this," he said, tears in his eyes. "You understand me? Ellen had nothing to do with it. Jane kidnapped Caleb. She kidnapped our only son! I should have known it all along! She was right there! Her store was closed, you saw it yourself! We just found him in a fucking sack in the middle of the fucking woods! It was her and her stupid fucking cult! Did you know there's a cult here? Huh?"

"Mr. Dreyer, please calm down and back away from that weapon," Cheryl said. She extended a hand and took two steps towards Aaron and the contaminated gun.

"Jane kidnapped Caleb! Are you not hearing me? She left him unconscious in a fucking sack! Left for dead! Then she came to our fucking house! She still wanted him! She tried to take him again!"

"Mr. Dreyer. I do hear you. I promise. Let's talk, okay? First, please put the gun down. Right now."

He threw down the weapon and put his hands in the air. "So, I shot her. You hear me? Ellen has been through enough. Caleb has been through enough."

Cheryl looked down at Jane. The brown robe she wore looked like some ancient sack a monk might have worn. Her arms were splayed out above her in a gesture that would have signaled surrender if she were standing. A thick, red halo of blood flowed steadily out from the remnants of her head, coating the golden grass in a dark stain of death. A lone fly buzzed through the air and landed on an area that might have once been associated with her right eye.

Ellen sat cross-legged and dazed in disbelief. Aaron crouched over a weeping Caleb, his small face was beet-red and soaked with tears.

"Listen to me," Cheryl said, one hand still on her unholstered weapon. "I understand more of what's going on. Is Caleb okay?"

Neither parent answered.

"Regardless of what happened or who did what, it's my duty to take you all into the station. Let's all go talk about this.

Let's get your son looked at. If you found him like you said you did, he's going to need immediate medical attention. Mrs. Dreyer, you know that better than anybody. Right?"

"Doctor," Ellen said.

"What?"

"It's Dr. Dreyer."

Cheryl pulled a zip-tie from her belt and corralled Ellen's wrists together, keeping her eyes on Aaron.

She steered Ellen into the back seat of her police cruiser. "Dr. Ellen Dreyer, you have the right to remain silent. Anything you say can be used against you in court. You have the legal right to a lawyer at any time before and during your questioning. If you cannot afford a lawyer, one will be appointed for you. If you decide to answer questions now without a lawyer present, you have the right to stop answering at any time."

She closed the door and turned to Aaron, pulling another zip-tie from her belt.

"What's gonna happen to my son? When can we get him treatment? He needs treatment now!" Aaron said.

"He's gonna get it right now, Aaron. Just calm down, please. We're all on the same side here. Now get up, and we'll get going. We're all going to the station. He'll get treatment there."

Cheryl read Aaron his Mirandas, cuffed him, and escorted him into the back of the squad car.

Although nothing in the material world would have led her towards closure, especially with another dead body to clean up, Cheryl couldn't help but feel some sense of resolution. Not full resolution, but it was a start. Something in her heart told her Duke's words were genuine, even if his motivations were as craven and misguided as she saw them. It ate at her that the sheriff hadn't told her earlier the truth of Bensalem's nature, that for whatever reason she wasn't worthy of the trust or ready for the responsibility. With his revelations so fresh in her mind, she still didn't quite know what to believe.

Cheryl approached Caleb, a withered and broken little child sitting alone in the meadow. "You're a very brave boy, Caleb. We're all very glad you're safe and back with your mommy and daddy. Everything's gonna be okay now. It's all over. You're very lucky to have a mommy and daddy who love you so much. Why don't you hop in the back here and sit next to them? Need some help up?"

He didn't. He crawled over Ellen and melted into the middle seat next to his parents.

Cheryl radioed Duke. "Sheriff? We need crime scene tech and paramedic at 12 Wickham Road. Please hurry."

"Oh God. Okay, ten-four, Deputy."

"I'm comin' your way with the Dreyers. All three of 'em."

"Ten-four. Guess that's the good news. Who'd you need the tech on?"

Cheryl paused. "I think you know, sir."

If Cheryl ever did become sheriff, she would run things differently. No matter what the town was grappling with, she would not sit idly by and allow things to continue a certain way just because that's how it had always been.

• • •

Hours later, a still zip-tied Aaron sat against the wall of the Bensalem Sheriff's Department. He twisted his head to peer out the foggy window above him.

Rain clouds rolled in from the north, blunting the bright

morning into an ambivalent haze. The temperature dropped, too, and Aaron felt a slight chill every time the rotating fan in the corner pelted him with a gust of air.

The clouds reminded Aaron of his bedroom window in the third-floor apartment he and Ellen had shared in Charlotte before moving to Bensalem. The day after they'd moved in, Aaron and Ellen had painted its walls white together. Every night, Cooper slept at the foot of the bed. They'd planned their wedding from that room. They'd conceived Caleb in that room. And when the southern air was thick with rain and clouds stretched across the northern sky, Aaron would often lie on the bed and watch them float away.

As sick as it made him to admit, he was glad to see Jane dead in the wheat grass after what she had done to Caleb. No longer could he see the sweet lady behind the counter in a country boutique, only the twisted, yellow-eyed night vision milking a crippled toddler, taunting him and channeling some mystic history he didn't understand. He wanted to believe that he'd been holding the shotgun, he wouldn't have hesitated to pull the trigger.

But he knew it never would have gone down that way if the roles had been reversed. There was only one Dreyer who possessed that kind of killer instinct and it wasn't him. Aaron was proud of his wife, and he didn't spend a second worrying about whether or not she could live with it.

He did, however, sneak an ask to Officer Monica Nelson to go check on Cooper, still locked inside the house since the final confrontation began. She didn't answer, but something in her eyes told Aaron she would.

After a long period of contemplation, the door to the interview room across the hall opened and out stepped Cheryl,

Duke and Ellen, holding Caleb in her arms. None spoke, but they all looked at Aaron, each with a different temperature in their eyes.

Cheryl strode towards him, hot with frustration and fatigue. Duke hung back in the doorway of the interview room, his eyes cold and his bushy eyebrows furrowed into a look of fatherly judgement. Ellen's wrists were untied, and she took soft steps towards the exit, exercising her right to remain silent. In her eyes, Aaron saw the same warmth and affection as the day they'd painted their old bedroom together.

Right before she opened the door and stepped out into the cloudy afternoon, she mouthed, "I love you."

• • •

Cheryl wordlessly yanked Aaron up by his zip-tied wrists and led him into the room his wife and son had just exited. She led him to the stool on the near side of the metal folding table positioned directly across from Duke, already seated. She sat next to the Sheriff.

"Gimme just a minute here," Duke said, scribbling notes on the side of a tape cassette in black marker. When he finished, he threw a half-second glance at Aaron before placing a new cassette in the black brick of a recorder sitting on the table. He pressed the record and play buttons together and the tape started rolling.

"Okay, this interview is with Mr. Aaron Dreyer of 12 Wickham Road here in Bensalem. The date is July the 18th and it's about half past eleven in the morning. Interview conducted by Sheriff Duke Quinlan and Deputy Cheryl McNamara."

Duke's fleshy old jowls shook as he spoke. Cheryl couldn't help but see an irksomely patronizing old man who'd hid critical truths from her but was now in the drivers' seat to gift wrap an open-and-shut case.

"Now, Mr. Dreyer, you and Deputy McNamara have gotten to know each other quite well over the last few days, haven't you?" Duke said.

Aaron looked at Cheryl, but she offered him nothing. "I'm not sure what that's supposed to mean, sir."

"She tells me you've been through a lot. Hank's death. Your son's disappearance. And now, covering up for your wife's crime that occurred in your own front yard. The Deputy tells me that your wife shot Jane Harcourt with a .22 but then you placed your prints on the gun to cover for her. Is that true?"

"No, that's not true. I was the one who shot her. I shot her because not only did she kidnap my son and leave him for dead in the forest, but then she came to our house to take him a second time after we found him."

"That's what your wife said. You are aware lying to a police officer is only gonna make your situation worse, right?"

"Well, I'm not lying."

Duke let out a dry laugh. "She said that, too. Okay, so your story is that you shot Jane because she kidnapped your son and she trespassed on your property. Did Jane have any reason to kidnap Caleb?"

"I told Deputy McNamara all of this already."

"Well, I'd like you to tell me, if you don't mind."

"You're never going to believe me."

Duke leaned back, and as he did, the overstuffed keyring lashed to his pants pocked jangled against the metal chair. He pressed the STOP button on the tape recorder. "Tell us what you saw."

"You really wanna know? It's amazing this police department has no idea what's going on in its own town."

"What did you see, Mr. Dreyer?"

"Well, there is this huge creature that lives in the woods by our house. I've been telling you guys this for days. It's some mythical creature Jane called a sentinel and her cult created it to protect us from some kind of ... I don't know ... some evil force that also lives in the forest."

"Okay. Is that it?"

"No. Her cult apparently created the sentinel by taking her young son and morphing him, performing some experiment like forty years ago. Jane told me that she wanted to, I don't know, kill him or rescue him or something. She wanted to use Caleb to create another sentinel. She had the audacity to tell me all of this in a dream just last night."

"In a dream?"

"Yes. I'm sure you won't believe that either."

"Uh-huh."

"Hey, you asked, so I'm telling you what happened. If you guys gave a shit enough to look around out there, we wouldn't have had to find our son ourselves and learn all this the hard way."

A scalding rage flared in Cheryl's chest and she felt her neck and cheeks flush with blood. She thought she had contained her physical reaction, but Aaron shot her a defensive glance.

Duke leaned forward and put his elbows on the table. "So just so I got this straight, and remember, the recorder's off, Jane wanted to kidnap Caleb so she could, uh, morph him into a monster? And she told you this?"

Aaron sighed. "You know what, you can laugh at me all

you want. We have our son back, and I'm sure you'll fucking try just like she did, but you can't take him away from us. I don't care. I told you why we shot Jane, she—"

"We?" Duke cut in.

"I," Aaron said. "I shot her."

• • •

After escorting Aaron to the station's holding cell, Cheryl found herself sitting in the same chair she'd sat in hours earlier. The rain outside and the stale air inside Duke's office left Cheryl marinating in a malaise of numbness and exhaustion as he spoke into his fossil of a desk phone.

"Yessir," Duke said. "Got two officers securing the scene now. That's a Officer Monica Nelson. Yessir. Mm-hmm. And a Officer Derek Brady. Mm-hmm. Mm-hmm. Yessir, that's Al Brady's boy."

In a normal week, Cheryl would've been much more concerned about Monica and Derek securing a murder scene together. She wondered which of them was taking the lead. Was it Derek, pride and joy of Bensalem? Or was it Monica, who, three days ago, had marched with Cheryl up the hill of hell to find Hank's mangled corpse? Cheryl hoped it was her.

Duke hung up the phone and sighed. "Well, VSP's on their way. They're gonna handle it."

"Do they know about this?"

"'Bout what?"

Cheryl glared at him. "All that shit you said last night. All that shit the Dreyers said. Are we really gonna prosecute them?"

"Have to. Don't mean they'll do time, but hell if I know. I'm not a judge."

"So, wait, all that shit Aaron said about a cult and monsters and rituals and God knows what else, that's all true, isn't it?"

Duke looked up at the drop-panel ceiling above him. He made a sound that was something in between a cry and a wince.

"Listen, I truly don't know the specifics. I've fought like hell to stay out of the affairs of that Order and just run the town. But ... I guess I wouldn't have a reason not to believe it's true."

"Well, who would know? Who's left in this so-called Order you all keep talking about?"

"Not many, I suppose. Hank, Jane, and her son did. They were all in it, but they're gone. Can't hardly believe it. Ethel Thomasin knew, we might be able to get in touch with her. There are a couple older folks in town, but Jane was the head or in charge of a lot of it."

"You need to loop me in on this, Duke. I need to know everything."

"I know. With Jane dead, I'm sure they'll be pokin' around to figure out what's next. I'll, uh ... I'll see if I can get in touch with them. Set up a meeting. Because Jane and them knew way more about this than I did. As long as that sentinel is out there and nobody messes with it, the town should be safe. But I don't know if there's a shelf-life on it or what. We need to figure that out. Which means we need to talk to the Order."

Cheryl closed her eyes. She dug her palms into the fraying armrests of her chair and sighed. "This is all so insane. I'm so goddamned mad at you for keeping this from me. Thank Christ that boy is back, but Hank and Jane are dead. This didn't need to happen."

Duke didn't respond. He set a rocky grimace on his face

and stared out the window as the rain poured. Seconds passed, then minutes, as the rain battered the building and Cheryl stared at the man she thought she knew.

After a long time, Duke spoke. His voice was soft and thin and scared. It was the voice of a man too old and too tired to conjure the courage to face his own demons. "I had this terrible dream last night. It was our wedding day. 1963. There were flowers everywhere, and the church smelled like a garden, and this beautiful light was comin' through all the windows. Everything was perfect. 'Cept, the roles were reversed. It was me standin' in the back, and Marcy was standin' up by the altar. And ..."

Duke paused, and the edges of his eyes began to glisten in the fluorescent lights overhead. "And nobody in the church ... had a face. Just these blank heads with no eyes or nose or mouth. Hundreds of 'em. Every single one, even the priest, even Marcy, they were all turned towards me, lookin' at me. And even though they didn't have eyes, I could feel their eyes on me, judging me, hating me. And it was so cold inside the church that I felt naked and exposed, like I was outside in win-ter in nothing but my underwear. Maybe not even that much. And I tried to walk to Marcy, but for some reason, I couldn't move my feet. I just couldn't move. I ... I couldn't do anything. The blank faces just kept starin' at me, not sayin' nothing."

The phone rang, knocking Duke back to earth. He picked it up. "Sheriff Quinlan," he said. "Well, hello there, Lynn, how you doin'? Zat so? Uh-huh. Yeah. Oh boy, yeah, you don't want that. No ma'am. Alright well, I'm 'bout to wrap somethin' up here, but we'll send somebody down this afternoon. Yes ma'am. You hang tight."

He hung up the phone and smiled at Cheryl. "Lynn For-rester's cat's stuck in the wall again."

She didn't return his smile. "Then what happened?"

"What?"

"In your dream. Then what happened?"

"Oh, well ... I suppose it just, uh ... it ended that way."

Cheryl pushed her chair back from the desk and rose. "I'll go deal with Lynn."

"Hey, well, listen, before you go. You know as well as I do, I won't be sittin' in this chair much longer. I messed up by not dealing with this sooner. After I'm gone, someone's gonna need to clean this up ... or keep it going or whatever they decide to do. If you think I was reluctant to trust you, I sure as shit don't trust anybody else. So ... if you want the chair ... I'll endorse, and I'll do whatever I can to help you get your arms around this ... situation."

"To be honest, I wanted it a lot more last week than I do now."

Duke chuckled. "Well, most weeks ain't this bad."

• • •

The man stepped off the bus at 1:14pm. He was late. Super late. He shoved his way through the tall revolving door of the building, and he looked straight past the security desk as he strode towards a corridor of elevators.

"Welcome back, sir," said the security guard.

But the man didn't respond, he didn't even notice the security guard as he mashed the UP button. Each second of the three-minute wait for the elevator and subsequent climb to the 110th floor crawled by at an eternal pace.

When he finally arrived, he strode down a long, impeccably clean hallway towards a pair of frosted glass doors. He buzzed the intercom, identified himself, and sat down in the lobby.

Gold-plated furniture, stout paneling on the walls. A fireplace that was always lit, even in the summer. The room smelled sacred and powerful because it was.

The receptionist, sitting behind an ornately carved desk, stood up. "He'll see you now."

The man made his way through a hall lined with dozens of closed doors. Portraits of stuffy old men adorned the wall spaces between them.

He was headed to the very end of that hall towards the gaping double doors that very few passed through. His fist fluttered with nerves as he knocked. A latch clicked inside the heavy mahogany, and he stepped inside.

"I'm sorry I'm so late, Grand Elder."

"Have a seat," said the Grand Elder. He stood where he always did, with his back to his guest and his hands folded behind him, firing his exacting gaze through the window blinds and onto the concrete jungle a thousand feet below.

The man, whose heart rate had soared from his commute and his lateness, practically ran to sit in one of two leather armchairs facing the Grand Elder's desk. The Grand Elder didn't sit. He didn't move.

"Sir, there's been a pr—there's a slight change," said the man.

"Not so slight, apparently. Otherwise, you would have told me over the phone."

"That's correct. I apologize, sir. I just wanted to be cautious. I arrived as fast as I could, and there's a, uh, a significant level of law enforcement activity in the area now."

"What happened?"

"Sir, the transition did not occur. The parents of the child found him at the entrance and recovered him. They stole him back before it could even begin."

The Grand Elder nodded.

"That's not all, sir. This might be a bit hard to believe, but the parents actually ... they killed the cleric. It happened just a few hours ago. They're in local police custody now. As soon as it happened, I rushed back up to Manhattan."

The Grand Elder unfolded his hands and stuck a finger through the blinds. "Were you seen?"

"I don't believe so, sir."

The Grand Elder swiveled his head slightly as he pried the hole in the blinds. The grandfather clock's rhythmic tick-tock moaned through the silence in the room.

"Sir," said the man. "Are you not upset?"

"Oh, I already know everything you've told me."

With a quick, tinny snap, the Grand Elder released the blinds and spun to face the man. As if he were struck by a bolt of fire, the man gasped in horror and dug his palms into the chair's arm rests — the Grand Elder's eyes were completely white.

"S—Sir!?"

"Don't be afraid, Deacon. The New King Salomon lives through me. I have seen all that he has seen. I see what he is seeing right now."

The man could muster no response.

"Do you know what he's looking at?" said the Grand Elder.

"No. N—No."

"It. He sees the Nothus Noctis. He's down there with it, right now, deep in that cold, hard earth."

Something about those white eyes gripped the man with such ferocity that all thoughts in his mind coalesced around them. They seemed to somehow glow, and then they expanded, white circles of light beaming in the middle of the Grand Elder's skull. Their brilliance was such that the man found himself squinting just to maintain the Grand Elder's gaze.

The Grand Elder put his hands on the desk that separated the two men and leaned in close. The man found his own head drifting off the back of his chair and slowly towards the Grand Elder, towards those white eyes. Then, with their faces just a few feet away, the Grand Elder's eyes shrank back to the dull gray pebbles they had been the last time they met.

"Cleric Harcourt never knew what she was doing. In all my years of working with the Bensalem chapter, our relations have been strained," said the Grand Elder.

The man sat back in his chair and his eyes traced the contours of the room, as if attempting to remember where he was.

"This is an opportunity. You're to go back. Not now, we'll let the police sort out what they need to. But when the time is right, you'll go back."

"To facilitate another transition?"

"No. You're going to do something we should have done a long time ago. Something the cleric refused to do." The Grand Elder returned to the window and clasped his hands behind him. He stuck his fingers through the blinds again, the same exact spot, and peered down through them. "You're going to end this once and for all. But you're going to need help to do it."

The man wiped the pad of sweat that had formed on his brow. He looked at his hands. "Of course, sir. Just tell me what I need to do."

"I certainly will, Deacon Pierce."

• • •

Ellen had deliberated for quite some time before swallowing her pride and calling her mother to come up and help. She didn't explain much on the phone, just that she needed help now.

"Everything's fine, I promise," she pleaded, "I'll explain when you get here."

But explain what? How could she explain Aaron was going away for a while? She'd have to be honest about that part. But how much of this would make sense to someone completely removed from it? Maybe her opinion would change in the moment and her mother would beat the truth out of her, but for now, Ellen resigned herself to a story that didn't involve dreams or sentinels or demons in the woods. No, Caleb had just been kidnapped by some old meth-head for money, and when she'd had the audacity to come dangle him in front of them, Ellen had snatched the boy and Aaron had shot her.

Fine.

A busy night of phone calls lay ahead. First, a criminal defense lawyer she and Aaron had attended college with. Ellen was already prepared to throw every penny of their net worth at a trial to free her husband. Next on the list was the child psychiatrist who had been recommended to her when she'd taken Caleb to the hospital.

Physically, Caleb appeared to be fine, but he still hadn't spoken, and all Ellen wanted to do was peek inside that head to see what was in there. She wanted to know what he had witnessed, and she wanted to claw the eyes out of everyone and everything he'd come in contact with since he'd gone missing. Finally, Aaron. Phone calls to Aaron as often and for as long as she was permitted.

She'd sleep on it and call the hospital tomorrow. At this point, she had no earthly idea what to tell work.

She stood over a boiling pot in the kitchen and watched the sun roll itself down the western range. She wondered if the sentinel was out there. She thought about how Aaron had said that thing was Jane's son, but she couldn't bring herself so far to think about her own son becoming one of them.

Whatever was happening out there was going to continue until someone did something about it. Would Ellen be able to resist the temptation to stay away? Would it be better to move? She didn't feel bad about Jane, but she did empathize with the idea that the sentinel was someone's son. After all, it was almost her son.

Jane had seemed to imply that her son was still in there. How much of him was left? Were there other ex-sentinels walking around town, or had Jane wanted to give him a proper burial?

There was only one way to find out. The temptation ate at her. She'd be able to resist for tonight, and possibly tomorrow. She gave herself the goal of trying to stay out of it until her mother left. Eventually, though, she knew she'd be out there again, studying it, trying to rationalize the irrational.

Caleb's cartoon about trains hummed in the background. That he wasn't speaking worried her sick. If he remembered everything — anything — how would he express it? Would he wake up screaming in the night? Would he walk into her bedroom and say cryptic, terrifying things? Would he ever speak again?

She hoped beyond hope that he wouldn't remember but began to prepare herself for the lifetime of emotional torture that was likely ahead.

Outside, she saw a fat, gray songbird dart through the back yard and land on the thin bough of a nearby dogwood tree. The bird leaned over a nest and began regurgitating into the mouths of a handful of hungry babies.

Ellen put her hand on her chest, and this time, she felt something.

She was back in her childhood house, up in the bathroom, feeling those tiny, crushed bones in the front pocket of her overalls. Tears welled in her eyes and a fire of anger, remorse, and love began raging inside her. It burned like a wildfire in a forest of dry trees.

She squeezed her eyes closed, sending streams of tears down her cheeks, and she clenched her teeth to keep it all inside. Careful not to scream, she focused hard and channeled the sudden rush of overwhelming emotion and clenched even harder. Only the softest of sobs got through.

She let herself burn. She embraced the hurt, the shame, and the confusion.

And then she told it: get the fuck out.

She turned off the stove, walked over to her son, and hugged him from the back. Holding him close was enough to shove the anger and remorse away and focus solely on the love.

"Never again," she said, not to herself, not to Caleb, but to the mother bird from so long ago.

• • •

Before riding out to Lynn Forrester's, Cheryl called Skylar. She didn't answer, of course, but texted back saying she was watching TV with Rick. Cheryl texted back that she'd be home in a few minutes and to save some bacon for her.

Lynn Forrester's house was a gaunt shanty on the side of a hill filled with overgrown weeds. Cheryl knocked on the aluminum frame door.

"I done told 'em to stay outta there!" bemoaned Mrs. Forrester, her voice muffled from inside the house. She opened the door. "But he ain't listen! That thang ain't never listen. It's my son's and he don't take care of it. Don't know why I even bother."

That cat didn't take long to coax out of the wall, and when Cheryl got back to her patrol car, an ocean of gray, engorged clouds had invaded the sky.

The route from the Forrester residence to her own took her north on State Road 639 and right through downtown Bensalem. She rolled to a stop in front of M&J Fine Gifts and sat there for a few minutes listening to the cicadas.

The store that had withstood so much for so long would surely die now. Another turning of the page from the past to the present. It would either get scooped up by a global conglomerate or sit vacant for years. Probably the latter.

From where she sat, it looked like there was broken glass on the ground in front of the store, and she suddenly recalled stepping on a shard of something, earlier that morning. A long, churning thunder roll erupted above her.

Cheryl turned off the car and climbed out. Holding her flashlight in one hand and a baton in the other, she stepped toward the door. The top pane had been busted. She shouldered the door open, waved her flashlight around, and broke the silence.

"Hello? Police!"

Nothing. No one was there. The perp had probably already left. She took a slow lap around the inside of the store to assess the damage. Everything was intact except for the jewelry cases, which had all been smashed open. Nothing was left in-side except a handful of loose silver beads that must have fallen from a bracelet or a necklace that snapped apart in the haste of the robbery.

But behind the register, she noticed a rumpled tapestry that had clearly fallen from its place on the wall. There was a small door right behind it.

The door was just slighty ajar, and something told her that opening it would show her things she didn't want to see. She took a deep breath and steeled herself for whatever lay in wait on the other side.

The door creaked loudly and sent a heinous stench sailing into her nostrils. It was so bad she had to cover her nose with the inside of her elbow.

Shining the light through revealed a short corridor lined with old brick, and it led to a giant, windowless room. The sight of it sent a chill racing through her entire body.

She jumped her light from corner to corner of the vast space trying to consume as much of it as possible. It looked like some kind of mad laboratory. There were tables lined with glass jars filled with substances of varying colors. The walls were covered in arcane looking words scribbled in what she guessed was some kind of black chalk. Phrases and words and even characters she didn't recognize ran in every direction and smashed into each other. It was as if she had climbed inside the mind of an insane person.

Something shiny caught the light in the back corner of the room: a solid gold cross that must have been eight feet tall. A red rose stuck out from the center.

Someone had been here recently enough to set up at least

some of the still boiling and buzzing glass beakers. There were thousands of them, arranged in what appeared to be no orderly fashion on long tables that ran the length of the room.

On her way out, she draped her light over the area above the door. Her heart jumped out of her chest when she saw a sprawling portrait of a man with a thin moustache, dressed in what looked like puritan clothing. In his right hand, he held a shining cross, and his left hand pointed towards the ground. The man's eyes were entirely white. His half-smile almost seemed to welcome her, content in the knowing of something she did not.

Although the room was silent, Cheryl did not feel quite alone. In fact, it was as if she was surrounded by many people, old souls, the way one might feel in a funeral home or an ancient church.

It was too much to take in. She'd come back tomorrow. She'd bring help. She'd do this the right way. But on her way out, she saw a large, leather-bound book leaning up against the wall by the door. She scooped it up and bolted past the counter and out into the street.

She tossed the book, which must have been at least ten pounds, onto the front seat of her patrol car. On its front cover was another gold cross with a red rose in the middle. The book itself conveyed an intense physical presence, as if it had brought that puritanical man with it. Cheryl glanced over to the back seat just in case.

She traced her wet finger along the heavy gold-plated lettering that ran across the bottom of the book. It was in a language she didn't understand but which she guessed was Latin — or something just as old.

GRIMOIRE PERANTIQUARUM ROSARUM.

She didn't open the book. That could wait.

Cheryl drove. She wouldn't go home yet. She didn't want this thing in her house. Right now, the patrol car was her haven, just as it had been so many times before. She texted her husband and each of her kids that she loved them. And she readied herself for what was about to come.

• • •

Aaron had spent the last eight hours lying on his cot, tracing the cracks in the ceiling of his jail cell with his eyes. There wasn't a window, but he knew it was nighttime. He also knew he was alone. His only company was the buzz of a fan in another part of the building, placed far enough away to have no impact whatsoever on the temperature of the cell.

Giving in to sheer boredom, Aaron sat up on his cot. A rat crept into the edge of his vision. He watched it slink along the cinder block wall in the hallway outside his cell. It moved in spurts. Starting, stopping, starting again. It sniffed the air. It turned around when it heard something, second-guessing itself but then continuing on. A creature with total freedom, and not the slightest idea what to do with it.

The bars of his cell interrupted his line of sight as the rat scurried. When it stopped and disappeared behind one of the bars, Aaron stared at the bar for a long time. A sturdy, round rod that ran from floor to ceiling, its gray paint chipped all over the surface, laying bare the battle scars it had endured from decades of inmate rage.

He remembered India. He remembered his friends. They'd all be well settled into their homes by now, coping with reentry into their own unforgiving realities. Was that trip a week ago? Two? A month? Aaron found himself unable to put times and events together. How would they react to the news that he was in jail for murder? Would any of them ever talk to him again? Probably not. He'd have to explain. His name would be in the news. This would follow him forever.

The fan clicked off and the room went completely silent. Even it didn't want to keep him company anymore. It was just Aaron and the rat, now.

Little movements. Micro-decisions.

Huge impacts.

Aaron wasn't conscious of the fact that he was now standing, facing the bars of his cell. His elbows were cocked, and his fingers were curled around the handles of imaginary binoculars. His thumb moved back and forth over an invisible focus. He rocked it back and forth, back and forth. He stood there holding the binoculars, replaying the events of that night in his head.

If only he had not put them to his face. If only he had gone to bed. If only he had left it alone. If he had not gone to India.

"Maybe none of this would have ever happened," he whispered.

The rat resumed its run. Aaron turned his head to follow it and saw what the rodent had been after the whole time. A thick smudge of peanut butter spread across the trigger of a mouse trap. When the bow came down, it released a thwack that reverberated off the thick, stone walls. The trap had severed the rat's head. Blood trickled out from both sides of its body while its hind legs twitched with the last reflexes of life. Another victim of biological urges and mundane curiosities.

The cell was silent again and now Aaron was really alone.

Even the rat was gone.

He tried not to think about Ellen, about Caleb. The healing would start tomorrow. Not tonight. He laid down on the cot and closed his eyes. He slept.

He did not dream.

END OF BOOK 1

AFTERWARD

Thank you for reading my debut novel! I hope you enjoyed your introduction to the world of Bensalem and all its heinous acts and creatures.

I'd so very much appreciate your support in the form of a review on Amazon, Goodreads, or whatever platform you purchased this book. It's the biggest thing you can do to show your support, and the more people reading and reviewing this book, the more our town of Bensalem is likely to truly rid itself of the horrors that haunt it. Speaking of which...

BOOK 2 "NOTHUS" COMING 2022!

It's been six months since tragedy rocked the rural hamlet of Bensalem, Virginia. Newly elected Sheriff Cheryl McNamara has vowed to uncover the truth about her town's dark history and drive out whatever terrors roam the woods that surround them. Her big break comes from an unexpected source: her teenage daughter, Skylar, whose fascination with the occult and unique ties to an ancient mystery, makes a remarkable discovery. But tragedy strikes, and when the true form of the evil is revealed, it is young Skylar who must confront not only the Nothus, but also the town's old demons that lay in its lair.

ACKNOWLEDGMENTS

A smart person once said that 'behind every successful man, there's a woman'. Well, if this book is in any way a success, it's because of five women who poured their hearts and their energy into this book at various points in time: my "agent" and first writing buddy Alanna Robertson-Webb, my first developmental editor Jessica Black, my second (and third!) editor Linda Nagle, my unflappable publisher Michelle River, and of course my wonderful wife and biggest fan Cara Marie.

I'd also like to thank Francois Vaillancourt for his artwork, along with Ross Tyson, Adam Davies, and all my beta readers for the mountains of feedback.

Last but not least. Thanks to Sergeant Joe Palkovic of the Fredrick Police Department for not only your incredible help in crafting this story, but also for putting your life on the line every day. I hope Cheryl did you proud.

An Amazon bestselling author of horror and dark fiction, Drew Starling is a husband and dog dad who loves strong female leads, martial arts, and long walks in the woods with canine companions. He would like to think his plots are better than his prose, but strives to make his words sound both beautiful and terrifying at the same time. He listens to Beethoven, Megadeth, and Enya when he writes, and he'd be absolutely delighted if you'd consider joining his mailing list at **drewstarling.com**. You'll receive THREE free short stories when you sign up! His only rule of writing: the dog never dies.

Made in the USA
Coppell, TX
19 April 2022